CRICKDAM

Prelude to HERONSMILL

Roscoe Howells

Gomer Press
1990

First Impression—1990

ISBN 0 86383 643 7

© *Roscoe Howells*

Printed in Wales by Gomer Press, Llandysul, Wales

JUL

For
MARGED
my *Cariad*

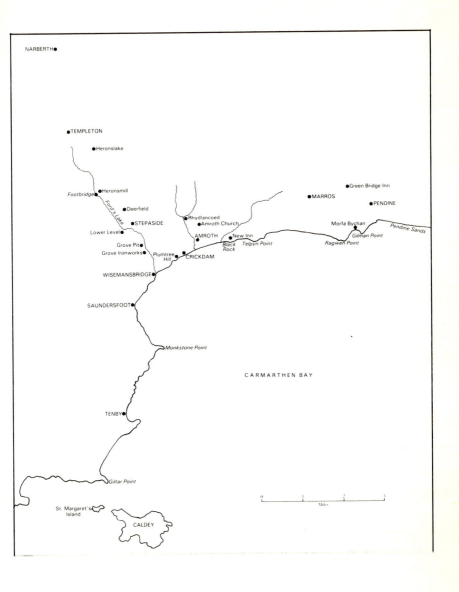

NARBERTH●

●TEMPLETON

●Heronslake

Footbridge ●Heronsmill   ●Green Bridge Inn

   ●Deerfield   ●MARROS

●STEPASIDE   ●PENDINE

●Rhydlancoed

Lower Level●   ●Amroth Church   Morfa Bychan   *Pendine Sands*

Grove Pit●   AMROTH   ●New Inn   *Gilman Point*

Grove Ironworks●   *Black Rock*   *Telpyn Point*   *Ragwen Point*

Plumtree Hill   ●CRICKDAM

WISEMANSBRIDGE●

Ford's Lake

SAUNDERSFOOT●

Monkstone Point

CARMARTHEN BAY

TENBY●

Giltar Point

St. Margaret's Island

CALDEY

0   1   2   3

Miles

I
Crickdam

'Tis virtue and not birth that makes us noble
Great actions speak great minds, and such should govern.

Francis Beaumont and John Fletcher. *The Prophetess*

1

All day it had been raining.

Across the bay the grey curtain shut out everything which lay beyond, with never a sight of the distant Gower coast and Worm's Head, or of Caldey nearer home. Not even a glimpse of Monkstone had there been.

At mid-day it began to blow harder from the south-west and the rain fell even more heavily. Down from the fields above, the surface water gathered and swelled into rushing brown rivers. The few bedraggled hens huddled under the cart, and the horse, head down, sought whatever shelter there may have been behind the pine-end of the pig's-cot.

As the chill November light began to fail, the gale, raging unabated now, lifted the white-capped waves high onto the rocks below and, momentarily, the curtain of rain rolled back a little out to sea, and the dim outline of Monkstone suddenly pierced the gloom.

In those last minutes of fading light Luther Knox caught a glimpse of the great ship, her top-sails already in shreds, as she battled to weather the storm. Saundersfoot harbour, built over the last four years, had now, in the year 1833, started to receive larger vessels, and this was the biggest ship he had ever seen in all his long life. And he had already passed his eighth birthday.

As he looked, darkness finally hid her from view and all about him the gale howled in demonic fury.

Before morning there could well be plunder. It all depended on what cargo the ship was carrying.

2

The damp ran down the walls of the thatched cottage as they ate their meal of potatoes and buttermilk on the white scrubbed table. The glow from the ball fire added a little light to that which was shed by the flickering candle.

Seeny, two years older than Luther, was watching their brother Will, nearly a man now, and listening to his every word. Their mother, Bronwen Knox, pulled her shawl more tightly around her as if that might protect her from the terrors of the night.

Will, with his coarse features and fair hair in sharp contrast
to his young brother's dark curls and clean cut nose and
chin, was glowering at the boy.

Will's eyes were hard and blue but Luther's were brown
and gentle.

'How do'st thee know' Will demanded yet again, 'that she
was full-rigged?'

'Because I seen her.'

'Ha'st thee ever saw a full-rigged ship afore?'

'No, never.'

'Then how do'st thee know?'

'Because I seen her.'

'How many masts?'

'I told thee that as well.'

'Then tell me again.'

'Square-rigged on the foremast and fore-and-aft on the
main.'

Will rose from the table and began to fasten a sack round
his shoulders.

'Ar't thee determined?' asked his mother.

'Of course I be. They said down the pit today as a big ship
was expected with a mixed cargo. With a bit of luck she'll
come in this side of Ragwen an' God knows how much food
and what else we might get out of her.'

'What if the Pendine people gets to her?'

'If she's this side of Ragwen she's as much ours as theirs.
And if she was where Luther said a seen her she'll be nearer
to Amroth. An' the Pendine people is lookin' for trouble if
they comes that far. They've had things their own way long
enough.'

'The Reverend Josiah Price said 'tis a wicked business,'
said Seeny.

It was the first time she had spoken. Her blue eyes had
none of the hardness of her older brother's.

Will glared at her. 'Shut thee thy mouth thou cheeky little
bitch.'

Grabbing her by the hair he dragged her to her feet. 'If I
hears one mewk about this out o' thee after tonight I'll. . .'
Here he jerked back her head and, as she cried out, Luther

grabbed the big knife and, dragging his lame foot, lunged at him.

Letting go of Seeny, Will gripped Luther's arm before he could strike, and then Mam Bron dragged him away, but not before he had pushed Luther to the floor.

'Right thou little bastard,' he spat down at him. 'Tomorrow I'll take a strap to thee an' tan the hide off thee. For thou'rt a bastard, an' after I've learnt thee thy place, like a bastard is how thee's'll be treated.'

Then he went out into the wild night.

3

As the storm raged all about them, Luther and Seeny slept in each other's arms, huddled together for warmth on a straw palliasse in the dingy loft above the one downstairs bedroom. Will's palliasse, unoccupied for the night, lay where the eaves of the thatch came down to the floor in the other corner. Between them a small window looked out from the pine-end of the cottage.

The events of the evening constituted one more bond between the two children.

Luther loved Seeny deeply. She it was who had run to comfort him and cradle his head in her arms when the tram had crushed his foot. That was when the Patches were still being worked, but they were closed now and times were as bad, so the older people said, as at any time since the wars with the French had finished.

In the cliffs between Amroth and Wisemansbridge there were four lots of Patches from which iron ore was dug and exported from the open beach. The boats came in to be beached at high tide, and loaded whilst the tide was out. Then they were floated at the next high tide, by men with long poles, and sailed across Carmarthen Bay with their loads to Pembrey to Thomas Gaunt's ironworks there.

All the families worked at digging out and picking the mine, as the iron ore was called. Hard work though it was it was better than having to go down the coalpit, and there was the compensation in summer of the sun and the sea and the blue sky and the golden sands and deep, inviting pools. They could all be seen even when their delights could not be enjoyed. Just to see them was better than the damp and dust and darkness of the coal pits where some of the children had to go. And they had to go because their parents made them. They needed the few shillings they could earn.

A special delight to Luther was to see the great sailing ships way out at sea. He felt somehow that that was where his place in life would be. Always the sea called to him although there was no talk of any seamen in the family. Their only interest in the sea and ships was to watch for the vessels driven in before a storm from the south-west, and be there to plunder and steal before the customs' men knew and could call the militia out to prevent them.

Now, the harbour had been built at Saundersfoot, and there was talk of the prosperity which this could bring. To Luther it meant seeing bigger ships in the bay than could ever come in for loading mine on the open beach below Crickdam.

Crickdam was the only Patch where there was a house. Just below the top of the cliff it was, with two small fields above, where the sloping ground ran down to the shore, and with the blacksmith's shop, halfway down, beneath it. That was where Patrick Knox, Mam Bron's husband, had worked. But he had died, something to do with his chest they said, the year after Luther was born. Luther could not remember him, but Seeny said she could.

A bit of a wild one they said he was, and Will took after him. Mam Bron had come from up the Welsh, somewhere in the north of the county, but Patrick's people had come over with the Irish. None of it was quite clear to Luther. He hardly knew exactly how many brothers or sisters he had. He had heard about Meg, who was the eldest, but she had gone away years ago, and there were two boys who had gone off to work in the pits up in Glamorgan. After that came Will, who was about nineteen now, and then two girls who had been out working on farms since they were nine years old. Even Seeny could not remember them. Then there was a gap of some years between them and Seeny, who had been christened Asenath, and Luther. In between there had been others. Some died when they were born, but one had fallen over a cliff and one had been drowned. It was no wonder, Seeny said sometimes, that Mam Bron hardly ever laughed or even smiled.

With dark eyes and dark straggly hair turning grey she looked a forlorn creature. Yet Luther, although often enough in his young mind feeling sorry for her, was never conscious of loving her like he loved Seeny. Nor was there ever any great show of affection by Mam Bron towards Luther.

In spite of this it was said, especially by Will, that Luther was spoiled and pampered. And he had the feeling, quite often, that he was the favoured one. There had been no great pressure on him, for instance, to start picking mine, but when he was old enough he went to be near Seeny.

He had not been picking mine for long when the word went round that Thomas Gaunt's works at Pembrey were closing and so the Patches would be closing down as well. It was in the last week's working that Luther's accident happened.

Dug from the tunnels driven into the cliff, the mine was run out in wooden trucks on rails and tipped onto the beach below to be picked over by the women and children. One of the pollers, as the women were called, had sent Luther up to tell her husband, who was filling, that there was some good coal amongst the mine and to ask him whether he knew.

'That's how 'tis with a accident' the man had said afterwards. 'If it don't happen quick it don't happen at all.' But it was small consolation to Luther. He could hardly remember how it had happened, except that he had slipped as he turned to avoid the truck which was being pushed out of the tunnel, and somehow or other the iron wheel had gone over his foot on the rail. He could remember crying out and he could remember Seeny cradling his head in her arms before he had fallen into a black pit.

When he came to his senses he was on Mam Bron's bed and there was a doctor there. Luther had never seen a doctor before. He had been sent by the people who were the bosses of the mine pickers. Luther was still vague about it but he could remember the pain and Seeny bathing his foot every day. Then, at last, he was able to hobble about on a stick and

Seeny had to go off early every morning for Stepaside to work down the pit. Luther thought it was hard for Seeny to have to work down a pit, for Seeny was still only ten, and his Seeny, he was sure, had been born for better things. She stirred in his arms and he held her more closely. Soon she would be struggling to get up in the darkness, bleary eyed and still weary, to pull on the rough clothes and hurry away in her bare feet to meet up with other children on their way to the pit.

4

At first light Luther clambered down the ladder from the loft and limped out through the stable-type half door which prevented the few animals from coming into the house. Except when the weather was bad the top half was left open, which meant that the hens could fly up and perch on the bottom door and see what food they could pick up from inside. There was little enough these days.

Mam Bron was already out milking Fronwen, the black cow. It was Mam Bron who had named her when she came to them as a calf. She had a little white patch on her chest and Mam Bron said Fronwen was a Welsh name which meant white breast.

There was no sign of Nap, the heavy Welsh cob, whose real name was Napoleon, and then Luther noticed that the cart had gone as well. He had no need to ask Mam Bron because he knew that Will would have taken Nap in the cart when he went off last night to see what could be had from the shipwreck.

He had not asked whether he should take the horse and cart. He never asked Mam Bron anything these days. He had become rough in his ways and language and he mixed with rough company. There had been no father's hand to control him since he was a twelve-year old and for a long time he had taken to doing much as he pleased. He had no great love for anybody, and for Luther least of all.

The storm had blown itself out, but great waves were rolling in from the bay, and along the beach was a litter of seaweed and flotsam. Not a soul was there to be seen.

Luther hobbled up the rough track to the field, where the going became easier for him. From the top he could see right along the wide sweep of coast beyond Amroth and Black Rock to Telpyn and Ragwen and the great stretch of Pendine sands receding into the distance. Under the cliff at Telpyn the stricken ship was on her side. Small ant-like figures could be dimly seen swarming over her, hacking and tugging. Along the beach, horses and carts were hurrying and people were running. There would hardly be much left of any value by the time the militia arrived. And it would no doubt be days before the bodies of her crew would be washed ashore.

It was late morning before Nap and the cart came down the track from the cliff road with Will. A stranger to Luther was leading Nap, and Will's dead body was in the cart.

Mam Bron knew the man and she said it was good of him to have done what he had done. Killed in a fight with the Pendine men Will had been, but two Pendine men had been killed, so maybe they would not be quite so ready to come so far down another time. There was more than enough wreck for them on Pendine sands. Far more than ever came ashore at Amroth. And, no doubt, the neighbours would see that Mam Bron had her share of whatever was to be had from the wreck.

5

The neighbours did not forget and, in due course, there was a roll of good cloth from the ship, a big tub of salt, and enough tea to last a couple of years, as long as it could be kept dry, as well as two sacks of flour.

When they came to bury Will in his cheap coffin they all put what they could afford in the bowl on the table. It was little enough from each of them, but it helped.

Will had to be buried in the churchyard by the parson, because that was the law, but it was the Reverend Josiah Price, dissenter, who came to comfort Mam Bron, for he had been good to them at Crickdam ever since Patrick had died. More especially he had been a great help and encouragement to Luther since his accident.

Luther had not been to the endowed school because he had started to work, but he had been going to the Reverend Price's Sunday school where he had learned to read and write and do sums and he had shown great aptitude at his books. After his accident he could not walk that far, especially in bare feet, and so the Reverend Price had called every week at Crickdam and given him a special lesson. He had set exercises for him to do by the following week and left books for Luther to read. And, knowledgeable in the ways of the wild creatures, he had instilled into Luther, early in life, a love of the countryside.

Above all, Josiah Price was a good man and, although he regarded himself as a friend of the poor, he condemned the stealing, the violence and the plundering of stricken ships driven onto the inhospitable coast.

Now that Luther was getting about again the Reverend Price said to him, 'You must apply yourself to your books because it is the only way you will be able to get a living. You will never be able to do heavy work.'

It was in the springtime following Will's death. Already the bees were busy amongst the early gorse blossom, and a pair of ravens, great croaking black devils, had their nest high in the inaccessible cliff. Who could afford to rear lambs for them to kill? Quite close on the full tide a ketch was putting about to make her run into Saundersfoot harbour against an off-shore wind.

'But when I'm old enough I can go to sea' said Luther.

Josiah Price, still a young man, although his hair was receding, wrinkled his kindly blue eyes.

'My boy' he said, ''tis the dream of many young lads to go to sea. But have you thought how you'd manage up in the riggings of a great schooner with that game foot of yours?'

'Ah, yes sir. But don't forget the steam-ships. Fancy crossin' th' Atlantic all the way by steam. That must be a powerful fine ship, that *Royal William*.'

'Luther, my son. One of the lessons we have to learn in life is to accept what the good Lord sends, whether we like it or whether we don't. As you grow older you'll find that acceptance makes a burden much easier to bear. Stick to your books, my boy. Stick to your books.'

Such was the general drift of many of their talks.

Luther worked at the books which the minister lent him, but he also spent many an hour on the beach and, on the good summer days, swam in the sea. He soon came to be a good swimmer and it was one of the pursuits where his damaged foot was of little impediment to him. And in the pools he caught prawns. The Reverend Price showed him how to bait a hook, and he contrived rough fishing lines which he would leave out overnight and on which he caught many a good bass. Mam Bron could hardly ever afford to buy butcher's meat.

One late summer the mackerel came. Of an evening it was, when Seeny had just come home from the pit, dirty and weary. But in the moonlight they ran, and Mam Bron with them, and scooped the mackerel up by the bucketful, pulling them in with the branch of a tree, jumping and splashing, all black stripes and silver. All along the shore the fish came in, driven, so folks said, by porpoises, and all along the shore from Saundersfoot and Wisemansbridge, along by Amroth and right up to Pendine, the people were scooping them up and driving them away in cartloads.

Absie Pugh was one of them. A tall boy he was, and not much older than Seeny. He did not work in the pit. He found what work he could on the farms and loved to be with horses, and one day, he said, he would have horses of his own. That night in the moonlight he drove his father's pony and went home with the cart loaded with mackerel as well as helping Seeny and Luther and Mam Bron to carry up their own fish. Seeny said it was kind of him but Luther said, 'Don't be daft. He got his eye on you.' And Seeny laughed. There was something to laugh about with all the fish that could be dried for the winter.

The following day Luther set to work with Mam Bron cleaning the pile of mackerel and laid them out to dry on the thatched roof of the cottage and anywhere else where the hens could not get at them. The guts went into the bosh, the big cask from which the two pigs were fed. Everything went into the bosh for the pigs. Old potatoes, sour milk, cabbage stumps, bad apples. The smell was nothing very choice but the pigs showed no objection. And it seemed a pity to waste good mackerel-guts. Those who were hungry were not in the habit of wasting.

Well, the Reverend Price had said they should count their blessings. Those who had gone away to the Welsh valleys to work in the pits had no pig or cow and could grow no potatoes. Certainly they were not there when the mackerel came. A blessing indeed were the dried mackerel, that winter. And God had been very good in making sure there was plenty of salt on board the shipwrecked vessel.

'Well, there 'tis then' said Luther. 'That's what the Reverend Price says, "Take what the good Lord sends."'

Mam Bron said nothing but just went on with her knife, cutting the heads off the mackerel, slitting them open and flicking out the guts. Mam Bron never did say much to anybody. Least of all to Luther.

That year, as it turned out, they were only able to keep half-a-pig because the calf died. Luther always thought it was strange to hear folks say they were killing half-a-pig, until he came to understand that, when they killed their pig, they would have to sell half of it to pay for the food they had bought for it and possibly a few other essentials. Mam Bron always sold one of the two pigs she reared. The other was killed and kept for their own use.

Luther was too hungry to have misgivings, much as he liked to hear the pigs grunt with satisfaction when he leaned over the wall of the cot and scratched their backs with a stick. Funny old things they looked with their heads held up to look with their piggy eyes from under their floppy ears.

He did not like to hear the screaming when they were killed but, after they had been scalded and scraped and cut up, there was good living for a few days. And he enjoyed the social round of giving, when Mam Bron sent him with little parcels of offal and griskin for frying, to those who would return the compliment some other day. He also enjoyed having the bleeze, as they called the pig's bladder, blown up to take it on the sands on his own to use as a football and imagine how he could have played had it not been for his injured foot. He could not play with other boys, but he could play a bit on his own.

That year, however, the calf died. It was one of those

things and, as Absie's father said, 'Where you got livestock you got deadstock.' Somebody else said ''Tis only them as got 'em can lose 'em,' but that thought was of small comfort.

What happened was that Luther found some useful timber on the beach and a piece had been used to repair the calf's cot and the calf had sucked and chewed at the timber as calves will. Then the calf took bad and died. Absie's father looked at it and said it was the timber because it was painted and it was lead paint, probably off a ship, and that was deadly poisonous for a calf.

Mam Bron said they would have to find the money from somewhere to buy another calf so they would only be able to kill half-a-pig that year after all. Then Luther knew what it meant to kill half-a-pig, because he was doing quite good on the sums. It meant being twice as short of bacon as the previous year. Lucky they had the dried mackerel. Perhaps God wasn't such a bad sort after all.

With Seeny down the pit all day, and Mam Bron having little mind to talk, Luther spent part of his time hobbling round the fields and calling at some of the many smallholdings. The Reverend Price said that they were lucky to have a bit of land and a cow or two. Most of them lived much better than the peasantry in the north of the county.

'Did the Reverend Price say that?' said Absie Pugh.

Luther nodded his head, 'If I never move from here alive again.'

'Then by damn they must be havin' it rough. They caught Jimmy Jack last night. Only a couple o'rabbats but it'll be over th'ocean for Van Diemen's Land.'

'Never.'

'Aye 'twill. They won't bother with gaol. Get rid of as many as they can to save the parish. 'Twas after dark see, so there 'tis. An' a've been had afore.'

'But there's no harm in Jimmy Jack' said Luther.

'That haven't got nothin' to do with it. An' it isn't all. They be gwain to take his place off'n an' pull the cottage down.'

'How?'

'Father says 'tis to do with this new law about votin'. Since th'owners no longer needs so many tenants to fix the votin' 'tis cheaper to pull down the cottages an' leave somebody else have the land.'

'Supposin' nobody else won't offer for it.'

'But they will. Th'owld shits.'

''Tis a bad thing. Reverend Price was sayin' last week like it says in Isaiah, ''Woe unto them as joins house to house and lays field to field.'' And what about Jimmy Jack's missus?'

'Don't talk dull, Luther. What do anybody care about her? 'Tisn't Sunday school people thee'rt dealin' with when that owld lot gets their hands on thee.'

It was more than Luther could understand, but he knew the truth of what Absie was saying. They heard so much in Sunday school about love and how to live, yet everywhere you looked it was quite different. There had just been a lot of talk about stopping the slave trade overseas, but nobody did anything to stop little children having to work down the pits with no shoes on their feet. There was something wrong somewhere.

Absie cut in on his thoughts. He said, 'Thee'rt lucky. How can thy gran keep thee home an' not work?'

'How do'st thee always call her my gran?'

'Well she is isn't she?'

'So some reckons but when I asked her she only said don't ask questions.'

'Well as long as she keeps thee home not workin' be glad of it.'

Luther was glad. He had no complaints. Although it was too far to walk to the endowed school he was at last able once again to hobble to Sunday school, and the Reverend Josiah Price now had him out to read in front of the others and was teaching him how to speak properly and how to pronounce certain words and improve his grammar, and shortly, he said, he was going to put him in charge of a small class.

'But I'm not gwain underground' Absie said. 'Father got a job for both of us drivin' stones for the new road they be buildin' through Stepaside an' they reckons as that'll last another couple o' years.'

Absie was always talking of what work he could get with the horses. He was tall and strong now and Luther had a fondness for him more than for any of the others he knew.

But most people were kind to him at the small-holdings where he called in. There was a bond between them all in their poverty. A word here and there sometimes would be let drop and he began to understand about his birth. But he did not know it all.

Since Will had been killed Seeny had taken over his palliasse. She was getting a big girl now, Mam Bron said, and it was better for her to sleep on her own. But sometimes she would creep across quietly to Luther in the darkness and they would cuddle up together for a bit of warmth.

It was on such a night in late summer, when the wind had been blowing hard for some days, that Seeny crept over to Luther and whispered so that Mam Bron below would not hear her.

'A 'ooman at the pit told me today about how thee was't born.'

'How?'

'Thou know'st Mam Bron is'nt thy real mother?'

'So they says.'

'But do'st thee know who is?'

'Who is?'

'Thou wou'sn't say if I tells thee?'

'No, not a mewk to a soul.'

''Tis our sister Meg.'

'That's never right is it?'

'That's what the 'ooman at the pit said. She reckoned as everybody knowed about it at the time.'

Luther went quiet for a while. The wind had died now and was moaning over the cottage roof and in the cliffs. A rat scuttled somewhere in the thatch above them. Suddenly out of the night there came a wild shriek as if from someone pursued by all the fiends of Hell.

'Christ in Heaven!' said Seeny, 'What was that!'

Luther jumped up and clambered down the ladder in his rough shirt and Seeny followed him.

'Mam Bron' he shouted 'What was that?'

He pushed open the door into her room 'What was that scream? What was it?'

'*Duw, duw,* boy. Go back to bed' she said from the darkness.

'But what was it?'

''Tis nothin' to trouble the livin' whatever. 'Tis only the tormented souls of them lost at sea. Go back to bed the pair of you.'

Settled again, they could hear the beating of the waves on the rocks, above the beating of their hearts. Twice again they heard the scream, but each time a little further out to sea. Each time they held to each other more closely. Then everything went quiet and all was silence for a long time.

At last, Luther said, 'Seeny.'

'What?'

''Tis right what people says then? Mam Bron is my gran.'

'She must be.'

Luther began to laugh quietly.

'What ar't thee laughin' about?'

'I've just thought of something. Thee'rt my Aunty.'

'Good God!'

Then Seeny began to laugh as well.

The following morning Luther went up to the fields to pick blackberries. Trying to hide itself in the long grass under the hedge was a bird such as he had never seen before.

Black, or sort of dark brown it was on top, and white underneath. It did not show any sign of having been injured, but it was unable to fly.

Luther picked it up and the bird tried, with its narrow, hooked beak, to peck at him. Yet it was a gentle bird, not as big as a wood-cush, and was soft and downy to the touch. When it fluttered its wings Luther held one out and could see that it was very long.

His first thought was to take it to Mam Bron, but then he thought more carefully and his instinct told him that she would probably wring its neck and put it in the pot. Hungry though they often were it would be a pity for that to happen. Overhead two carren-gulls were circling. Luther had seen what they could do, attacking newborn lambs, or ewes heavy in lamb that were on their backs and were unable to get up. It would be no good leaving the bird where the gulls could attack it. There was only one thing to do and that was to take it to the Reverend Josiah Price. He would know what it was and what to do.

On his way he crossed a small field of oats. It had been cut and bound into sheaves, and Absie's father was building the drying sheaves into large mows of fifty or sixty sheaves to each mow which would stand a long time against the weather before being carted and thrashed out by handflail on the floor of the barn. The stubble mattered little to Luther's bare feet because they were so hard from all the walking on rocks and rough stone roads. It was his lame foot which bothered him and slowed his going. But he pushed on with the bird under his arm.

'What's thee got there, boy?' Absie's father asked.

Luther showed him the bird. 'I don't know Mister Pugh. I found'n up in the field just now.'

Absie's father handled the bird. 'Well look at that' he said. 'A cockly-nave. I haven't saw one of them birds in years.'

'What is it Mister Pugh?'

'Cocklollies the fishermen calls 'em, but we calls 'em cockly-naves. They be main unlucky birds by all account.'

'How?'

'They reckons as they be possessed by the spirits of the sailors as have been drownded and roams the face of the deep in torment. Calls out somethin' terrifyin' with bein' possessed of dead spirits.'

'Is that right Mister Pugh?'

'Aye, 'tis boy. They screams like devils some nights.'

'Is that what we heard last night?'

Luther told him what they had heard.

'I shouldn't wonder, boy. I shouldn't wonder at all. Terrible unlucky they be.'

As Luther hobbled along, his mind kept turning to the night before, and how the screams had come to them from out of the darkness as Seeny told him something of the truth of his parentage. If Meg had been his mother, then who was his father? Nobody had said anything about that. And who was the spirit possessing this bird under his arm?

It was a great relief, on rounding a bend in the road, to see the Reverend Price coming towards him. Dressed in black he was, as usual, in his minister's long coat, but there was nothing sombre about him. Sorrowful sometimes, which he could hardly help being in such poor and hungry times, but he always tried to bring good cheer. And he was interested now, as well as cheerful, as he saw the bird which Luther carried.

'Well! well! A shearwater!' he said, as he took the bird into his hands.

'What did you call it?' Luther asked him. He was already conscious of trying to speak more correctly in front of the minister, remembering all the lessons he had given him.

'A shearwater. And where did you find it?'

'Up in the field, under the hedge. But Absie Pugh's father called it a cockly-nave or cocklolly or something.'

'So the fishermen call them. Round here they call them cockly-naves. Or sometimes they call them cockels after their call which they make at night. Sometimes they seem to scream. A most weird noise.'

'How do they do that then?'

'Why, you mean, Luther. Why. Well, that's interesting. You see how far back its legs are? That's because it is so much an ocean-going bird that the legs are used for driving it forward in the water. But it makes it rather helpless on land so that it can only launch itself off some high point.'

'Then how did it come to be in our field?'

'Blown off course. A young bird by the look of it. Blown off course with all the stormy weather we've been having lately. They breed on the islands off our coast, and when they come back from feeding at sea they call to their mate on the nest in order to know where they are. And because they are so clumsy on land they make sure they only come in by night when the gulls can't see them to kill them. Nature is cruel I'm afraid. Very cruel. But very inventive and a great adjuster.'

'I heard the bird calling last night, Mister Price.'

'And were you frightened?'

'Yes, I was. Terrified. Absie's father said the birds had been possessed by the spirits of sailors as had drowned and it's the spirits calling in torment.'

The minister shook his head. 'Oh, dear, what can you say in the face of such superstitious nonsense!'

He stretched one wing of the bird. 'See the length of it' he said. 'Their flight is marvellous to behold. Sometimes they glide on these long wings and tip from side to side to shear the tops of the waves. That's why they're called shearwaters I suppose.'

All the time he spoke the bird's brown eyes were bright and watchful, and he told Luther much more of how, during the breeding season, the fisher folk round the islands took the birds in nets, as they fluttered down to the sea, to use them for bait in their lobster pots or to eat them themselves. Sometimes, he said, they dried and salted them and then boiled them with cabbage. He had been to the islands as a young man and, as he talked about them, Luther felt again that fierce longing to put to sea. He also realised it was as well he had not shown the bird to Mam Bron.

As though reading his thoughts the minister said, 'And how is your mother keeping?'

'She's middlin' thank you, sir' said Luther. 'But I suppose you know she's not my mother really?'

'Oh, indeed? Then who is your mother?'

'My sister Meg. The one who went away.'

'But Mam Bron has been very good to you.'

'Oh, yes. Very good. But she's not my mother. Did you know that, Mister Price?'

'Well, yes, Luther, I had heard something about it.'

'Then did you happen to hear who my father was?'

'No, I didn't. I don't think anybody knows. And there is always much gossip when these things happen. We must not listen to gossip. ''Where no wood is, there the fire goeth out. So where there is no talebearer, the strife ceaseth.'' Thus saith the Lord. Now do you take this bird and return it to its own surroundings.'

'But how do I do that?'

'Take it to the top of the cliff and throw it into the air. It will take care of itself after that. And attend to your books, Luther. Do not trouble your head with idle talk.'

It was all right for the minister, Luther thought. It was not his mother or his father. But he took the bird to the top of the cliff above Crickdam. He held it in both hands in front of him and threw it as high as he could into the air. There was a fluttering of wings, the bird dropped, found its balance, and then scythed its way downwards towards the water's

edge and, skimming low above the waves, flew out to sea
and away towards the far horizon.

6

Try as he would, it was best part of a year before Luther
could find out any more of the story which he so longed to
learn. And, when the discovery came, it came, as so often
happens in life, by chance.

The new road through Stepaside had opened and the mail
coach now had a straight run through to the great harbour at
Pembroke Dock. It was the coming place they said.

Haymaking on most of the farms had finished and now,
before harvest was ready, on the first Friday after Narberth
horse-fair, it was time for Amroth Big Day. Even Mam Bron
cheered up and looked forward to it, for some of her own
people would come down from up the Welsh. Croggans, the
Amroth people called them.

This year there was more excitement than ever because
Queen Victoria, who was only a girl of eighteen, had just
come to the throne. It was always good to have something to
cheer about, for there was plenty of poverty and misery.
Everybody was still talking about the young queen when it
came time for Big Day.

A fine event it was. From great distances, even beyond
Narberth, the farmers and country people would come. For
some of them, it was the only day's holiday they would have
in the whole year, and they made the best of it. Rising early
to milk and feed their stock, they would set off for Amroth
shortly after daybreak. Every year it was a race to see who
could be first to the seaside and there was a steady stream of
traps and carts and gambos from an early hour. Boiled ham
and beef they would bring, and whole-meal bread and
cheese and butter. They were willing to share, too, and
many a hungry belly was grateful for Big Day.

Then there would be the big wash, for to 'wash in the tide'
was their way of saying to go for a bathe.

Of a winter's night Absie's father would sometimes tell of
the croggan who had come running up the beach one Big
Day shouting 'I've found my waskat. I've found my waskat.'

To his interested listeners he had told excitedly how at the previous year's Big Day he had gone to wash in the tide and, when he came to dress afterwards, could not find his new waistcoat which he had only just bought. All the year it had grieved him, especially as he had to buy a new one.

'This year' he was almost shouting, 'I come down again to wash in the tide. I take off coat. Take off new waskat I did buy in Cloth Hall, Llanboidy. Take off shirt. Then I go to take off vest and, *duw, duw*, there's my waskat that I lost last year under my shirt!'

Luther thought it was not a very likely story, but it was always good for a laugh, for many of them who came for Big Day even spoke a different language. Mam Bron could speak it and talked more on Big Day to her own people than at any time throughout the year. But nobody else he knew could speak the language.

After a good feed there were games on the sand, and it was then that Luther would feel out of things because he could not run about like the others. But he could have as much fun as anybody washing in the tide because he could swim with the next. Then there was another feed and a grand finish with a concert on the green.

Luther was standing with some of the children from Pleasant Valley and Stepaside when Seeny came up behind him and said, 'Here thee ar't at last. I been lookin' for thee everywhere.'

'I thought you was with Absie,'

'I was. But there's somebody here wants to meet thee.'

Standing behind Seeny was a young woman who had a strong resemblance to Seeny. A kind face she had, but her shoes were worn. Her hands, Luther noticed, were rough from hard work.

'Well, look at that' she said. 'Fancy a don't know his own sister.'

'I can guess' said Luther. 'It's Annie,'

'Well, bless my soul. Fancy a knowed.' She bent to kiss him and there were tears in her eyes.

A step or two away from her was a man who looked older than Annie. Luther had seen him before and knew he was the ostler at Rhydlancoed, the big house up in the valley, where Meg had been in service. Not very tall, Tom Jenkins was of wiry build with a cheerful face and a cap pushed well back on his head. When he took his hands out of his pockets they looked strong and capable. Absie had said he was a good man with a horse.

Before anything else could be said, three men who were the worse for drink, swayed past them. One turned and said in a loud voice, 'A don't look much like thee, Tom.'

The other two roared with laughter and one of them said, 'Nor a don't look much like the Squire neither.'

Tom Jenkins went white and clenched his fists. Annie took him by the arm and said, 'Leave 'em be, Tom. The more thee meddles with shit the more it stinks.'

The three went laughing and shouting on their way and the moment passed. But Luther looked at Tom Jenkins with a new awareness.

From stray pieces of conversation here and there Luther was able to piece the news together. Annie and Tom Jenkins were getting married and, instead of re-hiring in the autumn, they were going to America. The parish would give a grant. They wanted to get rid of people. At Narberth a workhouse was to be built. Those who wanted parish relief would have to go there to live and work, and people were terrified at the thought. Stories about these new workhouses were already spreading through the countryside. Luther knew something about them because the Reverend Josiah Price lent him the magazine every month after he had read it, and there was a story about a small orphan boy called Oliver Twist who knew nothing about his parents. Luther had a fellow feeling for him. He had been brought up in a workhouse and was suffering the most cruel hardships. Every month Mr Charles Dickens wrote of another episode in Oliver's dreadful story. Truly the workhouse must be a terrible place.

From his own earliest recollection of older people's talk Luther knew how hard things were for everybody. If a farmer did not pay his man enough, the poor man could go to the parish overseers for relief. So nobody was paid enough, and the parish had to keep finding more money and the farmers were complaining of the rates they had to find for that and for the church and the tithes. And the parish overseers were so worried because so many poor people were asking for relief that eventually there had to be a new law. So those parishes which could not afford to build a workhouse of their own had to form a Union with other parishes, which was why they were going to build a workhouse at Narberth. And everybody knew by now that the guardians of the poor were making life so hard for those who were sent to the workhouses that people would starve rather than be sent there.

Well, Tom Jenkins had been Meg's sweetheart once, but she had gone away to London after Luther was born, and now he was Annie's sweetheart and they were getting married and going to America. Some young couples said it was better to be married and have as many children as they could so that they could have more money from the parish, but Tom said that this new workhouse business would stop all that. Besides, he wanted to get away from all the talk and jibes now that he was marrying Meg's sister. And others were going as well. Boats could take them from the new harbour at Saundersfoot and put them aboard the big ships that crossed the Atlantic to America.

That night Luther had gone to the loft before Seeny came home but, tired though he was, he could not sleep for thinking of all he had heard during the day. Seeny's thoughts were far away at first, and Luther guessed she was thinking of Absie. But he plied her with questions.

It was not long before she showed him a piece of ribbon that Absie had bought for her.

'Do that mean you're his sweetheart?'

'Of course it do.'

Luther felt a pang of jealousy, but he was glad it was Absie. Seeny was fourteen now, so she was old enough to have a sweetheart as long as Mam Bron did not find out. And Seeny said she did not mind much if she did find out.

'Everybody got to have a sweetheart,' she said.

'How about Meg? Is it right she was Tom Jenkins' sweetheart?'

'Of course she was.'

'Then how is Annie his sweetheart now?'

'Because Meg went off to London and left'n.'

'How didn't she marry'n?'

'Annie said a offered to although a knowed a wasn't thy father.'

'Then who was?'

'Annie said she don't know, but the Squire helped Meg and she went to service in a house in London and 'twas the Squire as fixed that.'

'Was the Squire my father then?'

'Annie don't know that neither.'

'But that's what that bloke was shoutin' about today.'

'Thou do'sn't want to take no notice of tacks like that.'

'No, but 'twas funny for a maid to go off and leave a small babbie.'

'What else could she do? She couldn't keep thee.'

'I suppose not' said Luther. Maybe Mam Bron had had a rough time altogether. But he knew it was no good asking her any more questions. Seeny was the only one he really loved. She was the only one he could talk to.

7

It was just after Big Day that Mam Bron surprised Luther by saying he could have a pair of clogs.

Absie was coming to drive balls. This was one of their problems at Crickdam. The ball fire, which burned day and night, was all that enabled their old clom cottage to remain dry. The balls, the size of a lemon and shaped by Mam Bron with her hands, were made from a mixture of culm and slime. The culm was small coal, not much bigger than dust and of an inferior quality, but it was all the poorer people could afford. In some places it was mixed with clay, but at Crickdam, as in the Amroth and Wisemansbridge area generally, the cottagers dug slime from the beach. The slime came from the decaying tree trunks of the submerged forest. Hundreds of years previously, nobody seemed to know how long, the whole of the bay, so it was said, had been a huge forest, but the sea had come in and flooded it. Sometimes, when the cottagers were digging slime, they would come across the antlers of animals that had once roamed the area long, long ago. The forms of the trees could still be seen in patches here and there along the beach where they had fallen, and even huge tree stumps still stuck out of the sand in places.

It must have been a great forest at one time because, far out in the bay, a big ship had gone down and, at low water, her masts could still be seen quite clearly. That's how shallow the water was.

Once, the Reverend Josiah Price had shown him a very old book by a man called Leland who had written, 'I roade through a wood, not veri greate, but yet the fairest that I remember that I saw in Pembrokeshire.' Some people thought that was the sunken forest, but the minister said it referred to the ancient forest of Coedrath, and the submerged forest was in fact more than four thousand years old because flints and one thing and another had been discovered.

Well, however old the trees were, they made good slime now for mixing with the culm to make balls, and it was time to fill the ball-pit ready for winter.

First of all the culm was spread out on the ground and then the slime was mixed with it by hammering with a maddock, adding water all the time and walking the horse over it. After that it was turned by shovel and, when it was thoroughly mixed, it was stacked somewhere convenient for the winter. Then it would be fetched, a bucketful at a time, to be wetted again and made up by hand into balls which were put carefully on the fire. Once the heat began getting through the wet balls it only needed a hole or two to be made with the poker for the flames to rise and burn merrily. So it was possible at least to come down to the cheer of a fire in the morning.

Throughout the day the iron kettle stood on the hob of the fire ready to be hooked on to the chain above the flame. In the afternoon the big iron pot hung over the fire, boiling the hay-tea, which was made by filling the pot with the best hay and adding water. Mixed with skim milk it was useful for feeding the calf, which Luther usually did. He had an idea he would not mind being a farmer. He had already resigned himself to the fact that he would never go to sea.

Driving the culm and digging the slime and mixing the balls had, for a long time, been Will's job. When he was killed, Absie's father had helped out and, soon afterwards, Absie took over from him. Now, Luther felt he could surely do something to help and, so determined was he, Mam Bron said he had better have a pair of clogs.

He had never worn anything on his feet and he was now twelve years old. The clogs felt clumsy at first and the pain in his twisted foot was unbearable, so Mam Bron cut a piece out of the side of the clog and that eased it considerably. Come the winter and he knew he would be glad of them because in the wet or frosty weather the pain had always been a burden to him.

So, as well as reading, and being taught and encouraged by the Reverend Josiah Price, he was making himself useful. It was still only early autumn and he had spent the afternoon on the beach gathering suitable pieces of timber for the baking oven in the corner alongside the open fireplace.

On a Friday, if Mam Bron had any flour, even if it was only barley flour, she baked. The sticks were lit and the iron door was closed. When the oven was hot enough, the ash was raked out and the bread put in. Baking done, the sticks were put in the oven to dry so that they would burn readily next time the oven was needed.

That afternoon he had collected a good pile and stacked them above high-water mark. The sun had set and the lamp at the lighthouse over on Caldey had already been lit. But, although the daylight was fading, Luther could see a long way over the beach and was surprised to see a number of people walking from the direction of Wisemansbridge. Where one rock ran out further than others across the beach the people turned in towards the cliff and crossed over the wide, flat stones, and then turned out again to continue walking on the sand.

About twenty or more of them there were and, as they came nearer, Luther could see that they were walking in two columns and that the men in front were carrying a coffin on their shoulders.

He had never seen a funeral go along the beach before and had not heard of anyone dying. He was even more puzzled when he saw Absie and his father and some of Absie's brothers and sisters walking behind the coffin. Luther wondered whether he should speak to them or not, but they made no attempt to speak themselves and the procession passed on towards Amroth.

When Luther reached the cottage he said to Mam Bron, 'Who's dead then, Mam?'

She turned her wrinkled face towards him. 'What d'you mean then, who's dead?'

'That funeral.'

'What funeral you talkin' about then?'

'Just now. On the beach. Didn't you see 'em passin'?'

Mam Bron put down the pot she was holding.

'What is this nonsense whatever?'

''Tisn't nonsense. They just went by carryin' a coffin.'

'Who was it then?'

'I don't know who was carryin' the coffin, but Absie was walkin' behind it with his father and some of his brothers and sisters.'

Mam Bron went outside and looked along the beach towards Amroth into the gathering darkness, but no sign was there of a living soul.

'All right, my fine boy, which way did they walk?'

'Along the sands from Wisemansbridge.'

'So they will leave footmarks isn't it?'

'Not on the stones.'

'Which stones whatever?'

'Where they crossed by the rock.'

'Why do they cross by the rock then is it when the tide is out?'

'I don't know Mam. But that's what they did.'

The night was getting chilly. Mam Bron went indoors for her shawl to put round her thin shoulders. 'All right, my fine boy' she said, 'we'll go see their footmarks in the sand then isn't it.'

They went down the track together past the blacksmith shop to the beach. A flock of curlew flew wide out towards the water's edge, their haunting call clear and carrying far upon the stillness of this strange twilight.

Plain to be seen were the footmarks left by Luther's clogs.
But no other footmarks could they find. They went towards
the rock that ran out across the beach. There were no
footmarks anywhere near it.

'Dreamin' perhaps is it?' Mam Bron said. 'You wouldn't
make up lies whatever.'

'But Mam! I tell you! I saw them!'

'All right, *bach*. Perhaps it's the second sight it is. We'll
wait.'

She was still speaking in her sing-song Welsh voice and was
kinder than Luther could have expected.

She dragged her way back up the track to make some sort
of supper by the time Seeny came home from the pit, and
Luther followed her in silence.

                              8

It was not yet Christmas when the weather suddenly turned
cold and Absie's mother took ill and died. Then it started to
snow and, for a night and a day, and then for a second night,
it kept falling in great ghostly drifting flakes.

On the second morning the snow was sticking right down
to high-water mark where the little waves were lapping
gently, soft and silent. The cliffs were overhung with a great
undulating white mantle. A few wild geese and wild-duck
mingled with the gulls and oyster-catchers on the shore.

As the tide began to ebb Luther saw about twenty people
come walking along the beach from Wisemansbridge. The
sun was shining and the light was good. He called Mam Bron
and they watched in the snow as the people came to where
the rock ran out further along the beach. The tide was
lapping round it, so they turned in towards the cliff and
crossed over the wide, flat stones and then turned out again
to walk on the sand.

As they came nearer, the two columns, with the men in
front carrying a coffin, could be clearly distinguished. Absie
was walking behind the coffin with his father and some of his
brothers and sisters. They passed beneath Crickdam and
went on along the beach towards Amroth.

The explanation was simple. All along Pleasant Valley, and

up towards Summerhill, the snowdrifts were heavy and the roads were impassable. From Amroth up to the church the road had been sheltered by the overhanging trees and was fairly clear. So they walked along the beach with the coffin to Amroth, for the cliff road, too, was impassable.

That night it began to rain and, in the equable climate, the snows melted and were gone.

'It is the second sight whatever,' said Mam Bron. 'But be careful when it do snow. The snow will be a big time for you isn't it.'

The Reverend Josiah Price, when Luther told him, was more circumspect. 'Don't let your young mind dwell on it too much,' he said. 'The mind is a marvellous creation which we cannot begin to understand. There have always been happenings such as this. Fetch-funerals, some people call them. Have you never wondered how the primitive tribes of darkest Africa can send messages hundreds of miles purely by thought transference? You are never likely to understand these things. So apply yourself to your books, my boy. Stick to your books.'

9

It was always books with the Reverend Josiah Price, and the time came for Luther when the learning proved to have been worthwhile.

That time was one which neither he nor many others were likely to forget. It was the year in which he had his fourteenth birthday, if anyone had taken notice of such things.

For a couple of years the weather had been poor and the harvest worse. In January of that year a mob of country people had attempted to burn down the new workhouse at Narberth before it had even been completed, and soldiers had been sent there. Then, in May, farmers up in the Welsh had gone by night to a place called Efailwen and smashed a toll-gate which had just been erected to catch lime-carters who were evading the tolls.

It was all to do with the upkeep of the roads which were in a bad state. Those who owned the gates were supposed to maintain the roads but they, in turn, complained that the lime-carts did so much damage to the roads that they could not afford to repair them.

The lime season was just starting and the farmers needed the lime for their land. A cart-load of lime would cost about half-a-crown at the kiln but, before a farmer reached home with it, he would have to pay another five shillings or more in bills. To the men who were poor, and whose families were living on barley bread and whey, it was more than they could stand. Luther knew what hard times some of them were having, and when it came to Amroth Big Day there was further evidence of it. Not nearly so many people came and there was little of the boiled ham or beef to be seen. These things had to be sold to pay the rent and they were selling for precious little.

All through the summer it rained. Hay was cut and, where it lay sodden in the field, it went black and the new grass grew up through it. The corn was battered by the wind and, with the rain heavy upon it, the grain shed to the ground and began sprouting again. Everywhere throughout the countryside it was a picture of desolation. If people were hungry before, they were starving now. Corn was dear and there was little money to buy any.

These were all reasons which made it a time for so many to remember. But for Luther there was one extra reason.

In the autumn the Reverend Josiah Price told him he could find him a job.

'A job!' said Luther uncomprehendingly.

'Yes, my boy. A job.'

'But what job could I do, Mister Price?'

The minister smiled at him, 'You've kept at your books very well. You can read and write. You have a very fair hand indeed. You are quick at figures. So what sort of job could you do, Luther?'

Luther understood the minister that far, but he was still puzzled.

'Where could there be such a job, Mister Price?'

'You know of Mister Toby Protheroe, I suppose? The agent to Rhydlancoed estate who lives at Deerfield?'

'I've seen him go by on his horse.'

A very important man was Mr Protheroe. Few cottagers or farmers failed to doff the cap or pull the forelock when he rode past on his grey horse, and their children knew to do the same. He had no wife, but more than a few children in the neighbourhood had his sandy hair and blue eyes. That was no secret.

'I cannot say that I approve of his way of life,' said the minister, 'but the Lord said, ''Judge not, that ye be not judged.'' And he does have room for a young clerk in his office there.'

'In the office at Deerfield?'

'Yes. Have you ever been there?'

'Oh no, sir. Never inside the wall. But I peeped down the drive once when the big gates were open.'

'Well, how d'you feel about that?'

''Twould be a fair step for me to walk every day with my foot like it is.'

'I'd thought of that. Mister Protheroe would be willing for you to live in his household with the servants.'

Luther's thoughts were in a turmoil. Mam Bron. Clothes. Seeny. Not seeing Seeny every day. The thought of his ragged clothes.

The Reverend Price seemed to have read his thoughts. 'Oh yes,' he said. 'It's a big step to go out into the world. But it's an opportunity. And the apostle Paul said, ''As we have therefore opportunity, let us do good unto all men.'' Apply yourself to your work and you could one day find yourself in a position to help those who are sorely in need of it. I am sure your mother will settle something about clothes for you. And be ready to present yourself at Deerfield at ten o'clock next Saturday morning. Mister Protheroe will see you then and decide whether to engage you.'

Mam Bron was thoughtful when Luther gave her his news and all day she spoke little, but the following morning she said, 'Was anything said about money whatever?'

'No Mam. Nothing at all. Only to be there on Saturday morning at ten o'clock.'

'No mention of money, funny isn't it.'

There seemed to be something on her mind, but Luther knew better than to ask.

Later in the day she said, 'Well, it's to be a suit of clothes and proper boots now then isn't it. Better ask Jethro Pugh if we will go with him in his trap on Thursday is it.'

A new world seemed to be opening to Luther. A suit of clothes could only mean Narberth. And Mam Bron had said Thursday, which meant market day. In all his fourteen years he had never been as far as Narberth.

Mam Bron said nothing more on the subject of the suit but, when Absie's father came in the trap on Thursday morning, she was wearing her only decent coat and she had wrapped the roll of material which came from the wreck when Will was killed. Luther had forgotten it.

'What's thee got there Mam Bron?'

'Do not a body need somethin' to trade with whatever?'

It was as much satisfaction as she would give him.

Luther could have wished for a happier time to be making his first visit to the market town but, everywhere as they went, there was a brooding air of desolation over the countryside. The trees, after such a wet summer, were a riot of colour, of russets of many hues, to unfold a rolling panorama of rare beauty. But, although it had not rained all night and was not raining now, the land looked dreary and sodden and was like a sponge that could absorb no more. Hardly anywhere was there a haystack or a mow of corn to be seen. Here and there a few hungry-looking cattle stood desultorily near hedges or in muddy gateways. Where there were people to be seen they looked as dejected as their stock.

As if all this were not enough, as they came down the long hill and saw the town on the opposite bank facing them, the dreaded workhouse also came into view. A great grey building it was, cold and forbidding. Luther was glad when they had passed it.

Butter was taken to Narberth that day and was almost given away by tearful women. Horses and cattle were driven there and then driven home again because they could not even be given away to those who had nothing on which to feed them. Mam Bron, with her roll of material, fared rather better.

In a shop at the top of the town it was, where she and the man spoke all in Welsh. Not a word of it did Luther understand, but he was well satisfied with the result, because they came out with a good suit, three shirts and some collars and enough money on top of that to go down the street and buy a pair of boots. Good boots they were, too. Not heavy, but strong-looking and shining. And even after that Mam Bron had a few shillings left over.

So full of the new suit was Luther's mind, and so pre-occupied was he with thoughts of what lay ahead, that he paid little heed to anything else all day.

The next day Luther had worn his boots for short periods to get used to them, and in the evening when Seeny came home she teased him.

She did not come to him in the night now, and was more careful about dressing and undressing in front of him. He understood why, for he was only two years younger.

That night when he said his prayers he was tempted to pray for a fine day. It would be terrible if he had to walk all the way to Deerfield in the rain or with an old sack over his new suit. But he resisted the temptation because the Reverend Josiah Price had always said it was wrong to pray for such things as fine weather because somewhere some-body would be needing rain. Luther thought it unlikely in such a year as they had just experienced, but that's what the minister always said. Not pray for wants he said. Pray for our needs. There was a world of difference. And God knew our needs, so it was much better to leave it to Him. 'Thy will be done.'

Still, he thought a great deal about a fine day and some said that was much the same as praying.

Sleep lay but lightly on him all night and, long before first light, he was down and poking the ball fire into a flame before Mam Bron and Seeny showed any signs of stirring.

Outside, a fine drizzle was falling, and, hopefully, he recalled the old saying, 'Rain before seven, shine before 'leven.'

In the event the sun did not shine but, as dawn broke, the drizzle went out with the tide and it turned out to be a good day. Usually for breakfast it would be budram or hasty pudding, according to whether they had oats or barley. For days the meal would be soaked in water, then strained, and the gruel boiled to thicken it before adding a bit of sugar or treacle. This morning, however, Mam Bron did him a breakfast of bacon and the luxury of an egg, and well before nine o'clock he was on his way.

As he limped along through Pleasant Valley he was glad there was nobody much about to see him in his new suit. A funny feeling it was. Those few who did see him expressed surprise, but not unkindly. Word had soon spread that he was to work for the agent. Whatever others may think, it was something which, for his own part, he could not grasp.

He had already been lucky in not having to go to the pit. Originally it had been because of his injury but, when he began to get about somehow, Mam Bron had never suggested he ought to go. She had been good like that. On the other hand, he had, for quite some time, been in the habit of milking Fronwen. He had fed the pigs and the calf, worked in the garden, and contrived to do many odd jobs about the place. If he had not earned anything he had helped. In some ways he had helped to save, and the saying was that a penny saved was a penny gained. Living on top of the beach he had often been the first to spot the best timber coming in and stake his claim, and it was bartered for something that was needed, even if it was only goodwill which would stand in good stead for another day. His life had not been entirely useless.

Seeny, though, had been a slave. It grieved him to think of her underground, down on all fours in the darkness, with a chain and girdle round her waist like an animal, pulling skips of coal. Still, she was growing bigger and stronger now and next week she was due to start on the underground beam and druke, the windlass for winding up the coal and lowering and raising the other women and children on the log. Dangerous it was for the one sitting on the log, so they needed someone strong and reliable on the druke of the cutwyn winding them up and down. So, from next week, Seeny would be taking home four shillings.

With these thoughts chasing each other through his mind he was not so conscious of his new boots pinching, especially his injured foot, and he came at last to Stepaside to gaze up at the great new bridge, designed by the famous Mr. Telford, and over which passed the marvellous new road built by Macadam all the way from Red Roses through Kilgetty and on to Pembroke Dock. Although he had not expected him, he was not surprised to see the Reverend Josiah Price standing in the road under the bridge and smiling a greeting.

The minister ran an appraising eye over him and then, with a chuckle, doffed his hat and said, 'Servant, sir.'

Luther had to laugh. He was even more pleased when he learned that the minister would accompany him as far as Deerfield. A worrying thought it had been, picturing himself walking up the hill to the big house and coming face to face with Mr. Tobias Protheroe. But on that score he need not have worried. Toby Protheroe was, on the face of it, a cheerful soul.

The lawn and garden and flowerbeds, Luther noticed as they rounded the bend in the drive to approach the house, were tidy and well cared for. The door and windows of the house had been newly painted and there was an air of affluence such as never in all his life had he known before. His heart was pounding as the Reverend Josiah Price walked boldly up to the front door and pulled on the iron handle of the bell.

The door was opened to them by a servant girl who curtsied to the minister and looked speculatively at Luther. In the hall beyond the open door Luther saw handsome, polished furniture, and rugs upon the floor. A fox's mask looked down at them and there were prints of galloping horses upon the walls. He paid little heed to what was said but, as in a dream, followed the minister as the girl led them to a solid oak door with a brass knob. She tapped deferentially, a man's voice called out 'Come in' and she said, 'Mister Price, sir.'

Mr Toby Protheroe was standing on a rug warming his back in front of a log fire. A man of medium height, he was broad of shoulder and his suit was of tweed. About forty, Luther judged him to be. His sandy hair had not yet begun to thin. His eyes were bright blue, a little bit watery from the whisky maybe, and his complexion was ruddy.

Stretched out on the rug, enjoying the fire, was an aged black retriever which Luther had often seen trotting along by the big grey horse when Protheroe was riding. A lovely red and white spaniel, brown-eyed and friendly, a young looking dog, stood up and wagged his tail in greeting.

'Nice to see you, Price' Protheroe said. 'Sit down and have a warm.'

'No thank you, Mister Protheroe. I just came to bring young Luther.'

'So this is young Knox is it?'

Luther thought that perhaps something was expected of him so he said, 'Yes, sir.'

'How old are you, boy?'

'Fourteen, sir.'

'Sure you won't have a glass of something?' he said with a smile, turning to the minister.

With as big a smile Josiah Price said, 'No thank you. "They that be drunken are drunken in the night. But let us who are of the day, be sober."'

Toby Protheroe laughed heartily. 'Then come back some evening and get smashed. "Eat drink and be merry, for tomorrow we shall die."'

'Ah, no, Mister Protheroe. That is the point. Tomorrow we do not die. "Look not upon the wine when it is red. At the last it biteth like a serpent, and stingeth like an adder." And with that sobering thought I'll leave you.'

Protheroe put his hand on the minister's shoulder as he went with him to the front door and Luther heard him say, 'Well, thank you for bringing the boy.'

There was a carpet on the floor and the furniture was something which Luther had never imagined could exist. There were shelves against the walls with many books upon them. There was a rack with guns. It was all more than his mind could absorb. The spaniel came up to him and rubbed against his leg, mouth open and looking up at Luther foolishly. There had never been enough food to keep a dog at Crickdam. The best they had ever managed was a cat to keep the rats down or, at any rate, from over-running them. Luther put his hand on the dog's head and he wagged his tail happily.

'You like dogs?' said Protheroe as he came back into the room.

'I don't know much about them, sir.'

'That's Gipsy. Welsh springer. As good a dog as any man ever had. That's a good dog on the rug, too. Good dog for a bone. Sitter-and-pointer. Sits on his arse and points at the fire. But when he was younger he looked promising. I think he must have been influenced by all this talk of unions that's going on. Damned people ought to be shot or transported or something. You're chapel I believe?'

'Yes, sir.'

'Well, it can't be helped, I suppose. I don't care for these damned dissenters. But that man Price of yours isn't a bad sort. More sensible than most of them. And he says you can write well and you're quick at figures. Is that right?'

'I'll do my best, sir.'

'Right then. Sit at this table and copy out this letter. When you've done that, add up these figures.'

Luther sat down and Protheroe pushed some paper across the big table to him. There was a pen there and a bottle of ink. Luther's hand was shaking and his mouth was dry.

Protheroe walked out of the room and Luther knew a great sense of relief.

He had finished the writing and added up the figures, and was checking over them when Protheroe returned.

'Finished already?' he said.

'Yes, sir.'

Protheroe picked up the writing and looked at it critically. Then he ran his eye down the row of figures.

'Very good,' he said. 'Very good.'

He went to the sideboard, poured some whisky from a cut-glass decanter into a heavy crystal glass and added a drop of water. Then he took up his favourite position in front of the fire.

'Did the minister tell you what your duties would be?'

'Not exactly, sir. He just said clerking.'

'H'm. Well, I'm not sure myself. But he came to me and said you could be useful. Perhaps you can. Keeping accounts and copying out letters. Times are bad at the moment, but there's a great future for this area. There's renewed talk of building a tramline from here right down to Saundersfoot harbour. When that happens there's the possibility of doing something to make use of all the iron ore in the area. And there's talk of a brickworks as well. Whatever happens we want to be in on it. You can start next week.'

'Yes, sir. Thank you, sir. What day, sir?'

'Eh? What day? Oh yes. Monday. No, not Monday, I'll be out hunting. And we're shooting on Tuesday. Start Wednesday. Better come Tuesday evening, then you'll be here ready. Eight pounds a year and if you do all right I'll put you up to ten next year.'

Protheroe turned to tug on the tassel of a gilt rope hanging to the side of the mantelpiece and Luther heard a bell clang somewhere in the far recesses of the house. 'Missus Powell will look after you. Be clean in your habits and don't give her any trouble.'

'No, sir.'

Luther still had not come out of his dream when he found himself following the servant girl down a dark passage. Very smart she was in her white apron and cap. The hem of her skirts swished over her shiny black shoes as she walked, but she spoke no word to Luther. Very proud she was, as well as smart. Perhaps it was because she was so pretty. Still, she was no prettier than Seeny, and Seeny wasn't proud. But, of course, Seeny had nothing about which to be proud anyway, working down a pit with ragged old clothes and rough hands.

The maid opened the door into the large kitchen and said, 'The young gentleman has arrived. Mister Knox.'

Luther sensed the mockery in her tone and felt sure he was not going to like her. He suddenly felt self-conscious in his new suit.

A round-faced, well-fed looking woman, with grey hair which was piled high, skewered by a great bone hairpin and held up by a large slide, was standing by the table smiling. Luther knew this must be Mrs. Powell.

'Oh, come thee in honey' she said. 'Don't thee take no notice of th'Empress Josephine.'

The servant girl blushed and Luther could see she was tamping. Brown hair she had and it was done in ringlets. Her round face was pretty and she had striking, dark blue eyes. The cheeky way she looked at Mrs. Powell was quite different from the way she had curtsied at the door to the Reverend Josiah Price. But Mrs Powell didn't seem to mind.

'And how is poor owld Missus Knox gettin' on down there?'

'She's very well, thank you.'

'Good. Now when will't thee be comin' to live with us?'

'Next week, if that's all right. Tuesday Mister Protheroe said, so I can start on Wednesay.'

The back door opened and a younger girl came in lugging a can of water almost as big as herself. She was dressed in rough clothes, her hands were red and her dark hair was swept up under a mob-cap. Very old-fashioned she looked, and her brown eyes had something of the devotion of Mr. Protheroe's spaniel. Luther immediately felt sorry for her and knew he was going to like her.

'Don't stand there gawpin' like that Bessie,' said the Empress Josephine. 'Make a curtsy to the young gentleman.'

Bessie, however, ignored her and went on with her work.

Mrs Powell said 'Sit thee down then honey an' have a bite of somethin' afore settin' off back.' And the next thing Luther knew there was a pie on the table and a big currant cake and a big brown pot of tea.

He tried hard not to eat as if he had never seen food in his life before, and he knew the Empress Josephine was watching him. But it was difficult. Although he had had bacon and an egg this morning, that seemed a long time ago and he had walked a long way. Nor could he help thinking of the interminable diet of budram and boiled potatoes and butter milk, with occasionally some bacon, and hardly ever butcher's meat. Laura Powell had no inhibitions. She had lost her husband, never had any children and was glad to have somebody to mother. She plied him with as much as he could eat. The Empress Josephine ate stylishly whilst Bessie spoke no word. Luther thought Bessie was about his own age.

10

On his way home Luther tried to sort out all the thoughts
that were in his head, and the one that was uppermost was
the thought of eight pounds a year. He had never had a
penny in all his life. He had seen a gold sovereign, but to
have one for himself, to save or spend, was beyond his
comprehension. Then he did some mental arithmetic and
realised he would be earning nearly as much as Seeny. And
he knew from what he had heard that it was about as much
as a good farmworker could expect to earn living-in.

It was the living-in side of it which struck him almost as
much as the thought of the money. The pie and the cake
were still quite clear in his mind and it seemed a shame to
think of anything else. Such thoughts went a long way
towards strengthening his resolve to face up to the world.

The next day, being Sunday, Seeny did not have to go to
the pit and they walked on the beach together. As if to mock
at the weeks and months of terrible weather which had
brought such desolation, and would mean so much hardship
in the winter months ahead, today was a fox and the sun
shone in a cloudless sky. It was a better day than they had
known all through the summer.

Luther wondered how long it would be before he would
walk again on this beach which he loved. Perhaps he had
taken it all too much for granted until now, but he knew he
was going to miss it. He loved the smell of the seaweed and
the bleep-bleep of the sea-pyats. Lovely birds they were.
There would be no more looking for wreck, and the sight of
the big ships in the bay would now be only from the far
distance up at Deerfield on top of the hill, looking out over
Pleasant Valley to the sea. He wondered how much he would
be able to see.

The cottage at Crickdam was nothing much, but it was
better than some, and it was much less crowded than many,
with only the three of them there. He knew poorer cottages
with a dozen people in them, if you included children as
people. And it was his home. Now, he thought, he would
not have a real home, but he would have something to eat.
Maybe Seeny would not miss him greatly because she had
Absie. Mam Bron would miss not having to feed him, but he

thought she would hardly miss him for any other reason.
Not for love. Not in the way he would miss Seeny.

'What are't thee thinkin' about?' she said.

'Oh, nothing much. Only about going off to work and if I'll
do all right.'

'Of course thou'llt do all right. Thee'rt good at sums an'
writin'. An' thou'llt have plenty to yeat.'

'That's something isn't it?'

'Of course. A lot is gwain to be main hungry round here
this winter.'

'And I'll have the gracious company of the Empress
Josephine.'

Seeny stopped walking and looked at him. 'Who do'st thee
call that then?'

'She's the oldest servant girl there.'

Seeny's eyes crinkled into a smile in a way she had and she
burst out laughing.

'Where did'st thee hear her called that?'

'That's what Missus Powell called her.'

'Well, good God! It's right then!'

'What's right?'

Seeny laughed again. 'Ho!ho!ho! There's a joke if thee
likes. Bella Wills. Stuck-up bit of goods that one. Th'
Empress Josephine. I likes that. Wait till I tells 'em at the pit.
Do'st thee know how they calls her that?'

'No, I don't know. How should I know? I've never seen her
before.'

Seeny put her arm in Luther's. 'There's th' innocent boy
an' I loves'n. But thee'llt come wiser very soon now. Thou
know'st who th' Empress Josephine was? And they calls
Toby Protheroe Napolean at the pit very often because a's
such a hard man. Bloody slave driver! Most of 'em got a
cottage an' a burgage, but let 'em fall short with the rent and
then. . .look up!'

'He was very nice to me.'

'Hisht thee. Don't talk. Talk to the ones as lives in th'
estate cottages. But tell me some more about th' Empress
Josephine.'

There was nothing much to tell, but Seeny was still
delighted to know what Laura Powell had called her. 'If

Laura Powell called her that,' she said, ''tis bound to be right.'

'What's right, Seeny?'

'Good God, boy, a's tailin' her. A couple o' girls at the pit reckons as Napolean Protheroe is havin' it with her as often as a wants it. But nobody knows for sure, of course. Well, by damn. Th' Empress Josephine. That's a licker.'

Suddenly Seeny looked more serious.

'She's a fool, mind. The law have always been that if a maid claims on a bloke a got to prove a isn't the father. Very often 'tis difficult for a bloke an' 'tis cheaper to pay up an' not bother. By all account Protheroe have had a couple swore onto'n as a was never the father of, as well as them as was his. But under this new law they're talkin' about, they reckons 'tis gwain to be a lot different, an' now if a maid haves a babbie she got to prove a bloke is the father. So if Protheroe fills her I'll bet thee one thing. A'll never pay. It'll be th' workhouse for Bella if that happen.'

'I wonder who Meg claimed on for me then.'

'That's somethin' I don't suppose we'll ever know. An' don't thee worrit thy head about it neither.'

11

Luther settled in to his new surroundings better than he had dared to hope. His attic bedroom was clean and warm. The truckle-bed with its horse-hair mattress was luxury beyond words, and there was meat at least once a day and sometimes twice. To crown all, his window looked out over the valley to the sea and the ships out in the bay. It meant much to him to keep this link with the only life he had known up to that time.

Almost as big a luxury as the bed was the lavatory. He had heard about it but found it hard to believe. At Crickdam they had a bucket and lime, and the place was draughty in winter and smelly in summer with flies everywhere. Much of the time he would go off into the bushes somewhere along the cliff or even, if there was nobody about, down onto the beach.

Here, at Deerfield, there was a flush toilet. Nobody he

knew had ever seen one, but the talk was that some of the gentry were having them installed. There was one upstairs in the house which the servants did not use, but there was one for them across the yard from the back door. You gave a couple of good heaves on a pump by the side and everything disappeared.

Up on the roof there was a tank which collected rain water and there was also a big pump outside. When the rain water had run out Affie Day would have a spell on the pump every morning, before starting in the garden, to keep the tank full. The well never ran dry.

Whatever work Protheroe asked of Luther he attended to diligently. He copied letters and reports and kept account of money in the cash tin in the big desk. Eventually, Protheroe would tell him to write a letter and, having told him roughly what he wanted to say, allow him to compose it himself, and Protheroe always said he had done it very well.

The office was at the back of the house and, more and more, Luther came to regard it as his home. Eventually, when Protheroe was out hunting, Gipsy took to coming in and sitting by his chair. It was wonderful to have such companionship.

Bessie, too, began to be friendly with him. She would make sure his cup was filled at meal times and she offered to wash his clothes and sew buttons on.

It was of an evening that first winter that she said to him as the two of them sat by the big kitchen range, when Mrs. Powell was in her little sitting room, and Bella had gone to her bedroom with a headache, 'Would'st thee be willin' to learn me to read an' write?'

'If you like.'

'Is it very hard?'

'Not really. How much did you learn in school?'

'I never been to school.'

'Not even Sunday school?'

'No, never.'

'How was that then? Did you work down the pit?'

'No, I was a orphan on the parish an' I was put out to a farm when I was eight.'

'How long have you been here?'

'Only a year. The people where I was went to America. They was turned out an' I had nowhere to go an' Missus Powell heard about me an' got me here.'

Luther looked at her work-worn hands and thought of Seeny.

'Have you thought of working down the pit?'

'I wouldn't have nowhere to live.'

'You'd get more money. How much do you get here?'

'I gets two pounds a year.'

'That isn't bad, living in.'

'It's a lot more than I got on the farm, sleepin' in the tallet over the stable an' all we had to yeat most of the time was washporo. I knows 'tis a wicked thing to say, but I don't care if I never tastes budram nor hasty puddin' again as long as I lives.'

'You would if you were hungry again. But I was only joking about the pit. That's terrible to have to work down there. Yes, I'll teach you to read and write.'

She had her first lesson the following evening and Mrs. Powell was delighted, whilst Bella poked fun as usual.

On the rare occasions when Bessie bothered to take any notice it was only to say, 'Sticks an' stones may break my bones, but names will never hurt me. But when I'm dead an' in my grave you'll think of what you called me.'

'Don't take any notice,' said Luther, 'but remind me to tell you sometime what my sister Annie said when I met her at Amroth Big Day.'

'Oh, indeed Mister Knox! And why can't the young gentleman tell us now?' Bella asked. 'Do tell us what your sister said.'

'I couldn't my lady. It isn't fit for the ears of an Empress.' Bella coloured.

'Go on, Luther, tell us,' Mrs Powell said.

'I'd rather not, Missus Powell.'

'How not?'

''Tis vulgar.'

'Never mind about that.'

'Well, what she said was the more you meddle with shit the more it stinks.'

Mrs Powell turned away to the big kitchen range to hide

her amusement. There was no love lost between her and Bella.

'Fine talk coming from a Sunday School gentleman,' said Bella. Luther stuck a thumb in each of his ears, twiddled his fingers and gave her a sweet smile, but said nothing, and she went back to her sewing.

Before the spring Bessie asked Mrs Powell if she could go to Sunday school, too, and Mrs. Powell was very much in favour. Her writing was already quite good and from then on her reading improved as well. Luther was pleased with her success and felt it reflected some credit on him. For the first time in his life he also felt he had really achieved something.

Before the summer Bella was being sick in the mornings.

12

'Now then, Knox,' said Protheroe one morning in the autumn, 'we have a problem on our hands and I want you to talk to some of your chapel friends. Can you do that?'

'Yes, sir. I can talk to anybody.'

'But do you know what to talk about?'

'No, sir.'

'Then I must tell you. Certain people are starting to interfere, Knox. And they can be a nuisance. The latest information is that there is an inspector coming round to talk to the children working in the pits. It would be a pity if they gave the impression they were not happy at their work.'

'How can I help, sir?'

'Tell them, Knox. I believe Mister Isaac Dicks, foreman, is a bit severe when he uses the stick on them.'

'Yes, sir. He thrashed young Billy Johns last week for falling asleep when minding the doors.'

'Did he indeed? And how old is Billy Johns?'

'He's only six, sir.'

'Only six. A man who can thrash a child of that age for sleeping must be a hard man.'

'Yes, sir.'

'Yes, indeed, Knox. And I'm sure if Isaac Dicks, foreman, heard it back that they complained about his treatment of them he would be very hard on them indeed. What they must remember, Knox, is that these inspectors will not be there to stop Isaac Dicks, foreman, from wielding his stick on those who say things it would not be wise to say.'

Luther said nothing.

'You must understand, Knox, that it would be foolish if somebody stopped the children from working underground. Not only is it necessary to the better working of the pits, but the children's parents need the money. So, pass the word along, Knox. No word to the inspector about the beatings. For the children's own good, Knox. For their own good.'

Luther felt his temper rising, but he knew there was nothing he could do.

'Is there any other story of hardship that you've heard?'

'Yes, sir.'

'Indeed, Knox, and what is that?'

'Well, sir, Billy Johns suffers with chilblains. There was early frost and some snow last week, and walking to the pit in his bare feet Billy Johns went into Jethro Pugh's field where the cows were and rose the cows up and stood in the warm patches where they'd been lying down.'

'A sad story, Knox. I think it would give the inspector the wrong idea to hear that sort of thing. Pass the word along. I'm sure I can rely on you. Have you heard anything else?'

'No, sir.' Luther was saying no more.

'Very good, Knox. Now let me see. I think I promised you a rise of two sovereigns didn't I?'

'Yes, sir.'

'Well, you've done very well, and I hope with this problem facing us you'll do even better, so we'll increase it by three sovereigns, instead of two.'

Luther said, 'Thank you very much, sir,' and hoped nobody would ever call him Judas.

That evening there was a prayer meeting and afterwards Luther talked to Absie Pugh and Seeny. But there was more to talk about than the possibility of a visit from the inspector. Seeny wanted to know about Bella.

'I haven't seen her for two days,' said Luther.

'No, an' I can tell thee why, poor soul as she is.'

'It's the baby is it?'

'Of course 'tis. An' she've had to make for the workhouse. What have Missus Powell said?'

'Not a word to me. But I know she's upset.'

'That dam owld Protheroe. Won't pay nothin' an' Bella's gwain be left fend for herself.'

'There's gwain t' be trouble,' said Absie.

'What sort of trouble?'

'I heard Father say as they be gwain to give'n the wooden horse.'

'The *ceffyl pren* Mam Bron always called it.'

'Same thing' said Absie.

'They wouldn't dare.'

'Don't thee believe it, boy. A've turned a couple out o' their places an' some is only waitin' for the chance.'

'For God's sake don't get mixed up in it, Absie.'

'We can't help it, Luther. 'Twould be more than our lives would be worth not to turn out with the rest.'

'Who else is in it?'

'Jack Bowen for one.'

'But Jack's a quiet sort.'

'I knows that, but Sarah's the one. Jack got to do what she says. An' Protheroe treated her family bad.'

'But it's asking for trouble.'

'Look, boy, there's plenty as have had enough trouble without askin' for it. An' they'll use Bella Wills as a good excuse. They be only lookin' for the chance. So stay thee in thy bed for the next couple o' nights.'

Luther heard later that some of the hotheads had not been willing to wait, and perhaps it was just as well for Protheroe. In the event, the business was, as Absie said, a flat shot.

In the early hours they came with their public ridicule of the adulterer. There was much noise and banging of tins and, in the light of their torches, Luther could see them from his attic window as they milled around on the lawn. Their faces were blacked and, on a wooden pole, they had an effigy of Toby Protheroe.

Luther pulled on his trousers. On the landing he met Mrs. Powell, her hair tied with ribbon and a candle in her hand.

'What is it?' she said.

'I don't know, Missus Powell.'

'Come thee down with me then,' she said 'an' let's wake the master.'

There was no need for that, for Protheroe was already on the landing in a nightshirt and dressing-gown. He was carrying a gun.

'Put that light out, Missus Powell' was all he said.

Luther saw his silhouette as he crept low and gently raised the landing window. Then he pushed the barrel of the gun over the sill and fired. There was a deafening roar from the gun in the confined space and then a smell of gunpowder. Luther hoped the distance would be too great for anyone to be hurt by the shot, but it might frighten them. Such was the rabble's lack of organisation it was all that was needed.

13

To all Protheroe's questions the following morning Luther answered that he knew nothing.

'Then we must buy our information, Knox. We must offer rewards. The people say they are poor, so let them earn some money by telling us what we want to know. Get some notices out offering twenty pounds to anyone who can furnish information leading to the apprehension of any of these villains.'

Luther saw to the posting of the notices. Two nights later a letter was pushed under the front door and Luther found it. If Protheroe had been home Luther would have given it to him straightaway. But he was not at home.

For a long time Luther deliberated as he turned the letter over and over in his hands. When he found that it opened easily he followed his instinct and, for the rest of his life, was glad that he had done so, for the letter, a slightly illiterate effort, stated that the writer and his son knew all about the affair of the wooden horse that night at Deerfield if Mr. Protheroe would care to call to discuss it.

The letter was signed by Jethro Pugh. And Luther knew that neither Absie nor his father nor any of their family could write, because he did any writing they ever needed. So, somebody was no friend of the Pughs, and the letter went into the fire. He was quite sure he would remember the writing if another such letter came, but he kept the envelope just in case.

No other letter did come, however, and, when he saw Absie it was clear he knew nothing.

'I shan't say nothin' to Father' he said.

'Better not,' Luther said. 'It wouldn't do for it to get out that I opened and burnt a letter. But I'll keep my eyes and ears open.'

'Seeny was wonderin' ha'st thee heard any more about Bella?'

'Not a word. Nobody dare mention it.'

'All the talk is she've chucked the babbie down a' owld mine shaft.'

'Never!'

'Well, what else can she do an' where can she go?'

'God help her.'

'An' Protheroe goes away smilin'. Not that the lot as turned out that night is worrit about her, but 'tis hard on her all the same. 'Twas just a good excuse.'

'It's hard on everybody without that happening to them.'

'I suppose thou hasn't heard no more about the new tram line?'

'No, nothing lately. Only talk.'

''Twould be a wonderful thing if 'twould come. There'd be a lot o' drivin'.'

'I supppose so. But keep out of things like that wooden horse the other night.'

'To hell with 'em. Th' whole dam lot of 'em.'

Luther realised the extent of the bitterness when Chistmas came and, unlike the year before, there was no visit from the cutty wren. The custom was for a little wren to be carried round in a box and there were pies and drinks and good cheer. But nothing this year. Nobody came to Deerfield.

The new girl, Mary Ann, who replaced Bella, was very quiet and not much to look at. Word came eventually that Bella was working down the pit and then in the spring that she had gone off with a collier for America.

'Poor sowl,' said Mrs. Powell. ''Twas a bad end for her to come to.'

'Perhaps things will quieten down a bit now,' Luther said.

'An' maybe not, honey. There's a lot o' bad feelin' everywhere.'

It was about that time that the Reverend Josiah Price came to see Protheroe who, as it happened, was out shooting pigeons. Mary Ann answered the door and brought him in to the office where Luther was writing. Bella would never have done a thing like that.

'Well, my goodness, Mister Knox,' he jested, 'I hope I do not disturb you, and how comfortable I find you. What time will Mister Protheroe be back?'

'Hardly till after dark, Mister Price.'

'Well, never mind. It's nice to see you, and how are you doing?'

'Very well, thank you.'

'Maybe it's better for me to talk to you.' He lowered his voice a little. 'And how do you get on with Mister Protheroe these days?'

'Very well. I do my work and he has always seemed satisfied.'

'I'm sure he has.' He smiled conspiratorially. 'What about that foolish wooden horse business?'

'He was very annoyed about that.'

'But he has no knowledge as to who was responsible?'

'Not that he ever told me. Do you know who the ringleaders were, Mister Price?'

'The daffodils are a fine sight this year don't you think?'

Luther laughed. 'Perhaps it's as well for me not to know.'

'As well indeed, Luther. How right you are and growing in wisdom every day. ''He that keepeth his mouth keepeth his life'' saith the Lord, ''but he that openeth wide his lips shall have destruction.'' It is always fortunate to be able to answer honestly ''I don't know.'' And even if you do happen to know it's still not a bad answer.'

'But that isn't what you want to see Mister Protheroe for is it?'

'Oh no. Indeed no. I was just wondering about his temper these days. I want to ask a favour of him.'

'He thinks well of you, sir,' Luther said warmly.

'Well, that's kind of him. Kind indeed. But does he think well of my flock?'

'Not all of them I'm afraid. Those damned dissenters he calls them.'

Josiah Price laughed. 'Yes, well, the Word is the same for all of us. And the Word is, "Ask, and it shall be given you." So let us see. The time has come, Luther, when we must build a proper chapel. We have struggled in our poor building long enough. And I wanted to ask Mister Protheroe if the Squire might be willing to look favourably on a request for the little field where it stands.'

'The Squire is home at the moment.'

'So I understand. Will you tell Mister Protheroe of my visit?'

'Of course I will.'

'He might even be more favourably disposed if the request comes from you. I thought I heard some shots up in the wood when I came along and hoped I might find you on your own. Yes, I'm sure you'll make out a good case for us.'

Josiah Price was no fool, Luther thought after he had gone. And no man could have a better friend.

Protheroe, as it turned out, was in his usual good humour the following day when Luther told him of the minister's visit.

'They want to build a bigger chapel do they? Want a bigger place to have their damned meetings I suppose and stir up more trouble?'

'I don't think so, sir.'

'What makes you think that, Knox? Why so sure?'

'I asked the Reverend Price and he said he knew nothing.'

'Quoted the scriptures, I suppose?'

'Proverbs, sir.'

'What did he say?'

'"When wisdom entereth into thine heart, and knowledge is pleasant unto thy soul, discretion shall preserve thee, understanding shall keep thee."'

'Sounds like a lot of damned dissenters' nonsense to me. What's it supposed to mean, d'you know?'

'He didn't say, sir, but I was thinking afterwards that perhaps with the Government inspector coming round it would be a good thing for it to be known that land had been given for a new chapel.'

'H'm. Appeasement I suppose. All right. I'm going over to Rhydlancoed tomorrow. I'll see what the Squire has to say about it.'

'Thank you, sir.'

It was some small consolation to Luther for the price he was having to pay to his own conscience for having been coerced into making children not tell too much of the truth to the inspector. Protheroe would pay for that one day.

14

The home farm at Deerfield was let out, but Luther saw something of what was happening there, for they supplied the big house with milk and butter, and with fodder for Protheroe's horse.

Ben Humphrey was the farmer, and although he was not chapel he lent a horse and cart when he could for driving stones and sand for the new building. Mostly voluntary labour it was, although the money had to be found for the slates and timber. One cottager carried a stone on his shoulder each day. It was only one stone a day but, as Josiah Price said, it showed the spirit of help. The Hebrew word Ebenezer meant the stone of help and that was why the Israelites called the place Ebenezer when they raised a stone where they overcame the Philistines. And so the new chapel would be called Ebenezer.

Apart from all that, Dick Thomas worked for Ben Humphrey and was taking quite a bit of interest in Bessie. So, if Ben Humphrey was willing to lend the horse and cart, there was no problem to get Dick to do the carting because Bessie was strong chapel now. Church, Dick was. Outside pillar.

Throughout the summer the work on the chapel went on and the inspector, Mr Robert Franks, visited the pits. Mr Singleton, who was a steward underground, mentioned that the work in the pits was of a laborious kind but that the hours were generally short, probably not more than six hours a day or maybe eight. The children, not being such good scholars as the steward, were unable to work out how many hours a day they worked. They simply said that they started at six in the morning and worked until eight or nine at night and never finished before seven, Saturdays included.

Nor, without having been asked, did the children speak of their struggle to clean themselves when they returned, long after darkness had fallen on the cold winter nights, to the miserable hovels they called home. It was no easy matter to find enough warm water for all of them to have some sort of wash, stripped down in front of such fire as there may have been. Seeny would have accounted herself fortunate, no doubt, because she was the only one at Crickdam who went through this nightly performance. Luther had taken it all for granted at the time, but now, accustomed as he had become to the comfort of living at Deerfield, he saw that earlier miserable existence in a new light. And Seeny was still having to live like that. A pity the children could not have spoken about that.

Will Absalom, who was thirteen and old enough to know better, said to the inspector, 'The men goes away when they likes, for they works by the job. But we got to work whether we likes it or not, or else we gets the strap and they gives us plenty of it sometimes.' But he only said the men in general and not Isaac Dicks, foreman, in particular, so maybe that was not too bad. It could only be hoped that Mr Franks would understand the many problems and make allowances for children's fanciful stories.

In the autumn Mary Ann left. Bessie said to Luther, 'She've been gave a good character by Mister Protheroe and she's gwain to Rhydlancoed.'

'Who's coming here?'

'A maid by the name o' Rita Hier.'

'Is she? How's that then?'

'Her father spoke to Mister Protheroe about her. Don't say nothin' after me, but Missus Powell isn't very pleased about it.'

'How's that?'

'Her an' Hiers isn't very greet. Haven't spoke to each other for a long time. She don't like the family.'

'She's not the only one.'

'Do'st thee know 'em?'

'Yes I do. They've got the next little place to the Pughs. Misery Hill.'

'What about this Rita?'

'Smart piece, but they're all as sly as foxes and as cunning as a cartload of monkeys.'

Rita had not worked in gentleman's service before, but she had all the airs and graces and, in her new uniform, she was even smarter than Luther remembered her. She was a year or two older than he was, with copper-coloured hair, and would have been even better looking if her mouth had not been rather thin and hard.

Luther thought he would not willingly fall foul of her temper, but, to his surprise, and unlike Bella, she treated him with the same measure of respect as Mary Ann had always shown.

Throughout the winter Absie's talk varied between rumours of the possibility of the new tramway and stories of the hardships of farmers and cottagers. There was much unrest and bad feeling, and it was not far beneath the surface. The only thing that kept some of the colliers at home was the fact that they had a field or two and could keep a cow and a pig and grow their own potatoes. Up in the valleys of Glamorgan they could earn more money but had none of these advantages. And up there the miners were in the hands of the truck shops, owned by the colliery bosses, where they had to spend their money and be charged more than they could have bought the same things for elsewhere. Wherever you went, times were bad.

Up at Deerfield, Luther was cushioned from much of it. And all the time Rita was becoming more friendly.

The days were already lengthening in early February when one evening they were in the kitchen together. Mrs. Powell was in her sitting room, and work finished, Bessie was out with Dick.

Withoug any warning Rita came and sat on Luther's knee. She put her arm round his shoulder and smiled down at him.

'How do'sn't thee kiss me then?' she said.

Luther's heart was pounding and his face was burning.

'Thee'rt a real snib,' she said.

'No I'm not.'

'How do'sn't thee kiss me then?'

Luther pulled her head down gently towards him. Her mouth was on his and he felt the softness of her young body pressing against him.

'Not so bad,' she said, getting up and smoothing down her skirt. 'A bit o' practice is all thee'rt wantin'.'

'Have you had much practice?'

'A bit.'

'When can I start practising?'

'Don't sound so anxious.'

'Don't tease. When?'

Rita lowered her voice. 'Some nights after we've gone to bed Bessie creep down the stairs and slip out through the kitchen window to go out in the hay with Dick.'

'No she doesn't does she?'

'Of course she do. But don't say nothin' about that.'

'Of course I won't.'

'So next time she do that come thee into my bed.'

'Suppose Missus Powell should hear?'

'Hisht thee. Don't talk so dull. Thou ca'st hear her snorin' to shake the slates off the roof.'

'I can't hear her from my room.'

'That's better still then. So I'll come up to thy room instead.'

'Will you indeed? Promise?'

'Wait an' see. I'll learn thee a thing or two.'

15

A couple of years previously there had been much talk of the Penny Post being introduced and now all sorts of people who were able to write were sending letters and cards and pamphlets and messages. Every day the postman called at Deerfield.

Luther was not again alone with Rita after that evening in the kitchen. Each night he listened for any sound of Bessie creeping downstairs, but nothing happened.

Three days later it was Valentine's day and the postman brought Luther a Valentine card. Flowers and pretty stitches were all over it. There was no signature. The only writing on it was 'To my darling snib.'

Luther would have been delighted if it had not been for the writing. To make sure, he took the envelope up to his room. And the writing on the envelope was the same exactly as on the one which was supposed to have come from Jethro Pugh about the wooden horse.

Why, he wondered, should Rita be making a play for him? And why should she have written in Jethro Pugh's name in an attempt to get him into serious trouble with Protheroe? The Jezebel!

Luther compared the writing on the two evelopes again and pondered.

Jezebel? Why had he suddenly called her Jezebel? And who was Jezebel anyway?

A likely enough story was the story of Jezebel, wife of Ahab, who wanted Naboth's vineyard. And Jezebel had been willing to manufacture all sorts of lies and go to any lengths to ensure that Ahab got hold of Naboth's vineyard.

Jethro Pugh did not have a vineyard. But Jethro Pugh had a good field. His meadow, Shearing Hayes, was as good a field as any in the parish for early grass in spring or a crop of hay in summer. Bellman's Close was a nice little holding altogether, and Jethro Pugh worked hard. His best field, he knew better than anybody, was Shearing Hayes. And Shearing Hayes adjoined Misery Hill which would make something like a decent holding if Shearing Hayes were to be put with it. Luther seemed to recall having heard at one time that Cutty Hier had had a few to drink on one occasion and confided that he would like to have Shearing Hayes. And, if Jezebel was Ahab's wife, Rita was Cutty's daughter. A crafty bunch.

It could well explain the letter written in Jethro Pugh's name. But why was Rita now making a play for him? He was a couple of years younger than she was. Girls, apart from Seeny, had not interested him until now, and it was gratifying to think that a girl like Rita could see something in him, in spite of his lame foot.

She had always treated him with some respect. So had Mary Ann before her. Perhaps that was because he worked directly for Protheroe. All sorts of little responsibilities were being left to him. Without realising it himself, perhaps he was being thought of as a person with some influence on the Estate.

He had been much excited at the prospect of Rita coming to his bedroom. Now, he was not so sure.

Ah well, the old people had a saying, 'Brighter birds have sung at the top of the tree in the morning, but the cat have had 'em afore night.'

He had no intention of letting Rita get her claws into him. He would watch his step with that young lady.

It was the following evening before they were alone together and Luther said, 'That was a nice card you sent me.'

Rita smiled and said, 'What card?'

'That Valentine card.'

'I never sent thee no card.'

'Who sent it then?'

'I don't know nothin' about no card.'

'Oh, no? And I don't suppose you know anything about a letter that was supposed to have come from Jethro Pugh at the time of the bother with the wooden horse up here.'

Rita went red and looked flustered. 'I don't know nothin' about no letter from Jethro Pugh.'

'But I do.'

'How do'st thee mean?'

'You shouldn't have sent that letter. Mister Protheroe never saw it. And I've kept it. It'll be bad for you if that story comes out.'

Rita was deep. She had enough sense not to say any more.

Luther wondered how long it would be before Protheroe would get her into bed and what might happen after that. He would have to keep his wits about him.

Not surprisingly, his relationship with Rita became a little more distant.

16

The summer which followed was momentous. The weather was good and the crops bountiful. Unfortunately, the depression deepened and the farmers' prices stayed at rock bottom.

The good weather, however, enabled work to go well on the chapel and, in the autumn, it was packed for the opening service.

A fine building it was. Polished timbers were on the walls, and lamps swung out from the pulpit over the communion table. And there, sitting in the front, was Mister Toby Protheroe, who had been asked out of deference to come along and to read the lesson because the Squire had been so helpful and such a benefactor.

When it came time for Protheroe to read, Luther was greatly surprised to hear him read, from the First Book of Kings, the story of Ahab wanting the vineyard of Naboth the Jezreelite, and of how Jezebel, with her wickedness and cunning, had contrived the matter.

The Reverend Josiah Price's sermon was as good as anything Luther had ever heard from him. He took for his text the passage from the reading where Naboth had answered, 'The Lord forbid it me, that I should give the inheritance of my fathers unto thee.'

'What Naboth was really concerned about,' he said, 'was the lowering of standards. This belief in materialism rather than the principle of sharing. His were a people who for generations had lived in the deserts where each gave according to his ability and where each received according to his needs. The thought of acquiring anything to someone else's detriment went against all the traditions of his race. This commercialism was new to him. The vineyard was the inheritance which had come to him from his forefathers. But there was more to it than that. High moral standards had been handed down as well.'

There was much more in a similar vein. Luther thought deeply on it afterwards and saw much of the story in a new light.

Far more important to Luther that night, however, was when the minister said 'And now, my friends, the time has come for me to tell you that I shall be leaving you. The deaconite know of my decision. I have received a call and after much time in prayer I have decided to accept. I see a new challenge where I am going. A part of me and much of my heart will always be with you at Ebenezer, but I thank

God I leave you in good heart spiritually. There is nothing lacking spiritually in a fellowship who can strive to build a chapel like this in times such as these.'

There was a tremor in his voice, then he said, 'Like Naboth of old, stay true to your traditions, to the traditions of your fathers and of all those who have gone before you. And I pray God you will give the same wonderful support to whoever will be called to serve you here in my place.'

Whoever followed him, Luther thought, could never be the friend to him that Josiah Price had been.

17

The traditions of their forefathers were soon to change, however, because Mr Robert Franks had reported to some purpose and an act was passed by Parliament to prevent women and children being used as beasts of burden.

'It won't be much help to Seeny,' Luther said to Absie, 'but it's nice to know it'll help somebody.'

'Who's it gwain help?'

'Those little ones who won't be driven to work underground before they even know what time of day it is.'

'Look, boy. Don't talk so dull. People is so poor they got to have the money the childern can bring home.'

''Tis an evil thing, Absie. Even some of the gentry have spoken against it.'

'Only some of 'em. An' do'st thee know how that is? 'Tis the ones as can't get servant maids because they can earn a couple o' bob more underground.'

'Well, I suppose money counts.'

'It's what makes the donkey gallop as the old 'ooman said. An' with the new tramline startin' from Saundersfoot there'll be more drivin' than we'll know what to do with.'

'Protheroe reckons there'll be big developments all up the valley here.'

'The more the better as far as I'm concerned.'

'Don't be too sure, Absie. He talks a lot about iron, but everywhere else the iron trade's in decline. You heard the Reverend Josiah Price's sermon about Naboth and his vineyard. Never forget the land.'

'The land my arse. We can't sell our butter nor our couple
o' lambs, an' we're faced with keepin' a couple o' steers right
through the winter again because we can't give 'em away.
An' we couldn't put any lime on this year because we
couldn't pay the price to go through the toll gates.'

It was the toll gates which finally sparked off the trouble
that October before the harvest had been completed. The
rumblings had been there for a long time, with the feeling
building up year by year. What with tithes and rates, and the
threat of the workhouse, and poverty, and poor people
being sent to the hulks for transportation, it was bound to
come sooner or later. And it came with a mob turning out in
St Clears.

'You see Knox,' said Protheroe, 'this fine new road we
have through Stepaside has cost a great deal of money and
some of those damned people passing through Saint Clears
can travel a great distance on it without paying a penny
piece. Not at all the thing, Knox. Not at all.'

'But they reckon now, sir, that with two gates in Saint
Clears some people will have to pay twice within a mile.'

'That's their bad luck, Knox. Their bad luck.'

Only days later the word came that the mob had turned
out by night and, in the name of Rebecca, had smashed the
new gate and the old one.

'What's this business about Rebecca then Knox?'
Protheroe asked.

'It's from Genesis, sir. "And they blessed Rebekah, and
said unto her, Thou art our sister, be thou the mother of
thousands and millions, and let thy seed possess the gate of
those which hate them".'

'More of this damned dissenter nonsense I suppose?'

'I don't know, sir. They reckon that Carmarthenshire
people always have to make a bigger song and dance than
anybody else, but I think the feeling is very strong all the
same.'

'I hear this new man of yours at Ebenezer is pretty hot on
the condemnation. What's his name again?'

'The Reverend Erasmus Adams, sir. He's already been
nicknamed Suffering.'

'Suffering? Why Suffering?'

'Well, sir, his motto, they say, is all for misery and misery for all. He has condemned all ball games and sports and anything that is not for the glory of the Lord.'

'Oh, very good, Knox. Would you happen to know whether he's been saved?'

'Yes indeed, sir. And everything else that the Reverend Josiah Price wasn't. Hell fire is a certainty for most of us round here.'

'God almighty! What are we coming to?'

18

The following summer the trouble came nearer home. Gates were being smashed, toll houses demolished and ricks set on fire all over the place. Ricks belonging to the gentry, not the small farmers. Then a toll gate at Narberth was smashed.

'D'you know anything about it, Knox?' Protheroe asked.

'Nothing at all, sir.'

'That's unusual for you.'

'Not really, sir. I only know what others tell me.'

'And what have you been told, Knox?'

'My friend, Absie Pugh, said he was up at Ludchurch for lime last week and there were farmers there from above Narberth complaining bitterly about the tolls they were having to pay.'

'Absie Pugh? Is that Jethro Pugh's son?'

'Yes, sir.'

'From Bellman's Close?'

'That's right, sir.'

'They have a field called Shearing Hayes.'

'Yes, sir.'

'A good field they tell me.'

'Yes, sir. The best field in the parish by all account.'

'Good. I'm glad to hear that. I'm going to put it with Misery Hill.'

Luther was taken aback.

'You seem surprised, Knox.'

'Yes, sir. But it's not my business.'

'Let me tell you something, Knox. That Pugh family. Those friends of yours. D'you know something? They were the ones behind that damned nonsense coming here in the night kicking up hell's delight.'

'Who told you that, sir?'

'Who told me? Never you mind who told me. I'm telling you now.'

There was an old Pembrokeshire saying, 'Never let 'em say your mother bred a jibber.' There was another saying, 'In for a penny, in for a pound.' Absie was his friend who, one day, might marry Seeny. And Luther loved Seeny.

'I know who told you, sir. It was Rita.'

'What d'you mean?'

'Rita Hier. Her father has always wanted Shearing Hayes.'

'No doubt he can do with it.'

'Remember that lesson you read, when we had the first service in our new chapel, sir?'

'Lesson? Your chapel? Of course I don't remember.'

'It was about Ahab wanting Naboth's vineyard and how Jezebel told lies to bring it about.'

'What lies you talking about now, Knox?'

Luther took a deep breath.

'Rita says that she asked you about the field when she went to your bed. But her father says that if you put her in the same condition that you put Bella Wills they won't stop at marching round the lawn with your effigy.'

Protheroe went white.

'Is this right, Knox?'

'I'm only telling you what I've heard, sir.'

Luther just hoped that the Reverend Josiah Price would have agreed with him that sometimes lies could be told in a good cause.

At any rate, Shearing Hayes stayed with Bellman's Close.

19

On the fourth Sunday in Lent, Luther went home to see Mam Bron. *Dydd Sul y Meirion* she had always called this special day when servants, where it was possible, went home to see their parents and took some present, especially for their mothers. Sometimes, the present would be something nice to eat, and this year Luther had bought a fine piece of topside of beef. He thought this would be more than normally acceptable because he had just heard that his two brothers had suddenly turned up at Crickdam after years away in the valleys.

Ben Humphrey had lent him the little phaeton and the pony so that he could carry his present. It was the first time he had gone back to Crickdam other than on foot and it was a good feeling to be trotting along Pleasant Valley in the spring sunshine.

Along the road, Jack Bowen hailed him.

'You be gwain in main style today, Luther.'

'I'm carrying a bit of something to Mam Bron, so I couldn't walk.'

'She'll be glad of it I don't doubt. They tells me the two boys is home.'

'So I've heard.'

'Tis hard times on us all.'

On the small side, Jack was an inoffensive sort and his face showed all the sympathy he felt.

Hearing voices, his wife, Sarah, came to the gate. As tall as Jack, she was dark and not bad-looking. They had both always been kind to Luther when he was younger. Since he had been at Deerfield he had not seen so much of them. He knew Sarah's sentiments towards Protheroe and he could hardly blame her. He had given her people a rough time, but she and Jack were not tenants of the Estate.

'Gaw, boy,' she said, 'they've turned thee out smart this mornin'. Have Protheroe treated thee that well?'

'No, no, Sarah. It's borrowed plumes this morning. Ben Humphrey's.'

'I thought 'twas funny if Protheroe done it.'

'He's not bad to me.'

'Well I reckons a's a bad bugger. An' you'll find it if it ever suit his book.'

Luther had no illusions on that score, but he had more sense then to voice them abroad.

'Have there been any news up there about Lan'shippin'?' Sarah asked.

'No more than came out at the inquest.'

'Forty souls perished an' all through tacks like Protheroe!'

'How d'you make that out?'

'That Hugh Owen's every bit as bad as Protheroe and' they reckons they're big friends. So Sufferin' Adams says any road.'

'He comes up to shoot sometimes,' Luther said. 'But don't take too much notice of Suffering.'

'He complains because they're still workin' th' childern underground.'

'Everybody knows that, but that's the way the parents want it. They want the money. There was only one under age at Landshipping though.'

The area was still preoccupied with talk of the disaster at Landshipping where the Garden Pit had flooded a few weeks previously and forty men and boys had been drowned.

'Aye,' Sarah said, 'an' not one of 'em should ha' been there. They warned what was gwain happen, but they was drove in there. What did Hugh Owen care? Only a couple o' year ago a towld th' inspector as there was no need to stop young childern workin' underground as they was cheaper than bigger childern. What do the likes o' that care what happen? Him or Protheroe. There be nothin' to choose in addle eggs.'

Luther remembered only too well how Protheroe had coerced him into persuading the children who were working in the pit not to say too much to the inspector.

'No wonder folks is smashin' gates an' burnin' ricks. An' now some of 'em from up Merthyr way is comin' back 'twill be worse than ever.'

'How many are hiding down here from Merthyr?'

'Well, there's thy two brothers to start with.'

'Are they hiding?'

'Good God, boy! They haven't come back for a health cure nor look for work. They knows there's no work round here.'

Later in the day, when Luther talked to Seeny, he could not help but smile at the thought of his conversation with Sarah.

Mam Bron was pleased with the beef even if she showed little sign of being pleased to see Luther. And his two brothers were interested in him. They both had Will's fair hair and blue eyes but more of Seeny's gentleness than Will's hardness. And they both looked ill.

Although they seemed pleased to see him, however, neither of them had much to say. Patrick, named after his father, spoke hardly at all. What little conversation there was, came from George, who was younger and less withdrawn. It was walking with Seeny on the beach that Luther heard their story.

It was good to be on the beach with Seeny again and to feel the freshnes of spring with its quickening of life. Everywhere the primroses were in bloom and there were daffodils along the hedgerows. One field was a carpet of the lovely little local daffodils which the Reverend Josiah Price had once told him were not to be found anywhere else in the country. From the cliffs above came the mating call of the gulls. As soon as the weather turned a bit warmer they would be starting to lay.

He was taller than Seeny now, and with his better clothes, and the self-confidence he had gained, he felt older and protective towards her. He was nineteen and, as Seeny said, looking quite the gentleman.

'That's one reaon Pat and George won't say much to thee,' she said. 'They thinks thee'rt a bit of a toff. And they wouldn't want nothin' to get back to Protheroe.'

'I wouldn't say anything to anybody.'

'Oh, I knows that. But they don't. And poor Pat is beyond carin', God help'n.'

Luther could see her distress and held her hand.

'What's the trouble, Seeny?'

'God love'n. Last year. His wife and three childern all died with the fever. An' to think we never knowed nothin' about it.'

'Oh, dear God! And what's he doing now?'

'Him an' George got involved with the riots up in Merthyr. Well nigh everybody did as far as I can gather. So they thought 'twas best to make back here. But there's sowldiers and police from London all over the shop.'

'They're not after Pat and George are they?'

'I d'n know. On the way down here they fell in with a couple o' roughs with Welsh names. A John Jones was one an' some Dai Davies was th' other. But I d'n' know what their Welsh names was.'

'It wasn't Shoni Sgubor Fawr was it?'

'That's it. Do'st thee know about'n then?'

'And the other was Dai Cantwr I suppose?'

'Do'st thee know about 'em?'

'You should hear Toby Protheroe.'

'Thee'rt makin' it sound bad.'

'If they're in with that pair they're in trouble.'

'What they reckons was that they was afeart not to go with the rest. Not say nothin' mind but what's worryin' 'em more than about theirselves is the one who's hidin' with Jack an' Sarah.'

'Who's that then?'

'I d'n know. But a's in a real caffle. An' 'twas Sufferin' Adams persuaded Sarah to take'n in for a spell an' keep'n hid.'

'What's Suffering got to do with it?'

'Chapel. This Dai Cantwr bloke as you calls'n was a bit of a preacher at one time. An' a minister Sufferin' knows is in with 'em an' 'twas he sent this bloke to Sufferin'.'

'Sarah's a fool to get herself mixed up in these things.'

'But you got to help if people's in trouble.'

'Not this sort of trouble. Shooting off guns in the night and terrorising innocent people and setting fire to people's ricks just because some ruffian has a personal grudge against them.'

'Who's side you on?'

'Seeny, I know who's side I'm on, and so do you. But some of the crowd going about now are thieves and cut-throats.'

'What about Pat and George?'

'Just caught up in it I expect, like a good many more.'

'What's to become of 'em?'

'There's no work round here for them, and we both know that.'

'They was wantin' to get to Canada.'

'That costs money.'

'An' they haven't got none.'

'So I'll have to give it to them.'

Luther had said it without thinking.

Seeny looked at him. 'Say that again,' she said.

Luther smiled. It would dig deep into his savings but he could just about do it. And what else was money for?

'How much'll it cost?' Seeny asked

'If we can get them up to Liverpool they can go steerage for about five pounds each. I'll find out what boats are going up that way from Saundersfoot. Come to that, a couple of boats have started to go out foreign with coal from Saundersfoot. They might even be able to work their passage. But they'll need to shut up about it and not have a big send-off for everybody to know.'

He had little doubt about their discretion. Nor could he help smiling to himself at the thought of Sarah holding forth on the subject whilst all the time she was hiding somebody herself. And, by the sound of it, somebody in far more trouble than Pat or George.

'Ha'st thou saved that much money?'

'I've been saving ever since I started with Protheroe.'

'But it's a lot to give away.'

'Well, if you like, they can wait till they're caught and maybe go to Van Diemen's land for nothing.'

'Don't talk like that,' Seeny said and put her hands over her face.

'It's right enough isn't it?'

'I know. But they're not thy real brothers.'

'Maybe not. But they're your brothers.' Then he smiled and said, 'And you're my aunty.'

Seeny put her arms round his neck and kissed him and, not for the first time he felt a thrill which made him feel guilty, because he knew it was not the sort of feeling a brother should have for his sister.

20

For all his apparent concern for the poor in his willingness to become involved with some of the roughs who were now terrorising the countryside in other parts, Erasmus Adams had no tolerance for their simple amusements. Apart from the demon drink, and dancing, he turned his criticism that year to the Lammas houses.

'It's sinful my friends. It is sinful. And where there is sin
there will be eternal damnation.'

It was one of the disappointments in Luther's life that he
had never known the fun of the Lammas houses. When he
was younger his lame foot militated against his going. When
he was older and working for Protheroe he was outside the
circle of those who took part. But he knew all about them
and what fun they were and some of what went on besides.

Years ago the custom had been on August 1st, which was
Lammas day, to build the house with branches and fern
during the day ready for the party in the evening. By the
main pole in the centre there would be stones to form a
fireplace where the kettle could be boiled. There were apple
pies, because they were celebrating the ripening of the apple
crop. There was butter and cheese, and farmers nearby
would send milk and cream. At sunset, when the party was
over, they would set fire to the hut to light them on their way
home.

Eventually, the custom was to build the hut on the first
Saturday after Lammas day and then the younger
generation would continue with their revelries right through
the night and the occasion became one for them only. The
boys would build the Lammas house and the girls prepare
the feast. Then the boys from Amroth and Stepaside started
raiding each other's Lammas houses and trying to set fire to
them and the criticisms began. It was fertile ground for
Erasmus Adams to plough, and his denouncement was
strong. Rita Hier did nothing to help the cause by becoming
pregnant and, by all account, it had happened on Lammas
night. At least it was nothing to do with Protheroe.

Suffering was leaning over the pulpit as he deliverd his
harangue. His hair was straggly and his eyes in his pudgy
face were blue and watery. The corners of his mouth turned
down and he was the epitome of misery. Kill-joy was in every
word he uttered.

It was perhaps just as well that it was not a Sunday service
but a mid-week prayer meeting, for somebody had been
sufficiently foolish as to persuade Billy Drips to go. Billy was
eighteen and loved the fun of the Lammas house. But Billy
had also had a drop to drink before going to the meeting and

was feeling truculent. He was upstairs in the little gallery with some of his mates around him.

'It's here in the book,' Suffering was shouting as he thumped the big Bible. 'It's in the book. "The wages of sin is death".'

'An' the wages down the pit is bloody awful,' said Billy in a voice which was by no means inaudible. Most of those in the gallery heard it anyway. A couple of girls burst out laughing and tried desperately to stop giggling. Billy was encouraged.

There were some disapproving glances and some shush shushing, but those in Billy's proximity were clearly being treated to further extempore comment. As Suffering ranted on they held their heads down and their shoulders shook.

'My friends,' he said. 'Are we to stand by and see the traditions of our forefathers defiled and besmirched? Are we to stand by and see our young people taking this road to perdition and damnation? What is your answer going to be?'

Some orators would have said it was not entirely wise to ask a question with somebody like Billy Drips in the gathering. Especially with Billy in the mood he was in that evening. For Billy decided to answer the question.

Billy stood up and, in a voice which carried far beyond the confines of the little gallery into every corner of the chapel, said, 'Balls.' Then he marched noisily downstairs and departed from the outraged gathering.

Luther, sitting downstairs, had much sympathy with Billy's point-of-view, but he was as certain as it was possible to be in an uncertain life that the deacons would not have agreed.

21

'I hear,' said Toby Protheroe 'that one of your dissenters has been dissenting to some purpose.'

'Billy Drips, sir.'

'Drips?'

'Billy Parsons, sir. His father is Tom Parsons of Plumtree Hill.'

'And they tell me he actually shouted "Balls" in a chapel meeting.'

'Not exactly shouted, sir. But said it quite loud.'

'Loud enough for everybody to hear?'

'Oh yes, sir. Quite loud enough for that.'

'Ha, ha! By damn! Good young man. Pity there aren't more about like him. But I believe his father's had something to say about wages. A bit active with the union I believe?'

'He's not a bad sort, sir. Just doing the best he can as far as he sees it.'

'Then tell me, Knox. Why is it, if wages are so much better in other places, that some of the men round here don't cut their stick and go and get work there?'

'Two reasons, sir. Mainly, the ones round here have some land, or at any rate a garden. So they can keep a pig, and maybe a cow, and grow some potatoes. That's worth a lot to them. The other thing is, they reckon that those who work up in the valleys are very bitter about the company shops. They have to spend their money in them and the prices are high. So some reckon they're no better off by going up there to work.'

'A pity somebody can't explain that to that miserable interfering preacher of yours. He's upset the vicar very badly. Did you know that?'

'No, sir.'

'Did you not know, Knox, about that ruffian who came back from Merthyr to hide?'

'No, sir. I didn't know about that.'

Protheroe gave him a penetrating look. 'You know, Knox, for one as sharp as you are, and for one who is so often so well-informed, you never cease to amaze me at what you don't know sometimes.'

Luther recalled Josiah Price's advice. Even if you do know, sometimes to say don't know is not a bad answer. He certainly did not want too many questions asked about anybody who had come back from Merthyr to hide. Pat and George were safely away, but Jack and Sarah Bowen had been running a bigger risk altogether.

'His name,' said Protheroe, 'was Benny Sais. His real name was Hughes. But because he was from down this way and spoke no Welsh they called him Benny Sais up in the valleys. Sais is Welsh for English. Did you know that?'

'Yes, sir, I knew that.'

'Good. I'm glad you know something. But, of course, that sort of knowledge doesn't hurt you, Knox. Don't think I haven't a sneaking regard for your discretion, but be careful how you tread. Don't get involved with them. Some of them are much more than well-meaning reformers. This Benny Sais was one of the worst types in with that desperate pair Shoni Sgubor Fawr and Dai Cantwr. But Sais was never caught. Amongst other things, apart from certain acts of violence, he stole plate and vessels from a church as some sort of protest against tithes. The vicar was not pleased to hear of that. And he was certainly not pleased to learn that Sais had received sanctuary in this area and that Adams arranged it. Most assuredly if it ever comes to light who gave him shelter they'll be out on their necks. Whatever estate they're on.'

The fact was that people were being intimidated by Rebecca. They would risk imprisonment and transportation rather than refuse to comply. Protheroe probably knew that. Luther certainly did.

No more was said but, from subsequent occasional remarks, Luther knew that Jack and Sarah were under suspicion. For the time being Protheroe was more interested to talk of possible developments in the area.

'I know it's been slow, Knox,' he said. 'These things often are. But I told you when they built the tramline from here down to Saundersfoot harbour that this valley would have tremendous prospects. Well, I hear now that Sir Richard Philipps is commissioning a firm of surveyors to report on the iron and anthracite reserves in the area. We want to make sure that we get in on anything that's going. On top of all that there are rumours of a possible link-up from Tenby and Saundersfoot with the proposed South Wales railway line to Pembroke Dock. And there are big plans afoot to develop the cross-channel traffic from Fishguard to Ireland. The whole area is ripe for development and we must be in on it. There'll be money to be made.'

22

Toby Protheroe was not the only one interested in developments. Absie Pugh also thought the prospects were good. He had always been thoughtful. Now, in the hope of better days to come, he and Seeny were getting married.

A pit had been sunk at Bonvilles Court, near Saundersfoot, and much nearer home Mr Stokes of Hean Castle had built brickworks at Woodside. Far more important, a company had been formed to build a new ironworks at the Grove which eventually would have four blast furnaces. Fosters, the surveyors, had made their report and the Patches at Crickdam were being worked again. Seeny was one of the first to leave the pit and become a poller. All along the cliffs from Wisemansbridge to Amroth there was activity and excitement.

True, the potato famine in Ireland had had serious repercussions and had killed any hopes of the possible cross-channel developments from Fishguard. Ireland was a long way away, and so was Fishguard for that matter. But, somehow or other, it spelled out a warning for Luther.

'You see, Absie,' he said, 'how things which happen on the land can have far-reaching effects.'

'The land's all right, boy. And I likes farmin' all right. But there's nothin' in it. It's the horses makes the money doin' the drivin'. An' you knows better than me what plans there is round here.'

That was certainly true. Luther was by now privy to many of Protheroe's and the Estate's affairs and was becoming a person of some small consequence. He knew that the new company had been granted a lease for sixty years on the mines and ironstone in the two parishes.

'This bloke Vickerman,' Absie said. 'They reckon as a got a mint o' money. Do'st thee know anythin' about'n?'

'Only what I've heard. He's a London solicitor with an estate in England. But Protheroe reckons he has big plans for what he's going to do down here.'

'Well, we got horses drivin' from the Patches nearly every day now, so they can start the furnaces gwain as soon as ever they likes.'

Before that was to happen, however, Absie and Seeny were married.

The week before the wedding Eli Morgans, who was a well-known taler, came from Amroth to bid neighbours to the wedding. Since the inception of the penny post it was now more fashionable to send the bidding in written form, but there were still those who preferred the old customs.

Quite a wit was Eli and never at a loss for a word. He came to the home-farm at Deerfield of an evening, dressed in his white apron with a white ribbon in his button-hole, and carrying his bidder's staff. He had a bag slung over his shoulder, too, and it was plenty big enough to take as much bread and cheese as he was given at any of the farmhouses at which he called.

Mrs Powell was there as well as Bessie and Dick, with Ben Humphrey and his family, and Beth Harries, who had succeeded Rita and was a different proposition altogether. There was no nonsense with Beth. Not Protheroe or anybody in the world would get her into bed without a ring on her finger.

Under the new law they would not have to go to the church but would be able to marry in the chapel. Eli had it all there in his rammas and Luther found him fascinating to listen to.

Three times he knocked on the door with his bidder's staff and then, with due ceremony, having been admitted to the kitchen, knocked three times with his staff upon the floor. Then he began his rammas. 'I was desired,' he proclaimed, 'to call here as a messenger and a bidder. Absalom Pugh and Asenath Knox in the parish of Amarer in the Hundred of Narberth, are encouraged by their friends and neighbours to make a bidding on Saturday next. The two young people will start from the young woman's residence at Crickdam, thence to the chapel at Ebenezer to be married and return to the young man's father's house at Bellman's Close to dinner. They shall have good beef and cabbage, mutton and turnips, pork and potatoes, roast goose or gant, perhaps both if they are in season, a quart of drink for fourpence, a cake for a penny, clean chairs to sit down upon, clean pipes and tobacco, and attendance of the best; a good song, but if no one will sing, then I'll sing as well as I can; and if no one will attend, I'll attend as well as I can.'

His opening remarks were well received amidst much banter. Luther could not help but wonder where all this rich fare was to come from. Certainly not Crickdam. Then, of course, Eli continued with his rammas and came to the crux of the story.

'As a usual custom with us, in Amarer, is to hold a sending gloves before the wedding, if you'll please to come, or send a waggon, a cart or gambo, a horse and a colt, a heifer, a cow and a calf, or an ox and a half, or pigs, cocks, hens, geese, goslings, ducks, turkeys, a saddle and bridle, or a child's cradle, or what the house can afford. A great many can help one, but one cannot help a great many. Or send a waggon full of potatoes, a cart-load of turnips, a hundred or two of cheeses, a cask of butter, a sack of flour, a winchester of barley, a firkin of ale, or what you please, for anything will be acceptable; jugs, basins, saucepans, pots and pans, or what you can. Throw in five pounds if you like. Gridirons, frying-pans, tea-kettle, plates and dishes, a lootch and dish, spoons, knives and forks, pepper-boxes, salt-cellars, mustard-pots, or even a penny whistle or a child's cradle. Ladies and gentlemen, I was desired to speak this way that all payments due to the young woman's father and mother, grandfather and grandmother, aunts, uncles, brothers and sisters, and cousins, and the same due to the young man's father and mother etcetera etcetera must be returned to the young people on the above day. So no more at present. If you please to order your butler, or underservant, to give a quart of drink to the bidder.'

His thirst quenched, Eli went on his way to tell the tale. It was doubtful, they said, whether anyone would follow him as a taler. Printing and the post were killing all that. Times were changing. Nor was it going to be a horse wedding. There was too much boisterousness at those.

Even so, Seeny went in style in Ben Humphrey's best trap with Dick at the reins, and Luther followed with Mam Bron in the little phaeton with a fiddler going on ahead and everybody was very happy.

Everybody, that is, except Luther. If Seeny had to marry

anybody he would prefer it to be Absie. But he knew in his heart that he hated the thought of any man possessing her.

23

Another year was to go by before a start was made to build the ironworks. Luther did not witness the ceremony, but when the *Pembrokeshire Herald* arrived he saw that it had done full justice to the occasion.

'On Saturday last,' said the report, 'the first stone of the intended works was laid by Mrs Vickerman, of London, amid cheers of hundreds of anxious spectators, and firing of cannon, which must have been heard at several miles distance. There was a Dinner provided for visitors in a temporary booth on the spot, to which a number of ladies and gentlemen sat down.

After dinner John Longbourne Esq was called to the chair, who in a neat and appropriate speech, pointed out the great advantages likely to be derived by the neighbourhood. Several other speeches were delivered during the evening on the same subject. The evening was passed with the greatest harmony and good feeling, to which the ladies contributed in no small degree by their smiling faces and charming repartee—the whole savouring more of a drawing room party than a public dinner. The workmen and their families were also plentifully regaled with bread and cheese and ale at the expense of the Company. The cannon continued playing from the heights above through the entire day.'

Having referred in glowing terms to the qualifications of the engineer and manager, the report went on, 'Under the superintendence of such men, the Shareholders may rest assured that their interests will be attended to. From the report of these practical gentlemen we learn, that ore is of an excellent quality, and capable of being worked with great pecuniary profit to the Company. They say that the furnaces will be lighted in six months from the present time, when there will be employment for upwards of 1,000 persons.

There are brick works lately established at Saundersfoot, where fire bricks of a very superior quality are

manufactured, another circumstance favourable to the
Company in the erection of their furnaces &c.'

There was much more in a similar vein on the enormous
benefit to the area, which made Absie's enthusiasm seem
justifiable, but another summer had come before the Grove
was ready to go into production. By that time Seeny had
given birth to her first baby, a boy. For the time being, she
and Absie were living at Bellman's Close with Absie's family
until they could find a place of their own.

Absie was anxious for the furnaces to go into blast.

'The thing is,' he said to Luther, 'we been drivin' mine for
a good time now an' 'tis pilin' up. If we're not careful they'll
be screwin' us down on price.'

'Well I haven't heard anything. It's nothing to do with the
Estate, of course, but Protheroe's interested on his own
account. Chadwick called on him last week and they were
talking for a long time together. What about I don't know.
But after Chadwick had gone Protheroe went heavier than
usual at the whisky. There's something happening whatever
it is.'

'Chadwick hisself called on Protheroe?'

'Yes, Chadwick.'

'That's big stuff then. What about Vickerman?'

'Oh, no. He has nothing to do with Protheroe. It's his
money, but Chadwick's a trustee and very much in charge.
Vickerman's only down here now and again. Protheroe's got
money in it I think, but no more than other small
shareholders.'

'Well I wish to God they'd get on with it.'

Billy Drips was one of the first to be taken on when the first
furnace eventually went into blast.

'And that's their first mistake,' said Luther.

'A's all right,' said Absie.

'Yes, I know. But he's wilder than his father. They tell me
he's still shouting about too much mine and coal being
driven to the Grove in case there's a dispute and they'll be in
the manager's hands. You thought the same thing yourself
not long ago.'

'Ah, but that was different. They hadn't gone into blast
then.'

'Don't be too sure about things all the same. They may not go all that well.'

'Hisht fellah, for the Lord's sake. The Grove's the best thing as have ever happened.'

It was certainly true that there was great excitement throughout the area. People were optimistic that there would be even more work to be had. Already more people had found work at the Patches, and a young blacksmith had started in the blacksmith shop at Crickdam and was lodging with Mam Bron. The Company at the Grove had been lucky, too, because several of their first workers to be taken on were men who had come back from Merthyr, where they had worked as puddlers, shinglers and catchers in the iron works, and they knew the job well.

The first furnace had gone into blast early in the summer. The men on the land had started scything in the earliest hayfields. The lilac was already past its best, and the honeysuckle and wild rose were taking over in the hedge-rows. It was a good time of year and Luther knew his heart was far more in what was happening on the land than in all these industrial developments. They were certainly doing nothing for the scenery or the peacefulness of the area but, if it meant better times for the people, it was a price which would have to be paid. If it meant better times. If was a big word.

Things were still bad on the land, but the land was dear to his heart. The land and the sea. They were all he had known. And since he had worked at Deerfield he had seen even more of the land and the problems of those who depended on it for a living.

The first hint of trouble at the Grove came when there was talk of Vickerman coming down from London and kicking up a row. There had been a meeting apparently, and he had accused William Chadwick of mismanagement and fraud. Hosgood, the manager, had submitted a progress report, but work on the two further blast furnaces had been suspended, and it was also decided not to put the second furnace into blast although it was ready. In the meantime, an accountant was to be brought in to investigate the Company's affairs.

24

In that summer of 1849, when the Grove ironworks opened, Luther went for the first time to Rhydlancoed. It was to be a momentous summer.

The big house, where Squire Radley lived, was always spoken of with deference. Protheroe went there himself when there were Estate affairs to be discussed, for the Squire, so it was said, had little interest in the Estate. Luther had never seen him, for he had not visited Deerfield in the ten years Luther had been there. He spent much time in London and was generally spoken of as being a lover of the good life.

Luther knew he was home at the moment, and it came as a surprise when Protheroe told him to go to Rhydlancoed with a report which the Squire particularly wanted.

As if to explain his unusual request Protheroe said, 'The Squire may want to ask about one or two rents and changes of tenancy. And you've been handling them so you'll know the answers almost as well as I do. Better in some cases. Especially with some of the cottages. Take the pony and gig.'

Luther made no comment and asked no questions but, from what he had ever heard, he thought it strange for the Squire to have any interest in cottages when he had little interest even in the bigger farms. A still tongue, he thought, kept a wise head, and it was a good feeling to be bowling along the new road, with the pony trotting very nicely and the shafts of the gig balancing like weighing up a pound of sugar.

Along the way the countryside was rich with the growth of early summer. The bold red campion still lingered, although the white feathery flowers of the meadowsweet of a later season were to be seen here and there in the damper places. The occasional hayfield had already fallen before the reaper's scythe, but elsewhere the long grass waved gently in the breeze waiting for another week or two.

Apart from the day he had gone to Narberth with Mam Bron, Luther had travelled further than ever in his life before when, having passed the Cambrian Mailway inn and, knowing the way that he should take, he turned off the main road.

He eased the pony to a gentle walk as he found the hill, steep in places, leading downwards through a wood, until he came upon a place rich in fern and foliage and more beautiful than anything he had ever imagined could exist. Through the trees he caught the first glimpse of rhododendrons, now past their best, but even yet showing blooms of many colours.

Entranced, he stopped the pony and sat and listened to the silence of the woodland where it lay still and soundless as it slumbered in the shade of the summer sun. Then he heard the stream. Birds, silent since the pony stopped, burst forth again into song.

The gardens of the cottages near the house were a blaze of colour, and aubretia and snow-on-the-mountain tumbled and flowed and spread all over the stone walls. At the end of the valley Luther caught a glimpse of the sea, but the softness of this place was a far cry from the harsh winds and flying salt sea-spray of Crickdam.

The house was not as great as he had pictured it, but it was beautiful, and a place of dignity and good taste, designed, he knew, by the famous architect, John Nash. From what Luther could see, the gardens were extensive and magnificent, with rare and exotic plants flourishing, and the stream flowing through them.

Luther approached from the back and a young groom came out to meet him.

'Art thee from Protheroe?' he asked.

'Yes, of course. But how did you know?'

'Knows the gig an' the pony.'

Luther liked him and his face seemed familiar.

'Thee'rt Luther Knox.'

'Yes, I am. What's your name?'

'Well, never muv from here alive again, fancy thou do'sn't know thy own relations. I'm Absie's cousin. Nat Wilkins.'

'Ah, yes. I thought I knew your face. You were at the wedding.'

Luther could see the family likeness, but Nat didn't have Absie's fine physique.

'Aye, I was there. But I'll be fetched a kick up th'arse if I stays here talkin' to thee. What ar't thee wantin'?'

'Protheroe's sent me to see the Squire.'

'Squire? Thou wous'n't clap eyes on'n today.'

'How not?'

'How? I'll tell thee how. Because a's as tight as two farts tryin' to get out through one arsehole. That's how. Well a was last night any road. Had a big dinner party with some of the toffs before gwain back to London tomorrow. So today a'll be sleepin' it off I shouldn't wonder. But I'll take the pony. Go thee round that far end an' knock on the big door.'

Luther did as he was bade and limped off. The thought occurred to him that he was experiencing none of the apprehension as when he had approached Deerfield that day with Josiah Price to face Protheroe for the first time.

Turning a corner he came upon a flower border. In a recess in the wall there was a lion's head in stone. From the lion's open mouth cold clear water gushed to splash into a trough and overflow before disappearing underground. The alyssum and sweet williams he identified and also the catmint and sweet rocket. All round, in the cracks between the stones, masses of valerian were in bloom. It made a nice picture, but what caused him to stand and stare was the concentration of butterflies, fluttering everywhere over these nectar-rich blooms, and jostling for position. Never had he seen such a sight.

The red admirals, red and black velvet, seemed to predominate, but there were countless painted ladies and peacocks as well as many little tortoiseshells. There were other varieties which he did not know. The whole bright picture was of blue and red and white and gold, hypnotic in the warm sunshine.

'So you like my butterflies, do you?'

Startled, Luther turned suddenly at the sound of the cultured, gentle voice, and saw a girl, younger than himself, slender and with golden hair piled high. Green her eyes were, set wide and honest, her nose was straight and her chin was firm. Her brow, like her eyes, was wide. He took off his hat.

'If you're going to gaze at me like that,' she said, 'you'd do better to turn back to the butterflies.'

'I beg your pardon, miss. You startled me.'

'It's quite all right. But you did look in a bit of a dream.'

'I was fascinated by the butterflies.'

'They are very beautiful. I have this border with flowers specially for them. Are you interested?'

'Yes, miss. All country things. But I don't know as much about butterflies as I would like to.'

'Neither do I, but it's nice to have them about the place. When I come home to live I'll see about having more plants for them.'

So this must be Miss Eiry. No wonder she was so well loved.

'Excuse me miss,' said Luther, 'but would you be Miss Radley?'

'Yes, of course.'

'I've come to see the Squire.'

The girl frowned. 'Is he expecting you?'

'I don't really know, miss. I'm from Mister Protheroe at Deerfield. I work in his office and he's sent me with a letter.'

'Oh, I see.' There was a smile on her lips. 'Don't be too upset about it, but you're out of luck. Father is resting. Sleeping it off as they say. His liver wouldn't be too good, even if you were to see him. So maybe I'd better take the letter for you.'

'Thank you, miss.'

Luther handed her the letter and, as he did so, she said, 'I noticed you limping as you came along. Have you hurt yourself?'

'When I was young, miss. A tram went over my foot at the Patches. Picking mine. Iron ore.'

'What d'you mean, when you were young? You're only young now.'

'Twenty-four, miss.'

'Then how old were you when it happened?'

'About six, as far as I can remember.'

'Six!'

She closed her eyes. 'Six! And we talk such pious humbug about slavery in foreign parts. Six!'

'But things have improved since then.'

'Not before it was time. But children still go hungry don't they?'

'Times are bad, miss.'

'Are they? Then would you like me to give you an account of the food and drink that were guzzled in this house last night?'

'Yes, indeed, miss. There are things which seem very unfair. But it's not usually people of your class who talk that way.'

'And that's just another of the world's problems. But I'm keeping you. No doubt you'd like something to eat. I'll tell Miss Parfitt. She's the housekeeper. What's your name by the way?'

'Knox, miss. Luther Knox.'

'Knox? The name's familiar.'

'My sister used to work here a long time ago.' He hesitated. 'Before I was born.'

She glanced at him quickly, but gave no sign that it meant anything to her.

'I'm sorry about your foot,' she said. 'Is it very painful?'

'Oh no, not now. A bit of a nuisance. It hurts a bit in the cold weather sometimes. But it's awkward more than anything else.'

'And you work for Mister Protheroe?'

'I've been there ten years.'

'I'm going to London with my father tomorrow. Next year or the year after I'm coming home for good. I'd like to talk to you then about some of these things.'

'Of course, miss.'

Luther could think of nothing else to say, but he was soon made to feel at home, in what he took to be the servants' hall, because Mary Ann was there. Very smart she looked in her parlour maid's uniform, and it meant something to the kitchen maids to see her treat him with the same respect as she had always shown at Deerfield.

When he had eaten, he wondered whether he should linger, but, much as he hoped for another word with Miss Eiry, there was no sign of her, and then Nat came and said, 'I've fed and watered the pony. Shall I give thee a hand to put her in the shafts?'

Back in the stables Nat had time to talk, from which

Luther supposed that whatever urgent job had been waiting for him earlier had now been accomplished.

'You never seen the Squire?'

'No. Only Miss Eiry.'

'Did you see the Mistress?'

'No.'

'How did Protheroe send thee today then, boy?'

Luther saw no point in making a mystery of it. 'Tell you the truth I don't know.'

'Hasn't thee ever noticed this last year or two, a never seems to come much when the Squire's here? But a'll come to see the Mistress.'

There was a knowing smile on his face. Luther found it hard to believe.

'What you getting at?' he said.

'Ah, well, boy. Like th'owld chap said, ''If thou ca'st spell, I'll read.'' But I can see thee'rt a bit thick.'

'You're not serious?'

'Listen, boy. We knows here, a couple of us, but we thinks too much of her to spread it about. So keep it to thyself. Protheroe been ridin' her regular this long time when the Squire's away.'

'Never!'

''Tis right. They're cute about it mind. But 'tis right.'

'How d'you know?'

'Never mind how I knows. But I knows. An' don't thee say nothin' about it to nobody.'

'No, I shan't say anything.'

Luther had much on which to ponder as the pony took her time walking up through the wood, pushing against the collar, and moving naturally from side to side of the road to ease the burden of the steep slope.

He was not particularly concerned about Protheroe and Mrs Radley, surprising though it was. His thoughts were of her daughter. Eiry had made a deep impresion on him and he was strangely attracted to her. She had said nothing about Meg being his mother, even if she knew. Thinking of Meg it occurred to him that the place, beautiful though it was, had meant nothing to him. According to some people, with Meg being his mother and with it all having happened at Rhydlancoed, he should have been aware of a presence or some deep attachment. But he was not.

The only affinity he had felt was for Eiry Radley, and her lovely face and golden hair remained clear in his memory.

25

Only weeks later, in the month of July, there was a cut in wages for all the workers at the Grove and for all the colliers in the area.

It was no more than Luther had expected because, that same week, there had been a report in the *Pembrokeshire Herald* of the depressed state of the iron industry, a quarter of the blast furnaces in the country standing idle. Booker, a Glamorgan ironmaster, was complaining that he had just lost a contract at five pounds a ton which four years earlier he had obtained at twelve pounds a ton. At Dudley, in the Midlands, notice had been given of a reduction of sixpence a day in colliers' wages, which would bring their wage down to three shillings a day.

Nearer home, at the Grove, it did nothing for the men's confidence when, on top of news of wage cuts, there was a rumour that, following Vickerman's allegations of fraud, Neale, the Company secretary, had resigned and Lowden, one of the defaulting shareholders, had gone off with the Company's minutes and other vital documents.

In August, a report in the *Pembrokeshire Herald*, albeit far shorter and less fulsome than the account of the ceremony at the laying of the foundation stone the previous year, said it all. 'The Pembrokeshire Iron and Coal Company' it said 'have discharged about 200 persons from the Iron Works and 30 from the Coal Works, owing it is supposed to the depressed state of the iron trade. They have abandoned their former intention of blowing in the second blast furnace, which is ready for working. The furnace in blast makes upwards of sixty tons per week; therefore, with a large stock of ore on hand, they consider it more advisable to reduce their working than increase their make of iron.'

What the report did not say was that work at the Patches had been stopped back in July. What Absie and Billy Drips had feared had eventually come to pass. There was plenty of iron ore stock-piled.

People at a much higher level also had their problems. Negotiations with Chadwick were said to have broken down, litigation followed and, early in August, the Court of Chancery ordered the return of vital documents. Chadwick was sacked. Protheroe, up at Deerfield, whilst having no apparent or immediate connection, drank more heavily and became unusually morose and edgy.

A week or so later Luther heard him tell Mrs Powell he would be away for the night. Yet, when he went, it was on horseback, and he took no luggage. Luther watched him go. From his attic window he could see a long way and he saw Protheroe follow the road which could, and no doubt would, take him to Rhydlandcoed. Luther smiled.

'Damn old ram,' he thought.

That afternoon, Billy Drips came to Deerfield. In Protheroe's absence, Beth showed him into Luther's little office.

Gipsy, grey now round the muzzle and dim of eye, was stretched out on the mat, grateful to be there in the cool shade, out of the heat of the sun, where a gentle breeze came in through the open window. The old black retriever had gone to his rest long since, and Protheroe's gun-dog now was kept with the gamekeeper, Dan Sinnett, at Tuppeny Furze. When the retriever had died Gipsy had attached himself more to Protheroe, but he still came to sit with Luther when Protheroe was away.

'Protheroe not here then?' was Billy's form of greeting.

'Not today, Billy.'

'Ah, well, 'tis all the same. Thou ca'st take a message.'

'Aye, aye, anything to oblige a good tenant.'

'That's just it. I'm off.'

'Off?'

'Aye, off. Cuttin' my stick an' off for Pennsylvania.'

Luther was shocked.

'Good God, Billy. Don't rush into something like that.'

'No rush about it. When th' owld man died in the spring I made up my mind that if things didn't go right I'd be off. Thou know'st what have happened at the Grove. There's enough mine piled up there to keep 'em gwain for months. They can screw down the wages, sack who they wants an' there's nothin' nobody can do about it. If they can sack Chadwick they can sack anybody.'

'But Billy. You've got a good house and good land. Plumtree Hill's the best little holding on the estate. You must be mad.'

'Listen, boy. I don't argue with that. But if 'tis such a good holdin' how couldn't th' owld man afford to keep me home an' I had to go work down the pit?'

'I know all that. But times are bad everywhere. It won't always be like that. I've always told Absie not to forget the land. It's what I believe.'

'Absie don't do so bad with the horses. But a can please hisself. I'm for America.'

The thought occurred to Luther later that, if Billy had not called, he would not have opened the drawer. He had never given the matter much thought but, in all the years he had been at Deerfield, there was one drawer in the big desk in Protheroe's study which was always locked, and Protheroe always kept the key on him.

When Billy had gone, Luther began to look through lists of tenants and thought that maybe Plumtree Hill would be all right for Absie and Seeny. He looked through the rent books, but there was one account book missing. Search as he would he could not find it. Then he came to the locked drawer.

For a while he pondered. Then he tried some of the keys from other locks. One of them seemed to be nearly turning. He fiddled with it for a while, exerted a little pressure, and the lock clicked back.

Cautiously he opened the drawer. It was full of account books and papers. He removed them carefully so that he could replace them in their original order. The account book he wanted was there. It told him little he did not know, but other papers did. Protheroe had received money from Chadwick for timber and stone supplied to the Grove by the estate. Luther knew that neither had been supplied. Nor had the money been entered in the estate account. There were similar items concerning services provided by the estate by way of haulage and supplying casual labour. All of it was spurious. Protheroe, and no doubt one or two others, had been milking the Iron and Coal Company right from the start.

From what he could see at a glance Luther wondered whether some of the rent books would stand a careful scrutiny. Before he could look more carefully at them, a small bundle of letters tied with tape, at the back of the drawer, caught his eye. He picked them up and saw that some of them were addressed to Miss Louisa Lloyd. He did not know what Mrs Radley's maiden name had been, but he knew that her Christian name was Louisa.

Footsteps sounded in the hall. Without thinking, he dropped the bundle of letters in his pocket and quickly, but carefully, replaced the books and envelopes and documents. Try as he would however, he could not get the key to lock the drawer.

That was a complication he would have liked to avoid, but it went from his mind that evening in his bedroom as he poured over the letters.

Nice letters they were, from a man who was writing to his sweetheart and cared deeply for her. He signed himself Chris. He sounded a good man. Several of the letters had been written from on board ship, and some of them made reference to the child she was expecting. Something told Luther he should not be reading them, but he read on. There was mention of a gold coin the colour of her hair, and much more he did not understand. But he understood that the letters were incriminating, and he had a fair idea that Protheroe had probably used them as some sort of hold over the recipient.

He found some brown paper, wrapped the letters carefully, fetched a chair to reach up to the man-hole in the ceiling, hoisted himself up into the roof and hid them behind a beam. If the letters could be useful to Protheroe he might be able to make use of them himself. Life was very uncertain and often had some odd twists to it. He saw no reason for the thought to disturb his sleep.

26

Luther had begun to dispel any misgivings he may have
entertained when, a few mornings later, he knocked on the
door of Protheroe's study. As he entered, he knew a
sickening feeling as he saw Protheroe standing by his desk,
the one drawer open, and the account books, envelopes and
papers strewn before him.

Protheroe looked up, white-faced, and Luther saw the
unmasked rage in every feature. Yet, for some reason he
could never have explained, now that the confrontation had
come, he stood before the older man unafraid and feeling
strangely calm. He wondered afterwards whether it had
been an animal instinct which told him he had nothing to
fear.

Luther faced Protheroe, waiting for him to speak.

'Knox,' he hissed, 'you're a bastard!'

'I've known that nearly all my life. Nobody's ever let me
forget it.'

'That wasn't what I meant. You're worse than that. You're
a bastard in the lowest sense of the word. You're a prying,
thieving, treacherous bastard. I should have known what to
expect from you damned chapel-crawling scum.'

'If you want to know I only opened the drawer because I
needed the number three account book.'

'Why did you need that?'

'Because when you were off sprotting, Billy Parsons came
to say he's giving up Plumtree Hill and I wanted to check the
book against a tenants' list.'

Protheroe had winced at Luther's use of the word sprotting but made no comment.

He said, 'You could have waited till I came back. And it
does not excuse your taking of letters which do not concern
you.'

'It's no worse than you using such letters to get a lady into
bed with you.'

Protheroe was unmoved. Perhaps he knew that his
morality was too well-known for such a barb to bother him.

'Knox,' he said, 'don't get out of your depth in dangerous
waters. Just pack your few belongings and be out of this

house within the hour or, by God, I'll take the horse whip to you.'

'All right, I'll do that. Then I'll see that Mister Vickerman knows about the rest of what I've found out.'

It was not entirely a shot in the dark, but Luther was not prepared for the look of fear which came into Protheroe's eyes.

He was almost prepared to feel sorry for him. Until he remembered how this same man had been willing to make him sell his soul to frighten the little children working underground from telling their real stories to the Inspector. Luther had always vowed that Protheroe would pay for that one day, and it looked as if that day had come.

'You fool, Knox. Vickerman is only interested in hunting and cricket. He's a libertine.'

'What else are you? And the Squire if it comes to that?'

'That's different. We belong here. Vickerman's an outsider.'

'Maybe so. But he's brought his money here. And it could do a world of good for the working people. Or don't you care about them?'

'If that's how you feel why don't you go and work for him?'

'Maybe I'll be able to when I can get to him with what I know.'

Protheroe tried one last bluff.

'All right,' he said. 'Now get out.'

Luther turned and limped to the door. He had his hand on the door-knob when Protheroe, in a weary voice, said, 'All right, Knox. Come back here.'

As Luther turned, Protheroe was pouring himself a large measure of whisky. He took one mouthful, swallowed it, then said, 'What's your price?'

Long ago, Luther remembered him saying, 'Every man has his price, Knox.'

He had never thought of it like that. When he did not answer, Protheroe said again, 'I said, what's your price?'

It had been a good life in so many ways at Deerfield, with good food, warmth and a comfortable bed. The long hours had not bothered him. But in so many ways, too, he had been lonely, and he had missed Seeny so much. Suddenly he knew a fierce longing for a home of his own. He had saved his money steadily.

Without any forethought, he said, 'I want the tenancy of Plumtree Hill and to be appointed local agent to the Estate.'

He knew he was doing the work already, but the look of relief and incredulity on Protheroe's face made him wonder whether he should have asked for the moon to be thrown in as well.

'Is that all?'

'And I stay here until I move to Plumtree Hill.'

'All right. Now get out.'

'What about the letters?'

'The letters?'

'Missus Radley's letters.'

Protheroe grunted. 'Shove 'em up your arse.'

To that extent Protheroe had the last word.

On the other hand, Luther smiled to himself at the realisation that not once had he called him sir. And he knew for sure whose letters they were.

27

Billy was pleased when Luther saw him and told him that he would be going to Plumtree Hill. There was not much stock on the land.

'The furniture is the most I got,' Billy said.

'If you like,' said Luther, 'I'll do a deal with you for the whole lot.'

''Twould save me makin' a sale.'

'All right. I'll borrow Ben Humphrey's phaeton and come over on Saturday afternoon.'

Their bargaining did not take long. Billy knew what he wanted, Luther knew what he could afford to pay and there was little between them. There was no need to banter. Having made up his mind to go, Billy wanted everything cleared up and to be gone.

Luther still thought Billy was foolish to turn his back on such a good house and holding, but was pleased with his own good fortune in being able to take them over.

An old long-house it was originally, but it had been added to and much improved. An agent's announcement that it was to let would undoubtedly have referred to it as a superior residence with valuable land. But there was not to be any announcement this time. Nor was there any need for an announcement that Luther had been appointed local agent. He had been acting in that capacity for so long that most folks seemed to think of him that way without the formality of its having to be made official.

On his way back from Plumtree Hill he called at Bellman's Close. Seeny was in the kitchen, and little Seth, over a year old now, was toddling by the table. By the look of her round the waist Seeny had another one on the way.

Absie had heard Luther's arrival and almost followed him in. It was good to be with them again, and Seeny was glad when he said he would stay for supper. Absie's father, along with Absie's sister and her husband, had gone to call on another of his sons.

Seeny said, ''Tis the first time as we been on our own for a meal since I don't know when.'

Luther thought he saw Absie frown.

'Mind thee,' she said, 'Mary's very good. But 'tis her home more than 'tis mine, an' she got another babbie comin' as well. I don't know how we're gwain manage.'

'We'll manage all right,' said Absie.

''Tis all right for thee to talk like that, but we're gettin' on each other's nerves as 'tis. With two new babbies here 'twill be bedlam. Thou know'st how 'tis—''One dog one bone.'' Now I got to put Seth to bed an' then we'll see about somethin' to yeat. We don't want to burden thee with our troubles.'

When they were on their own Absie said, 'Ha'st thou heard about Jack Bowen and Sarah?'

'No. What about them?'

'I don't know if 'tis right, but I heard last night as thicky Benny Sais been took up in Glamorgan somewhere an' blowed the gaff on 'em.'

'What in the name of God would he do that for?'

'Tryin' to save his own skin. A was never no good to nobody.'

'Blowing the gaff on Jack and Sarah won't do him any good.'

'No, I knows. But it won't do them no good neither. The word have got back to the parson an' a've swore a'll have 'em on the road. Thou know'st what a is towards the chapel an' a knows that them hidin' him was Sufferin's doin'.'

Then they talked of other things until Seeny had put supper on the table. When the meal was finished, Luther said, 'What other news have you heard lately?'

'Billy Drips is gwain to America,' said Absie, 'but thou's'll know all about that.'

'Yes, I know about that. But have you heard who's going to Plumtree Hill?'

He looked at their blank faces.

'It's not a secret,' he said. 'I am.'

'Go from here,' said Seeny. 'Shut thee up with thy owld dull talk.'

'No, honestly now. That's right.'

'What ar't thee gwain do there boy?' said Absie.

'To tell you the truth I'd been thinking about trying to get it for you. But, out of the blue, Protheroe offered it to me and I had to make up my mind there and then.'

'Ar't thee gwain farm it?'

'I don't know. I haven't thought about it. Protheroe's also made me local agent for the Estate so I'll have plenty to do.'

'An' who's gwain look after thee?' said Seeny.

'I haven't thought about that either. But if you're so keen to move. . . if you'd like to come with me. . . well, there it is.'

Absie and Seeny looked at each other.

'I'm not asking you,' said Luther. 'I just haven't thought about it. And for God's sake don't come just to oblige me. But if you'd like to come, that would be wonderful. If it would suit you.'

'We haven't got no furniture of our own yet,' Seeny said, 'but we had over forty pounds gave us at the biddin' when we married. We still got that.'

'No need to bother about that. I'm buying Billy's furniture and it's good. But sleep on it.'

'How about the land?' Absie asked.

'We could work something out. I've always wanted to farm

a bit. But you could have your horses there and I could keep Billy's few head of stock on. I'll go on trying to find a place for you, so you needn't feel tied. And until you can get a place Seeny'd have the house to herself pretty well.'

'Let's go, Absie,' she said. 'For God's sake let's go. For Mary's sake as much as mine. For all our sakes.'

'It sound all right,' Absie said.

'Of course 'tis all right. An' I'd be nearer to Mam Bron an' could pop an' give her a hand now an' again. She's gettin' on mind. An' she's on her own there now.'

That was true, of course. The blacksmith's shop at Crickdam was idle again now that no mine was being dug at the Patches, and the blacksmith, who had lodged with her, had gone. Luther had helped her in different ways over the years, but in his heart he knew he had never really been as concerned for her as perhaps he should have been. Not in the way that he knew Josiah Price would have had him to be.

He thought often of Josiah Price's words, and little or nothing of what he heard from Erasmus Adams. He still went to chapel, if not as frequently. Protheroe was far from the mark when he called him a chapel-crawler. When Suffering started up Luther turned his mind to other things and counted the joints in the panelling under the pulpit and anything else rather than listen to what he thought for the most part was rubbish. Since Adams had come to Ebenezer two unhappy girls had been turned out of chapel because they had had the misfortune to be landed with bastards. The whole business sickened him. Adams, according to his own smug claims, may have been saved, but he was miles from being a Christian in the way Josiah Price was. Luther knew what that revered man's attitude would have been. And Luther, with great fellow-feeling, had infinite compassion for bastards and their unhappy mothers, whatever Adams and the narrow clique he had gathered round him had to say. Billy Drips had only struck a passing, ineffectual blow for sanity, and for Christ for that matter, when he had stood up and said 'Balls.'

Luther smiled at the recollection.

'What ar't thee laughin' about?' Seeny said.

'I was just thinking. Missus Powell has been wonderful to me all the time. But it could never be the same as having my aunty to look after me.'

'Ah,' Seeny said, putting her arm round him, 'he've always been my boy.'

28

Luther moved into Plumtree Hill during the third week in September. So much had happened during the summer, and it still seemed that everything was happening at the same time.

Mrs Powell was sad to see Luther go, and she was sad to see Bessie thickening round the waist. But there was no fear of retribution from Adams and his self-righteous pack of hounds, because Dick married her. Sad, too, though it was for Jack Bowen and Sarah to be turned out from Light-A-Pipe, it happened lucky for Dick and Bessie. Ben Humphrey, who was church, spoke for Dick and he was accepted as the tenant. Some folks said he should not have gone there, but they were mostly chapel people and, as Luther said, the place was coming vacant anyway. It was none of Dick's or Bessie's doing that Jack and Sarah had been turned out, hard though it was for them to have to sell their furniture and stock and move into a hovel.

Luther, for his own part, was more immediately concerned with his own affairs, and he felt he would burst with the sheer happiness within him. Never had he known such contentment.

Seeny sang in her new-found freedom and the knowledge of being mistress of her own kitchen. One cow was in full profit and kept the house well supplied with milk and butter. Seth, growing every day it seemed, was into everything and a delight to have about the place.

It had been a good year for the hay. Luther had taken over the two ricks which Billy had built in the haggard, and there was plenty for their needs, including Absie's horses, through the winter. A beautiful, satisfying smell it was when Absie was cutting it out with the great hay-knife, driving the blade down deep into the rick and carrying the tammats of sweet-smelling hay on his back into the stable.

Billy had also had a donkey, by the name of John Wesley. When he had bought him and brought him home, the donkey, who had just left his mother, stood out in the field and brayed for best part of a fortnight. At the time, Suffering Adams had been making much reference to the preaching crusades of the late John Wesley, who had, he said, had a great voice and preached in the open air. In a moment of irreverence Billy, no doubt hoping it would annoy Adams, if and when he came to hear of it, named his donkey accordingly. Luther had no use for John Wesley donkey, as far as he knew, but kept him just the same. It was typical of his feeling of well-being and expansiveness at that time. The world was a good place and he wanted others, including John Wesley donkey, to have a share in it.

He would still be going to Deerfield frequently, if not every day, and one of his first requirements would be transport. From Billy he had inherited a rickety trap and in this, with Absie's pony in the shafts, he drove to the hamlet at Heronsmill beyond Deerfield. The hamlet took its name from the Mill itself where Walter Harter was following in the footsteps of generations of his forebears who had been millers there before him.

It was funny, Luther would sometimes think in later years, how one thing would so often lead to another in life.

He had really had the idea of going to Heronsmill because it was from Watty the Mill, as Harter was known, that Billy Drips had bought John Wesley. He had about twenty donkeys there and used them for fetching corn in panniers for grinding at the Mill and for returning it to the farms afterwards.

Near the Mill, at a little holding called Rollin, Harter had a son-in-law, Tom Perrot, who was a skilled coachbuilder. Luther's intention was to ask him to make a small phaeton for him and this, in due course, he did. But, whilst he was there, the pony spread a shoe and he finished up calling at The Gangrel, where a young blacksmith, by the name of Jenkyn Griffiths, had just taken over from old man Nash.

There were, in fact, several other craftsmen in the hamlet
following such trades as saddler, mason, wheelwright and
shoemaker, and it was to the shoemaker that Jenkyn
Griffiths suggested Luther should go.

Luther knew most of these people from the years he had
spent at Deerfield, but he was more friendly with Jenkyn
than any of them. They were about the same age, and had
much in common in their attitue to life and country things.
Apart from that, Luther had first come across Jenkyn on
Amroth Big day when Jenkyn, who was a croggan from up
the Welsh, had also met old man Nash's daughter, Esther,
whom he had subsequently married. It was something of a
bond between them.

Already Jenkyn was falling into the dialect of the south of
the county, the Little England beyond Wales.

When he had fixed the pony's shoe he said to Luther,
'How'd you like me to have a go at that foot of thine now I'm
at it?'

Luther laughed, 'I'm afraid it's gone too far for anybody to
do anything about it now.'

Jenkyn took his pipe from his mouth and tapped Luther on
the chest with the stem.

'Shall I tell thee somethin'? There's many a true word
spoke in jest. You knows the shoemaker and clogger up at
Rushyland?'

'Jack Voyle?'

'That's it. Well, a've had young Tom Harter there learnin'
his trade an' I've never saw such work in all my life as that
crut can do.'

'Good is he?'

'Good? Look here. There's a owld 'ooman lives up in
Templeton name of Peg Leg Fluff. All her life, they reckon,
she've been heckin' about. Born like it an' gettin' worse all
the time. Well, young Tom Harter persuaded her to let'n
make here a special boot. Just to experiment a bit. An' can I
tell thee somethin'? I seen her last week, an' drop dead, the
way she was comin' walkin', a body would have said 'twas
the fairy queen.'

Tom Harter made Luther a pair of boots, after measuring
his injured foot with great interest and care. When he wore

them he felt a new man and immediately ordered a second pair. For the rest of his life he never went anywhere else for boots, and more than once was heard to say, 'And all because Billy Drips bought John Wesley donkey from Watty the Mill.'

29

The Grove ironworks had nothing to do with the Rhyd-lancoed Estate, nor did any of their other undertakings, such as the various coal-mines, actual and projected. It was simply the case that Protheroe, not as agent, but in his private capacity, wanted a finger in every pie. Luther had learned much of his attitude when he had said, 'Every man has his price, Knox.'

Because of Protheroe's personal interest Luther had been much aware of the various developments. Far more significant, however, was the impact all this enterprise was having on the lives of the people in the area, many of them being tenants of the Estate, farmers, smallholders and cottagers. More than fifty years ago the Pembrokeshire agent, Charles Hassal, had written of the harmful effect mining was having on the farm economy, and Luther continued to have his own doubts.

At that time a canal had been built from Stepaside down to Wisemansbridge, but it had been an engineering disaster and never functioned, whereas, Luther had to admit, the Grove ironworks, in spite of all its problems, had at least begun to function. He had heard much of the fine equipment with workshops and machinery. He had never been inside the buildings, but from the road it was possible to see their solid magnificence. Small wonder that so many could see these developments as holding out hope for a better future. Dick Thomas was one of them.

In the autumn, when Dick married Bessie and moved into Light-A-Pipe, he took a job at the Grove. That winter a new foundry was built near the brickworks at Wisemansbridge, the idea being that there would be a ready supply of raw material in the form of pig iron available from the Grove.

Whatever the hopes of the workers, however, the year closed with the iron trade experiencing a serious slump, and the decision stood that, although the second furnace had long since been ready, it was not worth putting it into blast.

In January, there was an explosion of gas and some of the machinery was damaged. The one furnace had to be blown out and iron-making was halted. Times were desperate for many. They and God alone knew how they managed to survive. Quite a few turned to poaching, as hungry people will. Again Dick Thomas was one of them. But unfortunately for him, and for Bessie and the newborn baby, Dick was caught. Worse than that, he was caught twice.

First of all he was caught with a rabbit and then, within weeks, and which was far worse, with a hen pheasant. Both by night. The fact that the pheasant being caught in the springle was a complete accident was neither here nor there. The verdict was a foregone conclusion and it was transportation. Because of his previous good character and the birth of the baby, he was shown mercy and sent for a mere five years instead of the more usual seven.

That summer, prices improved, but, although neighbours helped where they could, everything was too much for Bessie to manage on her own. Her baby was not well and took much of her time. In June she lost one of her two cows with the red water. Neighbours were good at haymaking time and had her hay in for her, but in August her other cow had garget. Although the cow lived, she lost all four quarters of her udder and, never going to give any milk again, was sold to the butcher.

Early in September Bessie came to Plumtree Hill, carrying her baby in a shawl. Luther was distressed to see how much older she looked, flecks of grey already in her dark hair, and her careworn features showing all too clearly how she had suffered.

'What do you want to do, Bessie?' he asked her at last when she had eaten the food Seeny had put before her, and she had told her sorry tale.

'What can a body do? I got enough to pay the rent this half-year, but after that God knows what's gwain happen. I got nowhere to go. If I waits to be put out it can only be the workhouse for both of us..'

A tear rolled down her cheek and she held the baby closer.

'No, don't cry. It hasn't come to that yet. We'll think of something.'

'That's why I come to see thee. I haven't got nobody else to talk to.'

'There are two things. First of all, we must find somewhere for you to live. Then we have to help you to keep going until Dick comes back again.'

'Oh, Lord sowls, do'st thou think a'll ever come back?'

'Why not? Others have.'

'Aye, but many have never been saw sight of again.'

'Not people like Dick. Don't ever doubt that.'

'But where can I go?'

'Leave it to me for a week and I'll see what I can think of.'

'I hopes thou do'sn't mind me comin' to ask.'

'What are friends for, Bessie?'

'Aye, but thou'rt a important man now.'

'Not really. And we're still friends.'

'The last words Dick said afore they took'n away was mind for me to come to thee if I was in trouble.'

'Don't worry too much, Bessie. The darkest hour's always before the dawn.'

Seeny, whose second baby, another boy, was the same age as Bessie's, was full of compassion. She had said little whilst Bessie was there, feeling that it was not her business, but, when she was gone, said, ''Tis cruel hard for some folks mind.'

'Yes, it is Seeny. But out of all suffering some good comes.'

'What good is there in this?'

'I don't know. But poor old Nanny Faggots died last week. Her son is coming over in the next day or two to clear out her few belongings and then her cottage will be to let.'

'Would they let Bessie have it?'

'Who d'you call they?'

'Well, th' Estate.'

'Who's the local agent?'

Seeny smiled and shook her head. 'Drop dead,' she said,

'I'll never get used to th' idea of thee bein' able to do things like that. An' thee only my baby brother.'

'Nephew. And I'll tell you what else I could do.'

'What's that?'

'I could put in a word for Absie and you to have Light-A-Pipe.'

'What?'

'It's a good place isn't it? Nice little house? Good land?'

'But they're church people. Thou know'st that. An' very difficult by all account.'

'That's right. I know that. Nobody knows it better. But my tutor, Mr Tobias Protheroe, always used to say, "Every man has his price, Knox. Every man has his price".'

Luther was not sure, but he thought the price in this case need not be too high. He knew the agent only slightly, but he was the sort of man who thought it might be no bad plan to oblige the young local agent to the Rhydlandcoed Estate. And when that young local agent showed willing to cement their relationship with a bottle of best French brandy he agreed that young Absalom Pugh would no doubt be a most suitable tenant for Light-A-Pipe. And, as Luther said, much better for his own family to be tenants on some other estate, not for it to look too much like favouritism. Just as if he cared.

Things had happened so quickly that Seeny hardly had time to think of the answer to another problem.

'Who's gwain look after thee?' she asked Luther.

'Well, I haven't thought much about it,' he said, 'but no doubt something'll turn up.'

Not that Luther was anxious for Absie and Seeny to go. Those twelve months together at Plumtree Hill he had known greater contentment than ever in his life. For his part, the arrangement could have gone on for ever, but he knew that Absie had always longed for his own place, and here was his chance. He hardly dared to think how much he was going to miss Seeny after the joy of being with her again, but her happiness and well-being were more important to him than he could have explained.

'Something'll turn up,' he said again, as cheerfully as he could. 'What was it the Reverend Josiah Price used to be so fond of saying? "Take no thought for your life, what ye shall eat, or what ye shall drink." Something'll turn up all right, you'll see.'

30

If Luther had any immediate ideas it was perhaps to ask Bessie how she would feel about moving in as his house-keeper. He had already told her that she could come to work at Plumtree Hill. Her cottage was only just down the road.

Seeny was not in favour of the idea.

'Thou know'st what people'll say,' she said.

'I hadn't thought of that.'

'Then thou's better think of it. A man in your position. Leave her move into the cottage an' come an' do somethin' durin' the day. People is bad for talkin'.'

People were already talking, and to some purpose. There was still a week to go before Bessie was due to move out of Light-A-Pipe and for Absie and Seeny to move in, and Luther had not made up his mind what to do for the best.

During that week he had an unexpected, but none the less welcome caller.

He had always had a regard for Sarah Bowen. As far back as he could remember, when he was a boy limping along in his bare feet, and she had come to Light-A-Pipe as a young married woman, she had been kind to him. Her kindness had no doubt been her undoing in giving shelter to Benny Sais after the Rebecca Riots and Merthyr troubles. Her kindness and her devil-may-care cheerfulness.

She had even managed to put a good face on things when they were turned out. She had never had any children—'Thicky Jack's no good,' she used to say cheerfully—and now, maybe in her forties, she was still not at all bad-looking, well-built, and appearing a bigger woman than she really was only because Jack was on the small side. But Jack was not with her when she came to Plumtree Hill.

'Mister Knox,' she said without preamble, 'I've called to apply for the job.'

'What job is that, maid?' said Luther.

'Go thee on. Don't tell me thou'rt gwain do for thyself.'

'Not if I can help it, Sarah. But I haven't fixed anything.'

'Aye, well, that's it, isn't it. Everbody's talkin' about what thee'rt gwain do. One says one thing an' another says somethin' else, but it's mostly owld lab with 'em, so I thought I'd come an' see.'

'What are you thinking of, maid?'

'Well, thou'rt gwain miss Seeny an' Absie. An' you'll need somebody to look after thee.'

'Bessie's going to come here to work.'

'Aye, but a man needs a'ooman about the house.'

'Would you and Jack come here to live?'

For the first time, a look of weariness came into Sarah's cheerful face.

'Name o' the Lord, thou know'st the state of the place we got!'

There was no need for her to say more.

'What about Jack?'

''Twould suit'n fine.'

Early in the summer the damage caused by the explosion at the Grove had been repaired, but there was no sign of the furnace going back into blast. Word went round that the Company were to concentrate more on their collieries, and it was even being said that, if they started iron making again, they might sink a new pit at the Grove in order to supply the ironworks direct. For the time being, however, they were concentrating on the collieries and Jack had a job hauling on a piecework basis.

'A could do a good bit about the place the same as Absie always done,' Sarah said. 'An' Bessie can milk, an' feed the calves, an' do a bit in the dairy.'

'You wouldn't mind working with Bessie?'

'How should I? She've never done nothin' to me.'

'She and Dick took Light-A-Pipe when you were turned out.'

'Lord sowls, boy. I never bothered about that. 'Twasn't their doin'. If they hadn't gone there somebody else would. An' Lord knows she've had enough to put up with, poor bugger.'

31

When Luther looked back in later years, he realised how opportune had been the timing of his move to Plumtree Hill and his more personal involvement and interest in farming. It had not been calculated but had come spontaneously from that confrontation with Protheroe. Luther had a fundamental belief that the land mattered, and it was merely propitious that his move coincided with a welcome and spectacular improvement in the fortunes of those who lived by the land.

The improvement was not immediate, but the signs were there, and it was to come in the course of a year or so.

As it happened, he was not in a position in those earlier years to take full advantage of the better times because his first responsibility was his job, and this occupied most of his time.Protheroe nowadays was often away from Deerfield. Luther did all that he had done before but, as local agent, took more decisions himself. It meant, however, that most days he went to Deerfield. More than once, with Protheroe not there to consult, he went to Rhydlancoed.

The first time it happened he had some misgivings. He knew the Squire was away but he had to talk to somebody.

The previous morning he had called by chance at Goose Meadow, where Owen Pugh, a relation of Absie's farmed. A sharp frost had followed some heavy spring rain. Winter was not quite over.

Luther found Owen trying to prop up the barn wall with some wooden posts.

'What's happened here then?' he said.

'Part of the damn owld wall have fell down.'

'I can see that. But how did it happen?'

'The frost I should think, on top of all the rain.'

Stones near the bottom at one corner had fallen out completely. To Luther it was evident that unless something were done, and done soon, the whole wall would collapse. And that would mean the roof collapsing as well.

'Why didn't you send to tell Protheroe?'

'Aye, Protheroe? A hell of a lot of good that would do!'

Luther knew it to be true. For years, ever since the wars with the French, the tenants had paid high rents, suffered from poor returns and seen their buildings being neglected. Protheroe was not alone amongst agents and landlords in his attitude, but he was among the worst for indifference to the plight of the tenantry as properties decayed.

With his own new phaeton, and Kit, a smart Welsh grey pony from the Preseli hills, Luther's confidence was increasing, but he had some doubts as to what his reception would be from the Squire's wife.

Mary Ann went to speak to Mr Ladd, the butler, and eventually came back to tell Luther that madam would see him.

He was shown into a room of no great size where a log fire burned cheerfully. Beautifully wrought miniatures were on the walls and there was an air of comfort about the deep armchairs and sofa. He took all this in as he waited. Then the door opened and he came face to face with Louisa Radley.

Her hair was golden, like her daughter's. Wide-browed and green-eyed, straight of nose and with the same firm chin, she was truly the mother of her daughter, but even more beautiful. There was a dignity about her which made it hard for Luther to believe that she could have shared her bed with Protheroe. Yet there was, too, a warmth and gentleness which stirred him and attracted him. He thought of the bundle of letters and he knew he could never do anything to hurt this woman.

'You asked to see me,' she said, and her eyes never left his face.

Luther felt foolish under her gaze.

'Yes, ma'am, and I'm sorry to trouble you.'

'It's no trouble, but what can you want of me?'

'Mister Protheroe is away, ma'am.'

'Where is he?'

'I don't know, ma'am. And I don't know when he'll be back. A tenant came to me yesterday. Part of his barn wall had collapsed. If it could be repaired now it would take a couple of masons two or three days. If it's left, the roof will collapse and the whole barn would have to be rebuilt.'

'And what does that have to do with me?'

'I really don't know, ma'am. But I felt something should be done, and I'm not in a position to authorise the work.'

'Would Mister Protheroe authorise the work if he were there?'

Luther hesitated. 'Maybe not, ma'am. No, I don't think he would.'

'But you think it should be done?'

'Yes, ma'am.'

She smiled. 'Then you see about it. As soon as you can.'

As she moved towards the door, she turned and smiled again. 'Thank you very much for coming to see me,' she said. 'And thank you for taking so much interest.'

The interview was over almost as soon as it had started. But Luther never forgot the warmth of that smile.

32

Luther did not bother to tell Protheroe of his visit to Rhydlancoed, or that he had had the work done on Owen Pugh's barn. Had he seen him at the time, he possibly would have done so, but the fact was that Protheroe had changed. He was drinking more heavily, had lost his air of levity, and now spent much of his time away from Deerfield. Something was on his mind.

The first inkling Luther had was in the summer, when Eiry Radley came home.

In haymaking time it was. At Plumtree Hill things were going well. Jack organised the work and there was no shortage of those willing to help. Sarah and Bessie cooked the food and served it and it was a satisfying life. Sarah was good in the house and saw to Luther's every need.

Not for one moment could he complain, and, although he missed Seeny's company, he was able to call in at Light-A-Pipe most days. His own affairs were prospering. It was the Estate which caused him far more concern.

A week after Miss Eiry came home he went to Rhydlancoed. Mrs Radley, as it transpired, and unusually for her, was not there. He saw her daughter instead.

Luther had been looking forward to seeing her again and had wondered whether she would be as friendly as on their previous brief meeting. In the event she asked him to have lunch with her. Confused though he was, his heart rejoiced, and he went through the meal, deferred to and waited upon, as in a dream. It was a far cry from boiled potatoes and butter-milk on a scrubbed table at Crickdam.

Afterwards, they walked in the garden and talked of country things and the hardships of the poorer people. They had much in common, and Luther felt a warm friendship towards her as she spoke of injustices which were anathema to her.

'On top of it all,' she said, 'the parson is as foolish and unfeeling as anyone could be. The very man who ought to be giving a lead if his belief in God meant anything to him. What do you think of the parson?'

'I don't know him, miss.'

'Never mind, let us sit here for a while anyway. And do you mind not calling me miss all the time. My name is Eurwallt. It's Welsh.'

'It's a lovely name. What does it mean?'

'It means golden hair. But everybody calls me Eiry. So if we are going to be friends will you please call me Eiry.'

'I would like to very much as long as nobody minds.'

'Who's to mind?'

'I don't know.'

'I'm twenty-one and if I wish to be called Eiry by you, I shall do so. How old are you, Luther?'

It was the first time she had used his name and it pleased him.

'I'm twenty-six,' he said.

'Then why don't you know the parson? Do you not go to church?'

'No, I go to chapel.'

'Oh, I see. That's interesting. Why do you go there instead of church?'

'I don't know. Brought up to it I suppose.'

'But there must be some attraction.'

The air was drowsy with the warmth of the afternoon sunshine. Even the birds seemed loth to sing, and butterflies lifted their wings lazily where they rested on the warm stonework. It was all so remote from the world of which they were talking.

'You seem very thoughtful,' Eiry said.

'That's because I'm thinking. You've just asked me something and I've never thought much about it before. But I suppose it's obvious really. Where do you sit when you go to church?'

'We sit in the front seat.'

'That's right. You pay for it and it's yours. And in the rows behind you they have their seats according to their social status right back to the peasants and labourers and paupers at the back.'

'And what do you do in chapel?'

'You can sit where you like. But more important than that, anybody can have the chance to become a deacon, to teach in Sunday school or even preach from the pulpit. That's a great thing with people who see themselves as being denied opportunity in other ways and oppressed. It's something to feel they matter. To be involved. You will understand their attitude I expect?'

'Yes, I do.'

Luther smiled. 'Even Mister Protheroe read the lesson on one occasion in chapel. When it was opened.'

'Ah, yes, Mister Protheroe,' she frowned.

Luther waited for her to say more. When she remained silent he said, 'Now you're being thoughtful.'

'M'm.' She looked sideways at him. '*I do not love thee, Doctor Fell; The reason why I cannot tell. But this alone I know full well; I do not love thee Doctor Fell.*'

'You may not know why you do not love Doctor Fell,' Luther said, 'but why do you not love Mister Protheroe?'

'I don't know. Truly I don't. But I know he is not a good man. He is dishonest.'

'How d'you know that?'

'Last summer, when my father was home, Mister Lloyd came to see him and I overheard part of their conversation.'

'Mister Lloyd?'

'Waldo Lloyd.'

'The solicitor?'

'Yes, the solicitor to the Estate.'

'I knew that.'

'Well, he seemed disturbed to say the least of it. But my father has no interest in the Estate. Only in the rents.'

Of a sudden she put her hand on Luther's and said, 'My mother was very touched that you should have come to see her to ask her advice. And she is very pleased at the interest you take in your work.'

'It's what I'm paid for.'

'I wonder what Protheroe is paid for.'

Eiry withdrew her hand and stood up. As Luther made to rise, she said, 'No, don't get up.' Looking down at him she said, 'When Chadwick was sacked as a trustee at the Grove, and Mister Vickerman made allegations of fraud, there was more in it than met the eye. Protheroe has had a very good run for other people's money, but I think his gallop is about to be reduced to a trot.'

Luther was to have little chance to ponder on this talk for he never saw Protheroe again. It was poor Mrs Powell who heard the shot that night and went upstairs to make the gruesome discovery that Protheroe had blown his brains out.

33

Luther had not intended going to Deerfield the following day, but when word came in mid-morning of what had happened he put Kit in the shafts of the phaeton and made haste. It was noon when he reached Deerfield, and Mrs Radley was already there. She was in Protheroe's study and it was evident that she had been through the drawers in the big desk. The one drawer remained locked.

'This is a dreadful business,' she said.

'Yes, ma'am, terrible.'

'How much do you know of Protheroe's affairs?'

'Very little ma'am.'

'Did you know he had shares in the Grove and was one of those who had been swindling Mister Vickerman?'

'No ma'am, I didn't know that.'

'Well, he was. Mister Vickerman met the Squire at his club in London and told him of it there. He said he had been having enquiries made for some time and that Protheroe had a finger in too many pies. Those were his words.'

Luther noticed she did not say Mister. It was just Protheroe.

'But that's not my business. Apart from that, he's been robbing the Estate for years.'

Her hands were restless and her eyes glanced from one shelf to another and back to the locked drawer of the desk.

'It will take ages to go through all these papers and books,' she said. 'The Squire will have to come home now, if only to see about this mess. His pleasures will have to take second place for a while.'

'I expect Mister Lloyd will know something, ma'am.'

'Mister Lloyd? Yes, of course. But we must have a look at some of these things now. Where is the key to this drawer, do you know?'

'It's Mister Protheroe's private drawer, ma'am.'

'Where does he keep the key?'

'He always kept it on him.'

Mrs Radley put her hand on the drawer knob and pulled.

'Maybe one of these other keys will open it,' she said. So intent was she, Luther wondered if she had forgotten his presence.

By some odd chance she picked on the right key at the first attempt. The lock clicked and she almost wrenched the drawer open. One by one she withdrew the account books, and envelopes of the Estate papers and documents, giving them scarcely a glance. When, at last, the drawer was empty, she stood there frowning and puzzled and Luther felt compassion for her in her agitation. Clearing his throat, he said quietly, 'You won't find what you're looking for in here, ma'am.'

She wheeled round and gave him a frightened look. 'What d'you mean, what I'm looking for?'

'The letters, ma'am.'

Her neck went white and Luther saw a vein twitch.

'What do you know of any letters?'

'I have them, ma'am.'

'You what?'

'I have them.'

He wondered whether she was going to strike him.

'I have not read them, ma'am. But I believed they were being used to hurt you. I meant no harm in keeping them.'

There was something he could not understand in the long look she gave him.

'You have not read them?'

'No, ma'am.'

'Where are they?'

'Hidden up in the roof ma'am. I'll fetch them for you.'

When he returned, a little dusty, a quarter of an hour later, Louisa Radley was still standing where he had left her.

He handed her the bundle of letters without a word and he saw that her hands were trembling as she took them.

'Do you give me your word that you have not read them?' she said quietly.

'I only glanced through them, ma'am, to see what they were.'

'And what were they?'

'I thought they were letters from a good, kind man to a beautiful lady.'

To his surprise he saw her blink back a tear.

Then she did an even more surprising thing. She kissed him gently on the cheek and said, 'I hope you will always be good and kind in life, too. Thank you for these and for your help. You may leave me now.'

II
Deerfield

There is a history in all men's lives,
Figuring the nature of the times deceas'd,
The which observ'd a man may prophesy,
With a near aim, of the main chance of things
As yet not come to life, which in their seeds
And weak beginnings lie intreasured.

Shakespeare
King Henry 4th, Part 2

Although Waldo Lloyd was no longer a young man, it was unexpected when he died soon after the sudden demise of Tobias Protheroe. It also caused considerable inconvenience and confusion for, apart from being a trustee of the Estate, he had always attended to its affairs personally. Whoever took over from him would have to burn a gallon or two of midnight oil sorting out the mess. Not least would be the daunting task of establishing what Protheroe's dishonesty had cost the Estate in hard cash.

'And that,' Luther said to the solicitor who came to Deerfield to see him, 'is something I don't suppose anybody will ever be able to do.'

Iorwerth Vaughan who, with the passing of Waldo Lloyd, had become the senior partner of Phillips, Lloyd and Vaughan, was a thin-faced , dark-visaged man of late middle years. Without disliking him, Luther did not immediately take to him. In a black frock-coat, tight trousers and black velvet waistcoat with a white silk cravat, he might have looked a dandy had he not looked so professionally prosperous.

'That may well be so' Vaughan had said. 'But we shall certainly have to establish what is left. How much can you tell me?'

'It all depends what you want to know.'

'To start with, then, what can you tell me about tenancies and rents?'

'Nothing that's not in the books.'

Going to the desk, Luther produced the ledgers, and the book with the list of tenants, farmers, smallholders and cottagers, together with a list of special agreements and clauses. He knew them nearly all and the background as to how they had come about.

'Here they are,' he said. 'I suggest you go through them, and if there's anything you want to know I'll tell you what I can.'

Vaughan turned the pages casually and sighed.

'This is going to be some job,' he said.

'It is indeed.'

'I'll have to take these books away.'

'Of course. But it will make things very difficult here without them.'

'Yes, I'm sure it will. But I'll see that you have them back as soon as ever it's possible.'

He turned over more pages, then he picked up an older book and began thumbing through it.

'What cottage is this? Who's Polly Gwyther?'

'She's the old midwife.'

'Doesn't she pay any rent?'

'No, she never has.'

Luther had never been able to establish why. Not that it was much of a cottage, but he had never known it to be in Protheroe's nature to run to kindnesses or favours of that sort.

'Maybe there'll be something in Carmarthen. In the Estate papers in our office. I know the old colliery papers are there.'

'That was before my time mostly,' said Luther. 'The Estate didn't do much with the colliery after the Act was passed. The pit depended on children for hauling the skips underground because the veins were thin and the mainways very low.'

'How much d'you know about the Grove Ironworks?'

'No more than anybody else round here. Mostly hearsay. But, of course, the Estate has had nothing to do with that.'

'But Protheroe did, I believe.'

'Privately, yes. You'll find some interesting references in that drawer.'

Luther smiled. 'Have a look through the papers first. Then it might be easier for me to explain some of it.'

Vaughan also permitted himself a slight smile. 'All right,' he said, 'I'll do that.'

He came to Deerfield again a week later, and this time Squire Radley was with him. It was the first time Luther had ever met the Squire, and it only needed one look at him to know why the drunk at Amroth Big Day had laughed and said, 'Nor a don't look much like the Squire neither.'

A mop of ginger hair he had. His freckled face was round, his blue eyes were round, and his belly was round. And, although he was not short, neither was he tall enough to look anything else but round. He wore a suit of heavy tweed, as Protheroe had invariably done.

Luther's face was fine and strong, his dark hair curled and his eyes were brown. Not by any stretch of the imagination could he ever see this one as his father, especially since Meg, so they said, had been the same colouring as fair-haired and blue-eyed Seeny and the rest of the family, who had all taken after their father, Patrick.

The Squire's speech was quick and impatient, as of a man who expected to get what he wanted when he wanted it. From the look of his petulant mouth Luther thought he would probably have had most of what he wanted ever since childhood. Reputed to be a good shot and a good horseman, it was no secret that his greatest interest was in the life he could lead when he went to London. And that was often, and for protracted periods. His tenants knew little of him. Many, like Luther, had never set eyes on him. Luther judged his age to be somewhere nearing fifty, and therefore a few years older than his beautiful wife. On looks alone, with a husband like this, maybe she could be forgiven for sharing her bed with Protheroe, whichever way he had managed to bring it about. The thought did nothing to besmirch the picture he carried in his mind of Louisa Radley. He felt a great compassion and tenderness towards her.

Cutting in on his thoughts, Radley said, 'Vaughan tells me you have a very fair knowledge of what's been happening on the Estate. You'd better carry on. Can't do any worse than that damned scoundrel Protheroe. Robbing me blind for years they tell me. Damned scoundrel. Pity he shot himself. Could have had him tarred and feathered. Ever seen a man tarred and feathered? Great sport. Not for the one who's tarred and feathered, of course. Haw, haw. By God no. They don't like it one bit.'

Luther made no comment, but Vaughan said, 'The Estate is in debt and the buildings have been neglected for years.'

'Oh, yes, I know that,' Luther said.

'But with good management something could be done. Perhaps we could set aside ten percent of the rent each half year to spend on the properties.'

Luther smiled. 'Ten percent would be about right if the buildings had been properly looked after over the years. As it is you'll need a mint of money to put them in shape first.'

'Where's the money to come from?'

'I've no idea.'

'We shall have to sell some farms as it is to pay off the debts.'

'Then maybe you'll have to sell some more to raise the money to spend on what's left.'

Squire Radley was not particularly interested.

'Well, you seem to have it sorted out between you. That's what I always say. No good having a dog and barking yourself. Not my line of business. Let me know if you want anybody tarred and feathered sometime and I'll show you how to do it. Haw, haw. More my line altogether.'

It began to look to Luther as if he would be the new agent to the Estate. Or what would be left of it. For the time being, at any rate, Mrs Powell and Beth would have to be kept on at Deerfield, and Affie Day in the garden.

2

It was not until the following spring, when the Grove ironworks had been idle for over two years, that the furnace was now to be put back into blast again and there was a return of workers to the Patches at Crickdam.

Absie, as always, was enthusiastic. Luther advised caution.

'Use what horses you have,' he said, 'but don't buy any more. See which way it goes first.'

'Well, things seem to be improvin' a bit with the farm.'

'Of course they're improving. But buy two or three more horses just to drive mine and if things go wrong at the Grove again you'll have nothing to do with 'em except feed 'em.'

He was nearer to the truth than he thought. The following year work began on the task of sinking the projected and much talked-of Grove Pit on the hill above the ironworks. The idea was that the coal would be fed down direct into the furnaces. Welcome though the development was, it was more than offset by the fact that the ironworks again closed down, and work at the Patches also ceased. At the same time there was talk of trouble in a place called the Balkan Peninsula.

A year later the trouble erupted into the Crimean War and Squire Radley bought himself a commission in the army. Nobody seemed to know what the trouble was all about, least of all Squire Radley, who was reported to have said that, as a good churchman, he was going out to see some of 'those damned infidels tarred and feathered.' Luther wondered whether it would make any difference when he discovered he was supposed to be on the side of the infidels against the Christians.

In the three years since Protheroe's suicide much had happened on the Estate. Luther's relationship with Vaughan had improved. Properties had been sold and Vaughan had agreed to much-needed work being done on those which remained. Luther saw no reason why that should not include Plumtree Hill. Spoilt by the luxury of a water-closet during his years at Deerfield, he had one installed at Plumtree Hill at the same time as he was having a new roof for the house and a new cowshed and stable.

Occasionally, it was necessary for him to go to Rhydlancoed. He did not always see Louisa Radley, but he usually saw Eiry and was always made welcome. They had much in common, with their interest in country things and in the affairs of the tenantry.

On one such visit he was having tea with both of them and he felt a warm intimacy about the occasion. The Squire had left for the Crimea some months previously and Luther enquired as to his well-being.

'There was a letter last week,' Eiry said. 'Nearly one whole side of a small sheet of paper.'

So confident of their relationship did Luther feel that he was emboldened to ask, 'Has he found out yet whose side he's on?'

Louisa Radley smiled and Eiry said, 'Not only that. He's made an even more important discovery. He thinks the Czar is one of those damned dissenters, which is worse than being an infidel.'

Her mother and Luther both laughed, and it was another little bond between them.

For the most part it was Eiry who did the talking, her mother seeming content to listen. As always, Eiry was interested in the welfare of the people.

'Is there any news of the Grove?' she said.

'I believe they keep running into all sorts of trouble sinking the new pit. But they keep pushing on with it.'

'I meant the ironworks.'

'Oh, no. Nothing at all. You keep on hearing all sorts of rumours, but I can't see them doing much there until the pit is working.'

'And how long will that be?'

'Goodness only knows. I don't know much about the iron business, but according to all that's in the papers it's in a bad way, and they say that Vickerman's already lost so much there he's short of capital.'

'Well, 'tis cruel hard on those who can't get work. But at least the ones on the land are better off.'

'Some of them don't know themselves after all the years of struggle and rock-bottom prices,' Luther said.

'It's good to see farming doing well again.'

'The amusing thing is though that some of them are simple enough to associate it in their own minds with me becoming agent.'

'But the improvements to the buildings are mostly to do with you.'

'Not really. Estate policy. But it's good for our relationship if they think so.'

Eiry's mother smiled. 'Do you think that good opinion is important?'

'I suppose it helps.'

'Then do you mind if I ask how the Bowens are doing with you?'

'The Bowens? Jack and Sarah? They're doing very well. And they seem very happy. But why d'you ask?'

'The vicar has a very poor opinion.'

'Of whom or what?'

'A very poor opinion of the Bowens and of the fact that you gave them shelter.'

Luther gazed at her blankly. He was saved from the need to say anything immediately because Eiry said, 'Oh, mother! Mortimer Strong is a senile, drink-sodden idiot. What's more, he isn't even a Christian.'

'But he's the vicar of the parish.'

Luther knew the answer well enough, but he asked, 'Can you tell me why it disturbs him so much?'

'I believe it goes back to the time when they gave refuge to a desperate criminal and, to use the vicar's words, desecrator of the House of God.'

Luther said, 'I don't condone what the man did and they were foolish to have concealed him. But I prefer to think of them as having shown compassion to a misguided wretch in his hour of need. What's more, it was all of ten years ago.'

'But the vicar has a very long memory.'

'And a very bitter one,' Eiry said.

'I think,' said Luther, 'I'll go and have a talk to him.'

He did not say what he had it in his mind to tell him. Nor did he say what it was in his mind to do.

He had a good relationship with Iorwerth Vaughan, who had every reason to be pleased with his stewardship. The time had come for him to buy the freehold of Plumtree Hill. He had the money. Maybe then he would go to see the vicar.

3

Before the transaction had been finalised Mam Bron died.

In the springtime it was, a treacherous time of year, when the churchyards always seemed to claim a good many unexpectedly.

Seeny had been good to her and she had wanted for nothing at the end. Luther believed he had done his duty by her, although he knew in his heart he had never had any real love for her. She was his mother's mother, which should have meant something to him, but somehow it never had. For her own part she had always looked after him as a boy and clothed him as well as she could, and not for the first time he wondered how ever she had managed to do as well as she had done. The burying of her would be his responsibility.

He and Seeny had sat with her that last night and Luther was glad of that. In the morning, almost as if she were expected, Polly Gwyther came and prepared her for her coffin. She was one of those Luther knew less well, and he didn't care much for the little he knew.

'Thee'rt lookin' main coppit and filty fine,' she said.

He was dressed as usual and saw no reason for any comment from this scraggy, unkempt old drabble-tail. When he looked more closely at her, he realised that she was probably no more than late middle age, and not nearly as old as she looked.

'They tells me as thee'rt a main important gentleman since Mister Protheroe have gone an' shot hisself.'

'Not important. I do what I'm told to do and what I'm paid for.'

'They wouldn't be tellin' thee to turn me out of my bit of a owld cottage, I suppose.'

'I don't see why they should, although you don't pay any rent. But I don't know why you don't.'

She grinned and showed her stained teeth, 'Don't thee worrit thy curly head about that, young Mister Knox. There's things as I could tell as lots of folks would like to know about. So don't thee try hawsin' me, young Mister Knox.'

He was glad when she went indoors to go about her grisly business, and more glad still when, her task completed, she went shuffling up the track towards the cliff road. That same morning he drove to see the vicar, with a firm resolve to say nothing on this occasion of any of his gratuitous comments and apparent attempt to cause trouble.

Even that early in the day Luther found him with his senses dulled by drink. He answered the doorbell himself, his black clerical suit turning green with age and his white, straggly hair uncombed. He looked at Luther without any show of friendship but asked him in. His study was dusty and untidy.

'I am having my morning drink,' he said. 'As a dissenter, do you have any objection to that?'

'None at all,' Luther said.

'I'm relieved to hear it. I thought that since you see fit to harbour the ungodly you might also go along with their ranting humbug about things of the flesh which uplift the spirit. Don't you ever read your Bibles in those places where you gather to rant and rave?'

'Which part do you have in mind in particular?'

'Which part? Any part you like. But as a starting point for a discussion, which was the first miracle Jesus performed?'

With an unsteady hand, with skin like parchment, he refilled his glass with sherry from a cut-glass decanter.

'As far as I remember,' Luther said 'it was when He turned the water into wine at the wedding in Cana in Galilee.'

'So you come to abuse me in my own home do you?'

'I hadn't intended to. But if you want me to I can remind you of something else concerning Christ and drink.'

The vicar glared at him.

'I won't insult your learning by offering you chapter and verse,' said Luther, 'but Jesus also said something about those who offered a cup of cold water in His name.'

He waited for the effect of what he had said to sink in.

'My dear man,' said the vicar. 'I do hope you will forgive me. Since the lights came into the sky my memory plays funny tricks.'

'The lights?'

'Ah, yes, the lights. You've seen them no doubt. But I don't expect you to be able to understand them any more than anybody else. That's a mystery which is given to few of us.'

For a long time he remained silent and Luther began to realise that he was not merely the worse for drink but that his mind was going.

'Why have you come here?' he said at last.

'To see about burying my mother.'

'Your mother?'

'Bronwen Knox of Crickdam.'

'Bronwen Knox? Crickdam? She's your mother is she?'

'She died last night.'

'I don't want to offend you, but would you take a glass of sherry with me?'

Luther was more or less a teetotaler. Not out of conviction, but out of a lack of interest in drink. He said, however, 'Indeed, vicar, I would be very honoured.'

The vicar seemed pleased, went to a cupboard for another glass, and poured Luther a stiff measure of sherry.

'About these lights in the sky,' he said. Then, for maybe twenty minutes, he rambled on incoherently with such lunatic talk as Luther had never heard. Luther's glass had scarcely been touched when the vicar stopped and said, 'Some more sherry?'

'No indeed, thank you, vicar. This is very nice. I'm enjoying it.'

'Are you really?'

'Yes, truly.'

The old man seemed foolishly gratified.

'Tell me about Crickdam,' he said. 'It's years since I was there.'

He did not wait for an answer. Instead, and Luther's heart almost stopped as he heard the words, he said, 'I baptised a little bastard child from there once. Should never have done it, of course, but pressure was brought to bear on me. The gentry can do that you know. No better than they ought to be, some of them. Imagine it. Me only a poor curate, and they made me baptise a little bastard.'

'Who was that, vicar?'

The old man seemed not to have heard the question. 'But I had my reward. Oh, yes. I had my reward. Years before I ever saw the lights.'

'Who was the child?'

'The child? Oh, this girl from Crickdam. A fine looking wench with beautiful fair hair and blue eyes. But she was a young hussy, of course. Should have been sent packing. But the gentry insisted, and curates who are waiting for their own living don't argue with the gentry.'

'Who was the child's father?'

'The girl was from Crickdam I tell you. I remember the entry well. It was so odd that she should have come all the way to my parish in Carmarthenshire to have her little bastard. I remember him too. Not a bit like his mother. Black hair and brown eyes. That's odd isn't it? I wonder why I remember that? There's so much I can't remember ever since the lights came into the sky.'

'What parish was that?'

'Oh, where the lights are. Where the lights are.'

For another half-hour Luther listened as the old man rambled on, interpolating with a question here and there, but getting no sensible response.

He was still rambling on when Luther let himself out of the house. He just hoped that 'the drink-sodden idiot,' as Eiry had so rightly called him, would be fit to conduct the funeral service.

In the event, it was the curate who did.

4

The day after the funeral, Luther went with Seeny to Crickdam, and Bessie went to Light-A-Pipe for the day to look after Seeny's children for her. Three she had now. Seth was six years old and growing sturdy, Jethro, named after his gramfer, was four, and little Hannah was two and into everything.

A delight it was to Luther to be with Seeny again, back there at this scene of so many childhood memories. Turned thirty she was now, but still beautiful. Gentle, as she had always been, yet full of fun.

Somehow she contrived a fire and boiled the old big black kettle to brew tea, and they sat on the wooden bench to drink it, without milk, out in the warm spring sunshine with a steady breeze pushing ripples across the blue waters of the bay. A big schooner was standing off Monkstone ready to come into Saundersfoot harbour and, as when Luther was a boy, the sight of her stirred something within him.

So content were they that they hardly spoke as they drank their tea. Then, as if by mutual consent deferring the depressing task of going through the cottage, they walked round the outside. Already there was an air of neglect. Nothing had been done in the garden since the previous spring and the few hens scratching round the buildings seemed to have little enthusiasm for life. There was no horse, no pig and no calf, but the old black cow looked as if she would be calving in a few weeks and so she was dry now and not having to be milked.

A good cow she had been and, as far as Luther knew, a grand-daughter of Fronwen, that grand old cow who had served the family so well in his childhood. A wonderful strain, Absie's father always said, Fronwen had come as a calf from down by Castlemartin below Pembroke where they had such a fine breed of heavy-milking black cows. Mam Bron's cow was hardly worth much at her age, but if she had a heifer calf it could be worth having.

'What's best to do?' Seeny said at last.

'There's nothing much we can do is there? There's only the two of us. You wouldn't want to live here, and I know I don't.'

The roof was in need of re-thatching, and the clom walls had started to crumble.

'Maybe if they started work at the Patches again somebody'd want it. But I can't see anybody wanting to come here otherwise.'

'What about the few things?' Seeny said.

'I wouldn't mind the old cow. See if she might have a heifer calf. I'd like to build up a little herd of black cattle.'

'You take her, boy. She'd be no good to us.'

'Aye, well, maybe I will. And Absie can have the cart and harness. He'd no doubt find a use for them.'

They came at last to the cottage. Damp ran down the kitchen walls which were cracking in places. It was dingy, and dank and miserable.

'Dear God,' he said. 'To think that we were happy here.'

'Aye, indeed,' Seeny said, 'we got a lot to be thankful for.'

The furniture, too, was sparse enough, but there was a good oak dresser, an oak chest and a couple of oak chairs. On the dresser there was a beautiful dinner service, a few lustre jugs and a handsome little tea-caddy. Shaped like a chest, it was about nine inches long and six inches high, made of polished walnut, inlaid with ivory, and with brass fittings and studs, and a brass handle for carrying. The domed lid lifted on brass hinges, there was a key to the delicate lock, and there were two compartments inside. It was reckoned to be anything up to a hundred years old. All anybody knew for sure was that it had come from a ship wrecked on the rocks below, as had the dinner service.

'You take what you want, Seeny,' Luther said. 'It's just us.'

Annie had married Tom Jenkins and gone to America. Patrick and George were in Canada. The other sister, Nancy, they had never seen. Years ago a message had come that she was going to New Zealand. She had never learned to read or write. That was the last they saw of her.

'But thou must have somethin'.'

'All right. I'll have the tea-caddy and jugs. You take the rest. Crockery, dresser, chest, chairs, the lot.'

In Mam Bron's bedroom there was nothing to speak of. Luther looked under the bed and pulled out a small wooden chest, which he carried out and placed on the kitchen table. The chest was locked.

'I knows where the key is,' Seeny said, turning towards the dresser and opening one of the drawers.

The lock of the chest opened easily. There were a few faded newspaper cuttings inside and there were some aged envelopes. There was also a tin. Luther picked it up and it was heavy. He opened it curiously and they saw the gold sovereigns. Seeny caught her breath.

'Christ alive!' she said.

Luther tipped them carefully on the table and counted them. There were a hundred and three.

He put the sovereigns back in the tin and said, 'There was a lot I didn't know about Mam Bron. And I certainly never guessed she was a miser.'

'Good God,' Seeny said. 'How could she manage it?'

'I often wondered how she managed as well as she did. Thrift and struggle I suppose.' Then he gave the tin to Seeny and said, 'Here, take this home with you now.'

'Don't thee be so dull,' she said. 'We'll share it.'

'No, indeed we won't. I've got more than enough and you and Absie can do with it.'

Seeny put the tin on the table and put her arms round him and kissed him.

'Thou wast always so good to me,' she said.

'That's because I've always loved you.'

There was no answer to that.

'I'll take the chest home,' Luther said 'and go through it sometime. If there's anything else there I'll let you know.'

He carried it out and put it in the phaeton. Absie could come back sometime for the furniture. Kit was in the stable chewing hay. She turned her head alertly as Luther came in. Then he heard a faint animal sound. Peering into the gloom in the corner he saw a pair of small bright eyes staring at him out of the darkness. He bent down and picked up a black kitten not yet half-grown.

Thin it was, and obviously hungry, but it purred at the comfort of Luther's touch. For some time he had been looking out for a dog. Gipsy had been the only dog in his life and he felt he would like a dog of his own. Instead he had acquired a cat.

5

Sarah, warm-hearted and generous, raised no objection to the new arrival and, in the twinkling of an eye, there was a saucerful of milk on the kitchen floor for him. When he had lapped it dry, he stretched out in front of the fire. Other cats must know their place and remain outside. But not Ham.

'Why Ham?' Said Sarah.

'Well, Ham, you should know, Sarah,' Luther said, 'was the black one of the children of Noah. Come to think of it, his descendants spread over a whole continent. I wonder what trouble we're storing up for ourselves.'

'Don't thee take no chances. Put his head in a jug an' out with 'em.'

'Sarah,' he said, 'you've got a nasty mind.'

'I knows what men are. Except thicky Jack. Sometimes I wonders if they put his head in a jug or somethin' like it afore he knowed what it was for.'

Sarah was always full of such nonsense and Luther sometimes wondered how serious she was. That evening, however, he gave it no thought at all as he went through the contents of Mam Bron's old wooden chest, after the meal had been cleared away. He had eaten alone, as was his custom. At first, he had not been happy about this arrangement, but Sarah had insisted. They would eat in the outside kitchen and, as master of the house, he must eat on his own. As time went by, he came to value this privacy.

A log fire was burning cheerfully, the oil lamp shedding its warm glow, as he put the chest on the table and, without any great enthusiasm, began to go through its contents.

Mam Bron had been much in his mind and he hoped the sovereigns would do Absie and Seeny some good. For her to have hoarded like that was beyond his understanding. The more he thought of the privations, the more intolerant he became. He had saved his own money, because that had been his training, but he hoped he would never make a god of it. He believed money was meant to be used. With hardly a thought he had given almost all his savings to Pat and George for their fare to Canada and a new life, and he had done it joyfully. What else was money for, he had said at the time. Yet here was Mam Bron, old, without comfort, clothes tattered, and probably often enough hungry in spite of whatever he and Seeny had done for her, and all the time with more than a hundred gold sovereigns in a box under the bed.

That was her nature, he supposed. Like that time they had gone to Narberth with the roll of cloth she had hoarded, and she had haggled and bantered, and come away with a new suit for him, and shirts and collars and new boots, and some change into the bargain.

He glanced at the newspaper cuttings and they were about the Rebecca Riots and the troubles at Merthyr. There was no apparent reason why she should have acquired these and kept them, unless she knew more than she had ever said about any part George and Patrick may have played in these affairs. There were certificates of births and deaths, and the usual sort of thing which could have been expected to be found in such a box, but their details did not register with him. His every thought was concentrated on the envelope of rather superior quality and the letter, in some clerk's beautiful copper-plate, which it contained from Waldo Lloyd.

It was short and to the point and set out the terms of the financial settlement on her to support Luther, bastard child of Megan Knox, until the age of twenty-one.

He read it and re-read it and then read it again. And it told
him nothing. Certainly it did not tell him who his father was.
Waldo Lloyd, of course, had been solicitor to the Rhydlandcoed Estate, but he was dead, and dead men, as the
saying was, told no tales. Not for the first time in his life he
found himself wondering how Meg could so heartlessly have
turned her back. Even for money.

Luther folded the letter at last and, as he did so, smiled to
himself, for it had told him something after all. It had told
him how Mam Bron had managed over the years, appearing
sometimes to spoil him and anxious that no harm should
befall him. He had been her meal ticket. The horde of
sovereigns was suddenly less of a mystery.

There was nothing else in the chest, apart from a little
velvet pouch. Luther opened it and found that it contained
a coin. But when he extracted it, he found that it was only
half a coin. Gold it was, in all its pristine brightness. For
some reason, which, for all he knew would remain a mystery
for ever, somebody had cut a spade-guinea in half, with the
cut running clearly from top to bottom of the spade on the
one side and the monarch's head on the other.

Luther put the half-coin back in its pouch and all the
contents back in the chest. For some time now, ever since he
had seen the vicar, a thought had been in his head. He must
find out where the Reverend Mortimer Strong had been a
curate before he came into the parish and one day, perhaps
sooner rather than later, he must go to that parish and see if
he could look through the church register.

6

Before Absie had a chance to collect the few things from
Crickdam, there blew up one of those wild equinoctial
storms to drive the white waves flying across the bay and lift
the spindrift high up the cliff-face and over the fields. Trees
bent before the onslaught, daffodils were beaten back into
the ground, and the deteriorating thatched roof was blown
off the cottage at Crickdam.

That same night the old black cow calved and had a lovely
heifer calf with a little white mark on her chest. Fronwen still

lived and, as the old house at Crickdam tumbled rapidly into ruins, the calf grew to be for Luther a link with his boyhood. On one occasion he found himself wondering whether Meg had ever milked that other Fronwen when she had been a girl at Crickdam.

He had been thinking much of Meg since finding the paper in Mam Bron's wooden chest. That crazy parson had said she was a fine looking girl. But no word had he let drop which as much as hinted that he knew who had fathered her child. Luther was certain it could not have been Squire Radley. Then why was Waldo Lloyd involved? He was not only solicitor to the Rhydlancoed Estate, but a trustee. Meg had been in service at Rhydlancoed. It was all too much of a coincidence. The Squire would have been a young blood at the time. His father had not long died and the young Squire had not yet married. To that extent he was free to father as many bastards and pay for their support as he wanted to.

One thing seemed fairly evident and that was, whoever his father was, he must have been one of the gentry, otherwise why all the fuss and secrecy and financial arrangement?

It was easy enough to discover the parish from which Mortimer Strong had come, because Eiry knew. Luther had never heard of such a place. It was called Llandeilo Abercowin.

'It's up beyond Saint Clears towards Carmarthen,' she said. 'Mother has a very soft spot for it. It's very old, they say.'

Luther said no more. It was as much as he wanted to know.

His first move was to write to the vicar. He said only that he had been told something of the church's great antiquity and that he would like to visit it. To his great delight he had a reply which was courteous and encouraging. The letter pointed out, however, that Llandeilo Abercowin was far off the beaten track and that, unless he had his own transport all the way, his best course would probably be to enquire at the Black Lion at St Clears for one Tom Davey, who had a trap for hire on the stage-coach route. The writer, the Reverend Ieuan Mostyn, would look forward to hearing when he could be expected.

Luther told Sarah that he was going to Carmarthen for the day. That, he felt, was enough for her to know. He knew a strange excitement at the prospect of this venture. Being a bastard was one thing. He had learned long ago to live with it and it troubled him little. The uncertainty, the complete mystery and the complete ignorance of any knowledge of his father were all vexatious to him. He dared not hope for too much, yet he felt that his mission had to be undertaken.

The dew was a mat of sparkling diamonds as the sun came up over the distant hills of Carmarthenshire that May morning, and Luther made his way in the phaeton out to the main road to meet the old Cambrian stagecoach at the Mailway Inn at the crossroads above Stepaside. He had always stabled Kit there for the day on the rare occasions when it had been necessary for him to go to Iorwerth Vaughan's office in Carmarthen. It made no difference that today he would be going only as far as St Clears.

He felt it was a good start to the day when the coach came round the bend and he saw that the box seat was available. Jimmy Wicks with his four-in-hand was no stranger to Luther. Unlike so many of his kind he was prepared to keep his mouth shut and mind his own business. The fact that his business happened to include the handling, on the side, of quite a few poached pheasants and salmon, was not Luther's concern. In any case, Jimmy always prided himself on the fact that he only ever handled them in season.

Luther knew none of the outside passengers and his conversation with Jimmy Wicks was confined to an occasional exchange of comment on the state of the crops and livestock as they passed. And, of course, Jimmy had his customary little grumble that things were not what they used to be.

'I knowed 'twould never be the same after the railway line come to Carmarthen,' he said. ''Tisn't three years yet an' things have changed altogether. The old Cambrian's as good as finished.'

'Never mind, Jimmy,' Luther said. 'It'll be a few years before the line comes down our way.'

'Aye, but it'll come.'

'Yes, I suppose it will.' Luther knew it to be true, and he

had a fair idea as to how it would transform their way of life. But it was not a subject to which he felt disposed to give much thought on such a lovely morning. He had more personal things to think of and he lapsed again into silence as the four-in-hand rolled comfortably along this fine new road at a steady eight miles an hour through the lovely countryside. They should reach St Clears easily in under two hours.

From the high ground towards Llanteague there was a fine view of the bay sweeping from Caldey way out to the Gower in the hazy distance. There were many more steam ships on the horizon now than when he was a boy. Soon, the coach had reached Red Roses, and then the road went into a gentle downward gradient and, for mile after mile, they travelled easily, down and down, never-ending so it seemed, through lovely woodland, broken only where the occasional cart-track led off and up through the woods towards unseen farms. The weary pull up on the way home in the evening would be another story, but Luther gave no more thought to that than to the coming of the railway.

The Black Lion lay near to the toll at the Mermaid, where the gate was open with no sign of a keeper anywhere in evidence.

'In wettin' his whistle with Tom Davey I expec's,' Jimmy said.

It made Luther's search a straightforward task. Not that it would have been too difficult, for it was not fair-day and there were not too many people about. Even the arrival of the stagecoach aroused little interest. The railway had already reached St Clears on its way through to Haverfordwest and the stagecoach had now become small beer.

Tom Davey was sitting cross-legged on the oak skew, his old hat pushed back on his forehead and with a pewter mug beside him on the scrubbed table. He stared as Luther entered the taproom and he rose to meet him. Before Luther could speak, he said, '*Bore da*, sir. Are you the gent then as the vicar said to expect?'

'Yes, are you Mister Tom Davey?'

'Yes indeed. Tom Davey it is.'

He still stared at Luther. '*Duw, duw,*' he said, as though unable to believe the evidence of his own eyes. '*Duw, duw. Duw, duw.*'

A pleasant man he was, of medium build, with an odd mixture, so it seemed to Luther, of cheerfulness and sadness. His clothes were the rough clothes of the countryman, and his hands were the hands of a man who had known much hard toil. Even when they were in his trap Tom looked sideways now and again at Luther with puzzlement in his blue eyes.

'*Duw, duw,*' he said again, 'You'll excuse me for asking sir, but was you some relation to Master Christopher?'

'Who was Master Christopher?'

'Are you not his relation, then?'

'I've never heard of him. What was his other name?'

'*Duw, duw,* I can't tell you that. I never heard it. You're not related then? But, *duw, duw,* you look just like him. Same build. Same features. When you did come into the Lion this morning I was thinking it was a ghost it was. *Duw, duw,* yes. Just like him. I would know you anywhere.'

'Tell me, then,' Luther said, his heart beating so loud he thought that Tom Davey must hear the thumping of it above the rattle of the wheels and the steady clip-clop of the horse's hooves, 'who was Master Christopher?'

'*Duw, duw,* I can't believe it. A lovely young man he was. Just your build. Tall and smart. Used to come up the river with his boat in the summer to Abercowin. Loved the sea he did. But he was drownded in the end somewhere out foreign. Friendly with Miss Lloyd he was at the time.'

'Miss Lloyd?'

'Miss Louisa. Beautiful lady. But he got drownded and she married one of the gentry from down your country somewhere.'

'How long ago was all this?'

Tom thought a while. '*Duw, duw.* All of thirty years I should say. Maybe more.'

'Tell me,' said Luther, 'what sort of place is this Llandeilo Abercowin?'

'Oh, beautiful place. But very lonely like. 'Tis easier to

reach from the water sometimes than from the road. Very, very old they do say it is.'

Unable to restrain his curiosity, Luther said, 'Thirty years ago, you said. Was there ever another young lady with Master Christopher?'

'What was her name?'

'I'm not sure, but I have an idea that it was perhaps Megan.'

'*Duw, duw*. Megan? Beautiful girl she was and lovely with it. Fair hair. But not a lady. A servant maid she was from down your country. Poor little soul came to Abercowin to have a baby.'

'Did you know her?'

'No, I didn't know her, but I talked to her a bit. It was me and Father brought her baby back.'

There was nothing for Luther to say. He only had to wait for Tom to collect his thoughts.

'I don't know what happened to Megan,' he said. 'Went off to London I think. But there was a servant with her. A nursemaid. I was helping Father in the boat that time and me and him took this servant with Megan's baby across to Laugharne and there was a coach waiting for them from down your country somewhere.'

'What was the servant's name?'

'*Duw, duw*. I couldn't remember that. I don't think I did ever hear it. Never spoke much but she was sharp when she did. Not bad-looking but keep out of her way like. I remember Father saying she could turn the milk sour if she looked at it twice. Did you know Megan then?'

'No, I didn't know her.'

'Thinking I was. You was too young. That's my little place over there.'

Luther looked to where he pointed and saw a trim white-washed cottage with a cow grazing in the field.

'Lonely it is, like.'

Luther sensed the sadness in him.

'You're not married?' he asked.

'Aye, *bach*. Married I am. Yes indeed. I'll always be married. But sleeping my little Annie is, down at Llandeilo Abercowin with our little ones, waiting for me. Gee up, then

Ianto,' he called and slapped the reins on the horse's back.
A gentle man he was and Ianto hardly bothered to change
his pace.

Tom fell silent then as they turned from the main road and
the village of Pentre Llanfihangel, towards the south, and
Luther sensed that he wished to be left with his thoughts.
Luther, too, had much to occupy his mind. Louisa Radley's
letters had been signed Chris, and Luther had assumed that
he would have been the father of the child she was
expecting. Now, he was not so sure and, even if he was the
father, it looked as if he could have been playing fast and
loose with Meg at the same time. A buzzard swooped low
and he became conscious of the rolling countryside through
which they were passing.

Everything looked prosperous. The cattle in their new
shining summer coats were sleek and fit, grazing rich, lush
pastures, and the condition of the lambs suggested that
some of them would soon be on their way to the butcher's
even this early in the season. In fields locked up for hay the
grass was already waving gently in the warm breeze. Though
neither bird could be seen, the rasping call of the corncrake
and the distinctive three-note whistle of the quail
announced that both species were present in considerable
numbers. Cock pheasants, far less wary now than earlier in
the year, were out in the corn fields, looking for grubs in the
still soft soil, whilst the hens, Luther knew, would be sitting
all along the hedgerows. It was a satisfying scene and good
to see the countryside so prosperous after the years of
struggle and poverty.

They crossed a bridge over the Cowin and eventually
began to climb until they came to a crossroads and once
more turned south.

Whereas for some miles the road had been poor they found
themselves now on the roughest of cart-tracks and, even at
walking pace, the going was uncomfortable. Away to their
right, and beneath them, the small river Cowin ran to meet
the Taf in a valley which Luther could see must be rich with
bird life.

The Taf, he knew, was tidal, and the tide was on the flood.
Shelduck, distinctive even at a distance, were everywhere to

be seen, and many other ducks, not readily identifiable so far away, were on the water with them.

At last, after something like an hour's travelling, when Luther wondered whether they would ever reach anywhere, they rounded a bend in the lane and he saw, below and ahead of him, Llandeilo Abercowin, situated on the confluence of the Cowin and the Taf, looking out towards the Taf estuary, and he felt instinctively that it was a place of great history. What he subsequently discovered to be the Rectory was the house he saw first, substantial and affluent. Opposite to it were the farm buildings, and beyond these again stood the little church. It had no tower but there was a bell at the west end.

As they approached, the Reverend Ieuan Mostyn came out to meet them and greeted Tom in Welsh. Luther got down from the trap, and the vicar held out his hand and said, 'I don't suppose you speak Welsh?'

'I'm afraid not, vicar.'

'A heathen and ungodly people you are. But we'll go on praying for you.' Then he laughed heartily.

A big man he was, round of face and exuding joviality, and Luther wondered if there had ever been anyone in his life who could have done other than like him. Again he spoke to Tom in Welsh, then turned to Luther and said, 'Now then, Mister Knox, you must be thirsty. A cup of tea first.'

Without waiting for an answer he led Luther indoors. A comfortable house it was, old and solid and with furniture to match. Ieuan Mostyn called 'Missus Rees,' in a loud voice and in no time at all the door opened and in bobbed his housekeeper looking more cheerful, if such a thing could be possible, than the vicar himself. Their exchanges were all in Welsh.

'You must excuse us, Mister Knox,' Mostyn said, 'but Missus Rees speaks only the language of Heaven. I, of course, have to hobnob with infidels and so it is incumbent upon me to know their lingo. But she will feed you as though you were one of the chosen race.' Again he laughed.

And indeed, as if by magic, a great pie appeared on the table followed by a fruit cake and wholemeal bread, golden butter and honey. There was more chatter in Welsh and smiles and bobbing, then the great brown teapot appeared. Luther remembered that first visit to Deerfield and Mrs Powell's welcome, and suddenly realised how hungry he was.

Ieuan Mostyn did not eat but had a large cup of tea. When Luther had finished eating, Mostyn took out a briar pipe and tobacco pouch which he offered to Luther, 'Do you smoke?'

'No thank you, vicar.'

'Perhaps you're wise. They say it's a killer. But I've smoked for nearly fifty years since I was but a callow youth. Don't ask me to justify it, for I can't. I just enjoy it.'

'I've never started,' Luther said.

'It's not that you have some odd chapel objection to it?'

'What makes you think I'm chapel?' Luther asked.

Ieuan Mostyn pursed his lips and suppressed a smile. 'Very quick of you. Very quick.' He paused, then said, 'We don't get many enquiries from people asking to come and see our church, so I was interested to find out who my caller would be.'

He paused again whilst he lit his pipe. 'Tell me, Mister Knox,' he said at last, 'what is your real interest here? The farmhouse opposite was once known as the Pilgrims' Lodge. Whether it offered shelter to pilgrims on their way to Saint David's is not known. There are three cells underneath believed to have been used by monks. Now they're in use as a dairy. The church on the opposite bank of the Cowin, near Treventy, is known as the Pilgrim's Church. Its real name is Llanfihangel Abercowin. Our church here at Llandeilo Abercowin is very old. It is believed to have been given to the venerable Saint Teilo and he died way back in the year five hundred and sixty something, so that puts it at near enough one thousand three hundred years. It is thought that certain alterations were carried out about three hundred and fifty years ago. So which of all this interests you?'

His cheerful face gave nothing away, but Luther knew that this bluff character was no fool. He had done many things in life by instinct. He said now, 'None of these things brought me here, vicar.' He paused, looked through the window towards the estuary in the distance, then turned back to the vicar and said, 'I am an illegitimate child.'

'Before you say more, Mister Knox, let me correct you. There is no such thing or person as an illegitimate child. Only illegitimate parents.'

'Put it more simply then. I'm a bastard.'

'So are many good men and women.'

'I do not know who my father was. Recently I talked to the Reverend Mortimer Strong. His mind is going, but from what he told me in his confused state, I have reason to believe that I could have been baptised in this little church when he was curate here. I was hoping you might let me see your church registers.'

Ieuan Mostyn put his pipe on the table. He said, 'Thank you for being honest with me. I thought it might have been that. The register is in the church, but I don't think it will tell you much.'

'Have you seen it? Is there an entry there?' His almost childlike enthusiasm was touching.

'Yes, there is an entry. But you shall see it for yourself.'

Ieuan Mostyn did not hurry as they walked down towards the little church, and Luther, even with his mind in something of a turmoil, could not help but notice and admire the sound condition of the buildings. In the haggard there were still two good ricks of hay remaining untouched from the previous winter. In the field by the church a flock of geese were grazing and they raised their heads as the two intruders passed.

Set into the church wall was a stone in memory of Sarah Bodel who had died in 1758 at the age of thirty six. Some of the headstones, Luther noticed, were even older and he was surprised how young so many of the people had died. But there were not many graves, and most of them were overgrown. Two of them, however, were well cared for, with flowers growing on them, and at these Tom Davey was working.

The church door was not locked and, as they entered, Luther was struck by the simplicity and austerity. It was nothing like he had expected. The floor was of stone flags and the seats were simple moveable benches with backs. Everything, from cheap table altar to pulpit, bespoke simplicity, and yet it was a prayerful place.

Going to a cupboard door beneath the pulpit, Ieuan Mostyn withdrew a wooden box and took a key from his pocket. He took the top register and handed it to Luther, 'That's the one you want.'

Luther's hands shook as he opened it. There were very few entries and it took him only moments to find his own. As Ieuan Mostyn had said, it was not going to be of any help to him. It said, 'Luther Knox, male, bastard child of Megan Knox, servant, of Crickdam in the county of Pembroke' and the year was 1825.

'Does it tell you anything?' Mostyn asked.

'Nothing at all, vicar. Nothing I haven't known for years. But thank you for the trouble you've taken.'

'No trouble at all my boy. Nice to see somebody from foreign parts. I lead a quiet life and it suits me. The parish work is light and I'm lazy by nature. I have my little boat which I enjoy in the summer, and in the winter, when the geese are in, the shooting is without equal. What more can a bachelor country parson ask of life?'

'How well d'you know the history of the parish?'

'What history do you mean?'

'Recent history.'

'Very little. Very little indeed. I came down here from Glamorgan.'

'Do you know nothing of the people at the time when I was born? Thirty years ago?'

'Nothing at all. But why don't you go back to Mortimer Strong?'

'His mind is going.'

Luther told the vicar as much as Strong had told him in his mixed-up rambling way.

'Go back to him then. I still think it's your best bet. Listen to his idiot talk and be patient till his moments of clarity return. Let us go out into the open where I can light my pipe.'

This done, the vicar said, 'But you've explained one thing to me.'

'Have I? You intrigue me.'

'Mortimer Strong was a fool. A lightweight. Had it not been for his family he could never have taken holy orders.'

'I don't know about that,' said Luther, 'but I don't think much of his Christianity. His attitude to the chapel people is shameful. I was much influenced in my boyhood by a good Christian nonconformist minister by the name of Josiah Price. He always maintained that, as well as believing, Christianity was also about living and about people and how we behaved towards our fellowmen.'

'Mister Knox, we all go off the track somewhere sometime. The Church is no exception. If you stay in business long enough, you'll find your nonconformist movement going off the track.'

'And what do we do then?'

'Simple, my boy. Simple. Come back into the church.'

'D'you really think it's as simple as all that?'

'I do indeed. We could heal the rift tomorrow.'

'Which way?' Luther asked.

'You simply close down your chapels and come back into the church.'

'That's very good. A good idea. But first of all, how would it be if you showed us how to do it by closing your own doors and going back to Rome? At least they know what they believe.'

Ieuan Mostyn laughed his hearty laugh, but he did not answer the question or make any comment. Instead, he took Luther by the arm and said, 'The time you can spend here is not long enough to argue that one out. But you were talking about what Christianity is supposed to be about. I won't even argue that one today either. But I'll tell you what life is about, and write me off as a cynic if you wish. It's not about what you know but who you know. I told you Mortimer Strong was a lightweight. But he knew the right people. He knew the Lloyds.'

'The Lloyds?'

'The Lloyds of Derllys in this county. Your Squire's wife is of that family. And I had always been told that it was they who had obtained his present very comfortable living for him. Now I understand why. Go and see him again, Mister Knox. Now I must have a word with Tom.'

Tom had moved over to the corner of the little churchyard where he was busy with a barrow and spade. Left to himself

Luther wandered slowly past the few graves, deep in thought. All his life it seemed, he had been collecting a snippet here and there without ever coming nearer to the answer. He did not hold out any great hopes of Mortimer Strong telling him anything more but, as Ieuan Mostyn had said, it was probably his best bet. He would go to see him and try once more.

Still deep in thought he stopped by the two graves Tom had been tending. There were slate headstones on them. The inscription on one read:

Sacred to the memory of
MARY DAVEY
daughter of THOMAS and ANN DAVEY,
Pentre Llanvihangel
who died jany 14th 1846 Aged 3 months
also
DAVID the son of the above named
who died Feb 5th 1848 Aged 5yrs.

The inscription on the other stone was:

Sacred to the memory of
ANNE DAVEY
wife of THOMAS DAVEY,
Pentre Llanfihangel
who died Nove 20th 1850 aged 43 years.
Cofia Yn Awr dy Greawdwr Yn
Nyddiau Dy Ieungtid Cyn Dyfod
Y Dyddiau blin

'We all have our own troubles and sorrows, my friend.'

Luther turned to see the Reverend Ieuan Mostyn standing behind him.

'We all need a little sympathy and understanding. Tom more than many. His story is a sad one, but he is a great example with his faith. An example to all of us. But, of course, the Lord only gives us as big a load to carry as He knows we can bear, and Tom bears his load very bravely.'

Luther understood now something of the sadness he thought he had detected beneath the cheerfulness when he had met Tom at the Black Lion that morning. Wife and children in less than five years.

'What does the verse mean?' he asked.

'It's from Ecclesiastes,' Mostyn said. ''Remember now thy creator in the days of thy youth, while the evil or tired days come not.'' By evil days it means old age. It's the twelfth chapter. Are you familiar with it?'

'I'm afraid not.'

''Tis no matter. In the same chapter The Preacher says ''Much study is a weariness of the flesh.'' If a man ever says he knows his Bible he's either a liar or a fool and as such to be avoided. But have a look at that chapter sometime and the one before it. They're a wonderful poem on youth and age. But I must not preach to you, because time is passing, much as I love a captive audience. Next time you come to see me come to Laugharne and I'll fetch you in the boat. It will give you longer here.'

'How far are you from Laugharne then?'

Ieuan Mostyn pointed down the estuary. 'It's just round the corner there. Ten minutes in the boat to Laugharne ferry. Think of the weary journey by road you would save yourself. Better still, get yourself a boat and come all the way.'

'Who knows? I might even do that. I've always loved the sea. It must have been bred in me I should think. I'd always suspected it, and after today I'm sure of it.' He smiled wryly. 'I believe I've made the journey across the estuary by way of Laugharne before now though, but I was too young to remember much about it.' Then he told Ieuan Mostyn all that Tom had told him that morning.

Deep in thought, Mostyn said, ''Tis a strange story, but I know nothing of the people or the happenings of that time. I'm new here and to the area. I only wish I could help you, but I can't. Try Strong again. He's bound to know more than he told you. And you have a little more to go on now.'

'Yes, I have indeed. Quite a bit more. I think I'll try our vicar once again. I might even learn more about the lights in the sky.'

They had been strolling towards the rectory as they talked and now they were greeted by a red and white Welsh

Springer bitch coming to meet them, wagging her tail and wriggling her body in sheer ecstasy at the sight of her master and the sound of his voice. She obviously had a litter of pups on her.

'Hello, my little girl,' he said. 'So you've come to tell us all about it have you?'

The spaniel sat down and gazed up at the vicar.

'There you are,' he said, 'I spoke to her in English out of courtesy towards you and you can tell by the look on her face she doesn't understand a word of it. Forgive me if we talk in the only language she knows.'

In flowing, lyrical, musical Welsh he spoke to her then, and she wagged her tail and barked joyfully. Then she turned and trotted off towards the rectory to return a few minutes later carrying a puppy in her mouth.

'A mouth like velvet,' Mostyn said.

Very gently, and with evident pride, the spaniel put the puppy down at his feet.

'This is the *cerdidwen*. The little one of the litter. But he's started on solid foods now and, mark my words, from now on he'll come on like a house on fire.'

Freed from his mother's grip the puppy explored the ground around him. Red and white he was, like his mother, with a white stripe down his face, and the bright intelligence of him was already there for anybody to see.

'Vicar,' said Luther, 'I've been looking out for a dog this long time. I've recently acquired a kitten which I didn't want, but which has taken over the household even so. But I still want a dog. Especially a Springer spaniel. Will you sell me this one?'

'Sell you this one? Most certainly not. I could not sell this defenceless soul like his brothers selling poor Jacob into bondage when I know he would be going amongst dissenters speaking in a foreign tongue. However much you paid me for him such money would be tainted. Truly then, if there is any truth in the theory of the transmigration of souls, he would rise before me in some other life and hail me as Judas. Take him, Mister Knox. I'll give him to you. And I'm sure you'll treasure him and give him a good home.'

Luther picked up the puppy and was lost for words. The puppy snuffled and made to lick Luther's hand.

'With your permission, vicar, I'll call him Mostyn.'

'It's the nearest he'll ever get to hearing his native tongue and I hope he'll forgive me. Have a cup of tea before you go.'

A cup of tea meant more pie and cake. Tom, it seemed, was eating in the Pilgrim's Lodge opposite where he was a welcome visitor.

The meal done, Ieuan Mostyn produced a neat little oblong basket with a lid which had a strap for fastening it.

'He'll travel better in this,' he said. 'Give it to Jimmy Wicks sometime to drop it at the Black Lion and Tom will do the rest.'

As Luther nursed the basket on the long journey up the lane leading from Llandeilo Abercowin, Tom was deep in thought. Luther had a fair idea what his thoughts might be and he was happy to respect his silence because he, too, had much to turn over in his mind.

The sea was now far on the ebb, the river was lowering rapidly and, where the mud flats were exposed, the curlews circled and lit to dig deep with their long curved beaks, then flew, calling their strange cry as they went, to alight a little way upstream and feed again. Over the marshland, peewits flapped their great wings in erratic flight. Ieuan Mostyn would need his *tarfgi*, as he called his Welsh Springer, if he went shooting in country such as this. And Luther's mind was away from the curlews and the lapwings and the shelduck and all else and back again at Llandeilo Abercowin recalling so much that had happened and been talked about during the day.

It was in the same faraway frame of mind that he reached the Cambrian Mailway Inn that evening and harnessed Kit for the last part of the journey home to Plumtree Hill.

Mostyn was his first concern. He ate the bread and milk he was given and then whimpered by the door. Outside he squatted down and piddled to his heart's content with a pleased and dreamy look in his brown eyes. Thus did Mostyn give notice that he was a clean little dog.

'How'st thee called'n Mostyn?' Sarah asked.

'He was given me by a parson by the name of Mostyn.'

'Aye, parson! An' ha'st thee heard anythin' about our parson today?'

'Not today. What's he done now?'

'Done? A've gone off his head at last, only now it's official an' a've been took to Amroth Castle. Should've been put there long ago.'

Amroth Castle had been a lunatic asylum for some years. Some of the inmates were private and some were kept there at the expense of the parish. Mortimer Strong was unlikely to be concerned in which category he was. He would know only about lights in the sky.

It was equally certain that he would remember less than ever of the events and people thirty odd years previously at Llandeilo Abercowin.

7

The introduction of Mostyn to Ham was not without its lighter moments. Ham had improved wonderfully during the couple of months in his new home. Black and sleek and a good bit bigger, he was still a kitten at heart. His first reaction when Mostyn waddled up to him was to spit at him. He arched his back and fluffed his tail, and then spat again. When this evoked no apparent fear in Mostyn, Ham scratched him on the nose. Clearly not liking this, and with his feelings evidently a trifle hurt, Mostyn flopped back on his haunches, put his head first on one side and then on the other, and then produced what was meant to be a bark. This, in turn, seemed not to deter Ham. For some time they stared at each other, then Ham, boxer-like, put out one paw to spar at the newcomer who immediately went down on all fours and wagged his tail.

That was as far as they went upon introduction, but Mostyn was not to be denied. Neither was Ham the sort of cat to resist for long the chance of some high-spirited fun, and Luther delighted to watch them. In a matter of days Ham was leading Mostyn out to meet John Wesley donkey with whom he had already established a close rapport. It was nothing, that summer, to see the pair of them snuggle up to John Wesley lying down in the field. He had an easier life than many. Between the shafts of his own small cart he did what was asked of him, but that was not much, and Luther knew it was only sentiment which kept him at Plumtree Hill. A gentle soul he was, with his long ears and dainty feet.

He seemed to know when he was well-off and caused no trouble. The general consensus of opinion was that he had brains, and some there were who suggested that they ought to send him out to the Crimea in place of Squire Radley. With the likes of him out there, it was said, it was no wonder that reports were coming through to the effect that everything was a shambles.

That same summer, Absie's sister Mary and her husband had the chance of a small farm of their own. Absie and Seeny agreed to move to Bellman's Close and old Jethro handed over the tenancy to them.

They were due to move in September. Before they moved, Luther went to see the agent concerning Light-A-Pipe. Luther knew that the place had always been something of a nuisance to him and now, without the crazy vindictive Mortimer Strong to create trouble, he was only too pleased to accept Luther's offer to buy it.

As soon as Absie and Seeny moved out, Luther had men to carry out improvements, including a new roof and windows. He was not surprised when Bessie said to him, 'What ar't thee gwain do with Light-A-Pipe, Mister Knox?' For a long time now she had called him Mister Knox.

'I thought to put a tenant in there, Bessie.'

'Ha'st thou got anybody in mind?'

'Yes, I've got a good couple in mind.'

'Aw,' she said, and her face fell.

She had suffered so much over the years that Luther felt it would be wrong to tease her.

'Don't you want to know who it is?'

'Well, 'tisn't my business unless thou wants to tell me.'

'Oh, 'tis your business all right.'

She looked puzzled, until Luther said, 'Isn't Dick nearly due home?'

'Oh, dear God,' she said, 'I'm afraid to think about it. The last I heard 'twas supposed to be afore Christmas. I prays about it an' I tries not to cry an' then I sees the look in little

Martha Jane's eyes when she keep askin' when is Dadda comin' home an' it nearly break my heart sometimes. 'Tis not knowin' as hurts cruel.'

'But we mustn't lose faith, Bessie. And you wouldn't want Dick to come home to your cottage.'

'Do'st thou really mean as we could go back?'

'As soon as the house is ready you can move in.'

'How about the land?'

'Wait till Dick comes home.'

'Supposin' he don't come?'

'We'll talk about that again.'

It was early in October that Bessie moved back to Light-A-Pipe. Before the month was out Luther was standing one morning, with Mostyn and Ham playing one of their interminable games in the warm autumn sunshine. John Wesley donkey was gazing through the bars of the gate, longing to be with them. Luther liked to stand outside for ten minutes of a morning, thinking things out for the day, and in a mood of thankfulness for the good things of life, especially in such prosperous times. Prosperous for farmers anyway. He was glad he had come to Plumtree Hill when he did.

He did not immediately recognise the man walking up the garden path towards him. Dick Thomas looked fit and brown, but he was older and his hair had gone grey.

'Dick!' Luther said as he grasped his hand.

'Where's Bessie?' he said. 'Is she here?'

'No, she isn't here.'

'I been to the cottage, but 'tis empty.'

'Why don't you try Light-A-Pipe? That's where Bessie is. She's working there.'

'Who for?'

'Some new people.'

'Who is it?'

'Go and ask her for yourself.'

Dick looked hard at him for a few moments, then turned on his heel.

Luther said no more and did not offer to go with him. He felt that he would not want to see a grown man cry, not even tears of such joy as he hoped Dick would know.

8

There was hardly the same joy of reunion the following year when Squire Radley returned to the bosom of his family at Rhydlancoed.

Luther had gone there on a matter concerning the Estate when Eiry gave him the news. Luther's affection for her had grown stronger whilst her father had been away. They shared so much in their love of country things and their concern for people. They were sitting, as they so often did, on their favourite seat in the garden.

'Father is back in London,' she said. 'He'll be coming home in a few weeks.'

'What else does he say? Does he have any plans?'

'Only for me.'

'What plans can he have for you?'

'He has arranged for me to marry in the autumn.'

'Good God! He can't do a thing like that.'

'It seems he's done it.'

'But who are you going to marry?'

'A gentleman, it seems, by the name of Mister Jonathan Allin. He's a rather well-to-do landowner from down below Pembroke. Father met him in the Crimea.'

Luther was about to say 'Doesn't he know about us?' But he did not say it, because there was nothing to know as yet. He said instead, 'I had hoped that when your father came home I might have spoken to him about us.'

Eiry turned her head towards him and smiled.

'Do you really feel like that about me?' she said.

'I don't know. Sometimes I think I do. I'm not sure.'

'Let me see. How old are you now? Thirty-one, isn't it? At that age you ought to be sure. If you're not careful you'll finish up a bachelor.'

'You haven't said how you feel yourself.'

'For one thing, you've never asked me. And don't ask me now, for it's too late. In any case, I know Father would never hear of such a thing. Mother has already told me I must not encourage you.'

Luther fell silent. Then he said, so quietly he could have been talking to himself, 'I should have known that it could never be. There's too wide a gap between us. Far too wide.

Money is not the only thing. The Squire Radleys of life can sire as many bastards as they like, but their daughters don't marry them.'

Eiry put her hand on his. 'Dear Luther,' she said, 'don't be bitter.'

Then she did a strange thing. As her mother had done some years previously, she kissed him lightly on the cheek and went into the house.

Miss Eurwallt Radley, the only child of Squire and Mrs Radley, officially anyway Luther told himself bitterly, married Jonathan Allin Esquire that summer. It was an occasion of some moment in the celebration of which Luther took no part.

'Funny they didn't send thee a invite,' Seeny said. But not even Seeny could he tell of his feelings. In fact, Seeny least of all. She was the one person in life to whom he could talk about almost anything. They shared many secrets together. Yet he could not tell his sister in other than fun that she was the only other woman he had ever loved. It was all right for Eiry to tease him about becoming a bachelor when the two women he had loved were both beyond him. There was nobody he could talk to. Instead, he limped up across the fields with Mostyn at his heels, which meant that John Wesley soon followed, and he stood, for a long time, gazing out to sea.

The ordinary working people were more interested in the fact that the new Grove Pit, talked of for so long, began to produce coal at last in September.

'Mark my words,' said Absie. 'When they puts the furnaces back into blast this time there'll be a main heap o' mine to be drove.'

'For once, Absie,' Luther said, 'there may be more hope.'

'Why aye, o' course I'm right. I been up there lookin' an' the way they got the coal comin' down th' incline to the top o' the furnaces is a masterpiece. They got the right idea at last.'

'Well, you've been bothering about horses and driving long enough. If you like, I'll come in with you on a contract for picking mine and driving.'

'What about the farmin' then, boy?' Absie laughed.

'Oh, the farming's all right. Jack does a bit and Dick Thomas is glad of a few days a week until he can get on his feet. In fact the farming's doing so well we have to put the money into something.'

'Aye, well, young Seth got a wonderful delight in it. Out there milkin' with Seeny mornin' and evenin' an not ten year old yet.'

'As the Reverend Josiah price would have reminded us, Absie, ''Wheresoever your treasure is there will your heart be also'' Make as much as you can with the driving, but don't ever forget the land.'

9

It was in the following spring that work began at the Patches. Of more moment to Luther, however, was the fact that Iorwerth Vaughan wrote to tell him that Squire Radley had decided to sell Rhydlancoed and move to Deerfield. Radley's incompetence and indifference, plus Protheroe's swindling, which Radley's own failings had facilitated, had cost the Estate dear. Whatever hopes he may have cherished through the marriage he had arranged for his daughter had not availed to save his now serious position.

Luther was glad he had bought the freehold of Plumtree Hill. He was independent now. It was useful being the agent to the Estate, but he could manage more than comfortably without it.

It was Iorwerth Vaughan who came to meet him at Deerfield to discuss some of the details of the move.

'First of all,' Luther said, 'it must be understood that Missus Powell remains here as housekeeper.'

'That is not for us to decide.'

'Indeed no. But if anybody decides anything else anybody is welcome to find a new agent at the same time.'

'The Squire won't like it when I tell him of your attitude.'

'Then the Squire will have to lump it then, won't he? There's nothing much of the Estate left, and where would they find a proper agent to take it on?'

Vaughan pursed his lips and then smiled.

'All right,' he said, 'I'll see to it that Missus Powell stays.'

'Quite. And don't try any more of this telling me the Squire thinks this or the Squire won't like that. You know as well as I do that the Squire is incapable of thinking, and you know as well as I do what he likes. In all the years I've been here he's never troubled a monkey's uncle what has happened and I don't suppose he's altered much.'

Vaughan frowned. 'So it's really a question,' he said, 'of who's going to run the Estate? You or me?'

'Oh you can go on running the Estate to your heart's content. You won't find me any more difficult than I've ever been. But if I want something done, it will be done. Especially about people. Missus Powell has been marvellous to me ever since the day I came limping up here as a terrified crut nearly twenty years ago. She's been more like a mother to me. But she's not as young as she was and I'm not going to see her turned out at her age. Beth is going because she's getting married. But Affie Day has done his best outside and he can stay as well. When it comes to any change of tenancies I'll consult you and the Squire as much as you like. And if you're sensible you'll accept my recommendations.'

'Quite some conditions,' Vaughan said dryly, but with a half smile.

'Not really. Just commonsense and getting it straight.'

Changing the subject suddenly, Vaughan said, 'I know you've done quite well for yourself and I'm genuinely pleased for you.'

'Yes, not bad. I can't complain.'

'And I know you have a fair idea of what's going on round here. How much do you know about the new developments at the Grove?'

'Only what I've heard.'

'Nothing from the inside?'

'No, nothing. All that stopped when Protheroe left us so suddenly.'

'What about their financial position?'

'That's fairly common knowledge. Most of the directors have pulled out. Vickerman is pouring money in there. He deserves to succeed, but I don't think he will.'

'Why not?'

'His attitude is wrong. They've started work on the

Patches again and they're already driving mine to the Grove.
It's no secret that I have a financial interest in that with my
brother-in-law. But they won't go back into blast until they
have stock-piled enough raw material to keep them going
over a long dispute with the men.'

'And what's wrong with that?'

'I suppose it's good business sense in some ways. But when
you go into a thing determined that there's going to be
trouble, then trouble is usually what you get.'

Vaughan was thoughtful. He said, 'So you won't be taking
up any of the shares which are being issued?'

Luther chuckled. 'Not on your life! If work stops at the
Patches my commitment will be very little. But as for putting
money into the Grove—not one penny piece!'

Vaughan was still looking uneasy.

'Look,' he said. 'I may as well tell you, because you'll soon
know. The Squire is putting money in from the sale of
Rhydlancoed.'

'Hm! Then the Squire's a fool. But that's something you
know and I know and everybody knows. And I said not
many minutes ago that I don't suppose he will have altered
much.'

Luther paused for a few moments, then he said, 'Now that
we're talking about all these arrangements, I think I'll move
the Estate stuff out of here and set up an office at Plumtree
Hill.'

As an afterthought, and out of courtesy, he added,
'You've no objections I suppose?'

'None at all. You're the agent.'

Luther did not say that, knowing some of the things he
did, and because of what had happened recently, he did not
want to be closer to the Radleys than he had to be.

10

It was another more than satisfactory summer. The corn and
cattle did well and sold well. And there was a steady stream
of mine being driven from the Patches to the Grove. The
cottage at Crickdam had long since tumbled into ruin, but
once more the blacksmith shop was working.

Dick was doing nicely and worked at Plumtree Hill three or four days a week and Bessie still helped. Even Seth, ten years old now, came and borrowed John Wesley donkey along with his cart and drove small loads of mine during the summer.

Jack, although continuing to do some work on the place, now did less hauling of coal and became more involved with the iron ore and working odd days at the Grove. By the end of the year, when the first furnace went back into blast, he was spending much of his time there.

Luther thought afterwards that what happened next was almost inevitable and, in the end perhaps, not entirely a bad thing. But it was to be some years before he could look at it that way.

He was alone with Sarah in the house of an evening before Jack, who had gone back for a few hours 'To do somethin' with the pigs' Sarah said, came home.

The pigs were the moulds which led off from the main sows taking the white hot molten metal from the furnace to make the pig iron.

'Don't let on as I've said anythin',' she said, 'but Bessie's up the spout again.'

Luther smiled. 'Is she pleased?'

'O' course she is. Didn't take Dick long to fill her did it?'

'Long enough. Two years.'

'Well that's a sight better than thicky Jack. A got no more interest these days than a pig got in a holiday.'

'He's working hard, Sarah.'

'Aye, well, a 'ooman wants that sort o' thing sometimes, same as a man.'

Luther laughed. 'Good Lord, Sarah, I thought you'd be past that by now.'

'Aye, past it? Hisht thee. I'm only forty-five. Like the maid as asked her Granny how old a 'ooman was afore she lost interest in it an' her Granny said, ''Lord ha' mercy, maid, ask somebody owlder than me, I'm only eighty-four.'''

'You're a terrible case, Sarah,' Luther laughed.

'What I ought to do is change the bull. Too late for that perhaps, but don't talk about me bein' past it. I tell thee now, there's many a good tune played on a owld fiddle.'

'I wouldn't know about that.'

'Then how do'sn't thee try me sometime then?'

'Don't talk like that, Sarah. Tormentin' a poor bachelor man. You know you don't mean it.'

'Don't I then? If there was anythin' in thee thou would'st ha' done somethin' about it long ago.'

'I've never had a chance.'

'Chance you wants is it? Well, listen then. Jack have had th' offer of workin' th' odd night at the Grove to help with the furnace. The money's good an' I said take it.'

'When?'

'One night next week.'

Before Luther could make up his mind whether she was really serious they heard the back door open.

He tried not to think about that conversation with Sarah during the next few days. She so often talked like that. It was difficult to know whether she had been serious or not. Once or twice she winked at him knowingly, but not in front of Jack.

On the Saturday at mid-day Jack said, 'I'm gwain have a couple hours nap this afternoon. They've offered me a chance night at the Grove an' I'm gwain back tonight.'

Luther hardly knew what to say or how to face him.

'There's nothin' much to it. Mostly a question o' bein' there an' the money's good.'

'Oh, good,' Luther said. 'What d'you have to do?'

Then he took in little of what Jack was saying as he talked on about sows and pigs, blast pipes and tapping holes, charging holes and bellows. He had never been interested in this aspect of the Grove. And now his mind was suddenly on the possibility that Sarah could really have been serious, and he was conscious of a quickening of his pulse.

It was after supper when Jack wrapped up and said, 'I'll be off then. I'll be home afore breakfast in time to feed the cattle.' Then he was gone.

Sarah gave Luther a knowing smile but said nothing. For an hour in the sitting room he tried to read, but saw nothing as he turned the pages. Mostyn and Ham stretched on the mat in front of the fire, oblivious to the tension within him.

At last he put his book away, went into the kitchen and said to Sarah, 'I'm off to bed.'

In a quieter voice than usual she said, 'Ar't thee comin' into my bed?'

It had really begun to look as if she were very much in earnest. With his heart beating wildly he said, 'Go on, girl. Don't be daft. I couldn't do a thing like that.'

'Then I'll have to come into thy bed won't I?'

'Aye, aye,' he laughed, 'that'll be all right. You do that.'

Luther turned the lamp low as he got into bed. He had left his door ajar.

After a while he heard Sarah slide home the bolt on the back door and then heard her go to her room. For what seemed a long time he lay there listening and hardly daring to breathe. He had already decided she must have been joking after all, and he was wondering whether he dare go to her room, when he heard her come quietly along the landing. His door opened a little wider and then she stood inside the room. In the dim light he could see that she was in her night-dress and that her hair was down over her shoulders.

Without a word she came to the side of the bed, pulled back the clothes gently and eased herself in beside him. She reached out and turned out the light.

He lay there in the darkness afraid to move. Then he felt her hand moving up under his night-shirt and he turned and took her in his arms.

Afterwards they lay together breathing heavily and sweating under the weight of the bedclothes. Sarah was the first to speak. She said, 'Ha'st thou never had a 'ooman afore?'

'No, never.'

'I thought not.'

'How could you tell?'

'Thou was't so quick.'

'Was that no good for you?'

'Aye, you was wonderful. But by-an'-by you'll be ten times as good.'

She laughed quietly in the darkness and she felt for his hand and put it on her breast.

'But it's all wrong, Sarah,' he said.

'Is it? What's wrong with it?'

'What will Jack say?'

'How? Art thee gwain tell'n then?'

'Good God, no!'

'Then do'st thee think I will?'

'You might.'

'Ar't thee real dull?'

'You don't think he'll know somehow?'

'Why no. Nobody misses a slice off a cut-loaf.'

The only time he had ever even kissed a girl was Rita that time at Deerfield when his hopes had come to nothing. After this experience with Sarah he realised how little he knew and how much he had missed.

'Thou ha'st a good bit to learn yet,' she said.

'Have I?'

'How did'st thee like it?'

'Wonderful.'

She snuggled up to him and he felt her hand gently rousing him again.

It was long after the grandfather's clock downstairs had struck midnight before she went back to her own bed and, sated at last, he fell into such a deep sleep as he had rarely known.

11

Whatever misgivings Luther may have had, and however much he dreaded the thought of facing Jack, his worst fears were dispelled when he saw Sarah's attitude in the morning when Jack came back from his night's work. She gave him a specially large breakfast and was more solicitous towards his every need than Luther had ever seen her. Sarah herself seemed fulfilled and happy.

Luther did not feel quite so good again later in the day when he went to chapel and, as luck would have it, Suffering Adams was holding forth on the subject of adultery. He cheered up only slightly when he recalled that someone, and it was certainly not Josiah Price, had once said that the most important commandment of all was the eleventh, which was, 'Thou shalt not get found out.'

His conscience troubled him deeply at what had happened the night before, and yet he knew that he could hardly wait to learn when Jack would be going back again at night.

He did not have to wait long. Nor for the next time after that. Sometimes, when the opportunity offered, they did not even wait for Jack to be going to the Grove at night.

It was to Sarah's credit, Luther thought, that in their working relationship her attitude towards him did not change. She was as cheerful as ever, often full of good-hearted badinage, but always respectful. And always in front of others, including Jack, she addressed him as Mr Knox. Only in bed did she call him Luther.

Before the following summer they were taking their illicit relationship for granted.

12

It was early the next summer that Dan Sinnet, the gamekeeper, called at Plumtree Hill.

When Luther thought back to the visit he could not remember why Dan had called. His only clear memory was that Dan had offered a good price for John Wesley donkey.

'I couldn't sell John Wesley,' Luther said.

'Why, fellah, a's eatin' his head off here.'

'What would young Seth do without John Wesley?'

'Well, there 'tis. I've made thee a good offer. I likes the little donkey.'

'You know 'tis unlucky to offer to buy animals people don't want to sell.'

'No, no. The bad luck is to refuse a good offer.'

'So it's your bad luck this time, Dan, for I'm not selling, no matter how much you offer.'

'All right, then,' he laughed, 'but give me first chance if thou should'st ever alter thy mind.'

'Yes, all right Dan, I'll do that much. But don't build up false hopes.'

Only a few weeks later, one evening when some much-needed rain had followed warm weather, and Luther was limping contentedly in the garden, delighting, as always at the prospect of growing things, he heard Mostyn barking furiously. He whistled to him and Mostyn ran into the garden still barking.

Mostyn was not a barking dog, but now, even when Luther spoke sharply to him, he would not desist. Instead, he kept trotting away, coming back and barking, then trotting away again as though asking Luther to follow.

It was just then that Jack came in from the yard and said, 'Where's John Wesley then?'

'I don't know,' Luther said, 'I haven't seen him since this morning.'

As on most mornings, John Wesley had come up to the gate and Luther had pulled his great long ears, scratched his face and stroked his velvet muzzle, what time Mostyn and Ham had indulged in their own particular fun close by. Luther had been out most of the day since then.

Mostyn's barking suddenly assumed a new significance.

By lane and field he led them up towards White Leys until they came at last to some growth where a level from one of the old pit workings sloped away into the bank and there he stood barking and looking back at them.

Later they found the gap in the hedge where John Wesley had pushed his way out of the field in search of some fresh grass, but nobody was ever able to explain how he had come to reach the old level and go exploring it.

It was whilst Luther and Jack were wondering what it was all about that young Seth came running and said that he had been to tell his father, but his father wasn't there, and he had seen John Wesley go into the tunnel and he had told Dick, and Dick had gone in and Mostyn was with him and he heard a noise like falling rock and he shouted and couldn't get an answer and that's when he ran for his father. So it was no wonder Seth was out of breath and something distressed.

'Take your time now, Seth,' Luther said. 'Who went into the tunnel?'

'Dick went in after John Wesley.'

'What about Mostyn?'

'He went in, too, but Dick towld me to stop outside.'

'What happened then?'

'I heard the noise.'

'What sort of noise?'

'Like a rumble. And then Mostyn come out barkin'.'

'What did you do then?'

'I went in a bit an' called, but everythin' was quiet in there an' I couldn't hear nothin', so I ran home, but Father's off.'

Just like Absie had looked, as Luther so well remembered him, at that age, Seth was growing into a fine lad, tall and strong, but there was something of Seeny's gentle look about him, too. Thank God Dick had told him not to follow him.

Others came then and they brought lanterns and went in and began to dig but knew it was no use. Then somebody made a rough guess and they went down to the Patches and dug in from that side, where the workings stretched so far back underground from an old disused tunnel at the foot of the cliff.

Dawn was breaking when they brought out Dick's mangled body, but they left poor John Wesley donkey where he was with the weight of all the ages upon his crushed and broken frame.

13

Bessie took the news as bravely as any woman could be expected to take such news with a three week old baby boy at her breast and eight year old Martha Jane crying her eyes out. So much hardship Bessie had seen right from childhood and now, when it seemed as if she had won through, the road ahead still looked like being uphill.

'We'll stand by you, Bessie,' Luther said.

'I got to keep gwain for the childern's sake I suppose, but God knows what'll become of us.'

'You've always had your faith, Bessie. It's at times like this you have to draw on it.'

She had had two wonderful years since Dick came back and was looking so much brighter.

'We're still young people, Bessie. You've still got your life before you.'

'What about the place?'

'What about it? You stay here. I'll see to that. There'll be help with haymaking and everything else you want. Apart from that, just trust in the Lord and leave it all to Him. Any time you can't pay your rent you know who your landlord is, so there's no worry on that score. You can't see me bothering you. We've been friends a long time and anything you want you let me know.'

Bessie was still weeping quietly when he left her, but he had a feeling she would cope. Materially, things were better for her than they had ever been. And what was it the Reverend Ieuan Mostyn had said when he was talking about Tom Davey's sorrows? 'Of course,' he had said, 'the Lord only gives us as big a load to carry as He knows we can bear.' Well, if that were true, the Lord must have a pretty high opinion of Bessie.

It was funny, Luther thought, how such sayings, and occasionally texts of sermons, or quotations of some sort, would stick in the mind and come back at times like this. He must write to Ieuan Mostyn and tell him of the progress of his canine namesake.

He wrote a week or two later and, to his great delight, Ieuan Mostyn replied 'If the hill will not come to Mahomet, Mahomet must come to the hill.'

It was no use, he said, waiting for Luther to take him up on his eminently sensible suggestion to visit Llandeilo Abercowin by boat, and so he would do something about it himself. It was, he reminded Luther, four years since his visit. If the dog Mostyn was all that Luther said he was, then he should be bred from. Ieuan Mostyn had a most promising young Springer bitch and he would like to turn her to the dog Mostyn. He knew when she was due to come on heat and had worked out the times of the tides. Given fair weather he would sail his boat to Crickdam, beach it there at about ten o'clock in the morning, and be away when it refloated at about six o'clock in the evening.

'Sarah,' Luther said, 'we must kill the fatted calf.'

Not that there was any need to bid Sarah to feed the traveller or the hungry. And these days particularly, even if Luther was the only one to know the reason, she was contented and full of goodwill towards the human race. To that extent he had a clear consience.

Early in the morning Luther was up in the fields and gazing along the sweep of the bay. Eventually he saw the sail of

Ieuan Mostyn's boat as she came beating down the coast off Ragwen, and there was no shortage of hands to drag her a yard or two out of the water when Mostyn ran her ashore on the sand below Crickdam.

It was a great joy to Luther to have Ieuan Mostyn's company for the day. The bitch was introduced to the dog Mostyn with much whimpering and sniffing, tail-wagging and cocking of ears and, no doubt to the delight of each, they were left together in the barn for the rest of the day.

Luther told his visitor something of the working of the Patches and the Grove. In the afternoon, he said, he would show him something of his livestock.

'With your fierce love of all things Welsh, vicar, I'm sure you'll be pleased to see a young Welsh black cow I have. She came to me as a calf from my mother, as I sometimes referred to her, at Crickdam, and I've already had a couple of nice heifers from her.'

Ieuan Mostyn was delighted.

'And I've heard no more since the quest which brought me to Llandeilo Abercowin four years ago. Mention of my mother reminded me of that and I thought you'd like to know. You heard, no doubt, what happened to Mortimer Strong?'

'Yes, I heard. And my advice to you is to leave it at that. If the Lord wants you to know, it will come all in His own good time.'

They were at table, and, though he drank little himself, Luther had provided wine for his guest.

'Yes,' he said. 'I think it may well be so. To tell you the truth I've tended to forget about it.'

'Very wise. Very wise. It is natural and right that a man should be interested in his roots. But it can be a great mistake to dwell too much in the past. Sometimes I fear that is the trouble with poor Tom. You remember Tom Davey, of course?'

'Indeed I do. A splendid man I thought him. How is he?'

Ieuan Mostyn sipped his wine appreciatively.

'Tom? He's well. In many ways he's well. He's looked after himself and not let himself go as many men in his case might have done. But he spends too much time weeping at the grave-side. As Christians, Mister Knox, we know that the grave is empty and therefore we should be rejoicing, not weeping. For a time I humoured him. But it's nearly eight years now since his wife died. The memories are sweet I know, but life is for the living. Our Lord himself said, "Let the dead bury their dead".'

'How old is Tom?'

'Let me see. His wife was forty-three when she died and Tom was a couple of years younger. So he won't be fifty yet. Far too young to be still grieving as he is. And he's much worse now than when you met him. What he needs is a change of scenery. Start a new life somewhere. I can't see any other way to take him out of himself.'

With that instinct which so often prompted him Luther said, 'I can find something for him.'

'You can?'

Luther thought a moment, smiled, looked at Ieuan Mostyn and said, 'I wonder if he'd feel like lodging with a very tidy and respectable young widow woman?'

Then he related Bessie's story.

'I haven't asked her yet, mind. But I think she might be guided my me. It would be useful for her to have a man about the place, and I can employ him here and on the Estate.'

Ieuan Mostyn had just finished filling his pipe and was lighting it contentedly. He blew a great puff of smoke and said, 'Truly indeed did the hymnest say "God moves in a mysterious way His wonders to perform." If you say this young widow will be guided by you I have every reason to believe that I might have some small influence with Tom. I rather like the sound of your Bessie, dissenter though she may be. A brave soul. And moral courage is a great virtue, Mister Knox. Take me to see her and let me ask this favour of her.'

Tom Davey came to Light-A-Pipe in September. The following spring, hardly able to contain his happiness, he told Luther he had a message from Bessie. She wondered whether Luther would be willing to give her away in marriage.

14

Farming was still prosperous, in spite of the repeal of the *Corn Laws* more than a decade earlier, and the corn-growers were still protected from serious competition from the great corn-growing lands beyond the Atlantic to the west because of the distance. The iron and coal trades, however, were experiencing a depression, and that spring, when Tom and Bessie married, discontent was simmering in the area amongst the colliers and small number of ironworkers employed by the Iron and Coal Company.

A ten percent cut in wages was followed at haymaking time by a mass meeting of workers on Kingsmoor Common near Kilgetty. Whilst the employers and their friends went to church, many a sermon of denunciation was preached from chapel pulpits. The Reverend Erasmus Suffering Adams had much to say upon the subject. Generally speaking, according to his book, the employers were unfeeling and ungodly, whilst the workers were saints and martyrs in a great and noble cause. Certainly not consciously did he do or say anything likely to improve the climate or bring peace.

It so happened, however, that the time also coincided with a massive spiritual revival and there were those who flocked to worship who, for many a long day, had refrained from darkening the doors of church or chapel. The chapels were packed to overflowing and souls were being saved in great numbers. Amongst them was a noteable sinner. She said so with a public declaration in chapel. She was a sinner and had come to be saved.

With the outward show of prosperity at the Grove there had also been a roaring trade at the Stepaside hostelry known as the Pan and Handle. On pay nights the quarry workers from the limestone quarries near Ludchurch came down to fraternise at the Pan with the colliers and ironworkers of the Grove. On such occasions it was not unknown for certain ladies of the area to mingle with the assembled gathering. Not necessarily because of the ladies, it was not unknown also for the gentlemen to come to blows. In fact it was unusual for them not to do so and, when they did, they applied themselves to the task in hand with a fair measure of enthusiasm. The ground for salvation was fertile.

Luther was more interested than a good many to have word of this particular molly-hawn, her public declaration and her salvation, because he had often wondered how he might have fared and whether his life would have changed in any way if he had, all those years ago, succumbed to Rita's charms.

Rita had five children, only the eldest of them, so it was said, being by the husband who had at last left her and started a new life for himself over the ocean. And now, in the autumn of that troubled and momentous year, Rita stood up in the packed chapel and, along with several others, went forward and was saved. Suffering Adams was delighted, and richly rewarded and filled with joy and gratitude to the Lord.

It was in the following spring that it became known how truly rewarded he had been, and how complete was Rita's conversion, when the news came that she was again with child. That, in itself, even in the absence of a husband, was not particularly newsworthy. What really caused the comment was that she was naming the Reverend Erasmus Adams as the father.

'It can't be right,' Luther said. 'I know she's a liar from years ago.'

'Don't thee be too sure,' Absie said. 'I knows it won't look good for the chapel, but Seeny reckons as Rita's eldest maid is gwain swear as she caught Adams on top of her on the bed an' a can deny it as much as a like.'

'Perhaps that's what Rita's told her to say.'

'Well, let's wait an' see.'

Justice, however, was not allowed to run its course. Even the deacons had no time to have a say in the matter or ask any questions, and nobody ever knew for sure.

Squire Radley was home from London and he sent word to Adams that, having given the land for the chapel in the first place, he would now like to make a substantial donation to chapel funds if Adams would care to go along to Deerfield that evening.

Affie Day saw everything because he was called upon to assist.

'Poor bugger,' Affie said to Luther the following day when

he had asked him how it had happened, 'I couldn't help feelin' sorry for'n although I was laughin'.'

'Did you know what was up?' Luther asked.

'Good God, no! I was innocent. As God in heaven's my judge if I never muv from here alive again I knowed nothin'. The Squire sent me with the message an' Sufferin' come up all smiles an' pleased about it. Thought it was all part o' the big campaign. Missus Powell said she never thought nothin', but a couple o' toffs was there the night afore an' she heard 'em talkin' an' the Squire said about bein' tarred an' feathered an' they said they didn't know how to do it an' the Squire said as he'd show 'em.'

'And what was it about?'

'Why, we didn't know. But we can see it now. The toffs is mad about Adams an' what a been sayin' about the wages, an' this business about Rita was a good excuse otherwise they daresn't have laid a hand on'n. As far as the Squire was concerned a only wanted a bit o' sport. But by damn, I can tell thee now, Sufferin' looked comical by the time they'd finished with'n.'

'Did you see it all?'

'Aye, every drop an' feather. They gripped'n by the arms an' before thou could'st look about they had his clothes off an' one of 'em had this tub o' pitch an' a long-handled lime brush an', drop dead now, a plastered'n from head to foot. in his ears an' all over his cock an' everywhere. Then they had this sack o' goose feathers.'

Here Affie began to laugh again. 'Good God, don't talk. Laugh! A had one big quill feather stuck on the end of his cock like a Red Indian, an' then they turned'n out but a wouldn't go, so the Squire fetched a sword an' started pokin' the point in his arse.'

'Where is he now?'

'I don't know no more than you do. First light this mornin' a couple o' blokes on their way to the Grove seen'n down by Ford's Lake tryin' to wash, but so soon as a clapped eyes on 'em an' them shoutin' an' laughin' a took off up the wood an' a haven't been saw by nobody since.'

Nobody else did see him until an hour or so after dark when there was a timid knock on the back door at Plumtree

Hill. Sarah answered it and Luther heard a half scream followed by hysterical laughter.

'It's him,' she kept saying in between great gusts of laughter. 'It's him.'

Jack took the lantern and Luther went with him.

They found Adams standing and shivering round by the back of the house. He had found an old sack somewhere and this had prevented Sarah from seeing for herself whether the already famous quill feather was still in place. A sorry spectacle he was. His watery blue eyes were bulging, his straggly hair was matted with pitch and goose down, and his podgy body was covered.

'Mister Knox,' he said 'you must help me.'

'I don't know about must, but I will.'

'Out of Christian charity.'

'Don't let us talk about Christianity just now because our views are poles apart. What do you suggest Jack?'

'Paraffin an' cart grease. I can't think o' nothin' else.'

'I'll try anything. Anything.'

Luther went indoors and found some clothes which he thought would fit Adams. Luther's boots would be no good to him and Jack's were too small.

'That does not matter,' Adams said later when his appearance had been somewhat improved. 'I can get to my house and clean myself up before daylight.'

They were in the kitchen where Sarah had prepared him a hurried meal.

'I thought you said there were people waiting outside your house?'

'There are indeed. But they will not jeer when they see that I am clean and properly attired.'

'But you will have to get away.'

'I fear so. My ministry is finished.'

Luther wanted to say it was a pity it had ever started but, instead, asked him into the sitting room.

'I must be away before daylight if I can,' Adams said.

'Are you not going to deny the charges being made against you?'

'I cannot face up to any more lies.'

Luther knew nothing of the affair, but he said, 'I have proof from a number of sources that you had carnal knowledge of the woman who is naming you as the father of her child.'

'Proof?'

'Yes, proof.'

Adams' shoulders sagged. 'Human flesh is very weak and she was a temptress.'

'So you will not go on denying it? And like your namesake, the original Adam, you have to blame the woman.'

Whatever Rita may be, he despised him for that.

'I don't know how you could have found out, but if you say you have proof it's no good trying to deny it. What is your proof?'

'Never mind about that now. But I knew something of the wiles of that young lady long ago. You'll need money.'

Going to a drawer Luther took a key from his pocket and, opening the drawer, took out a cash box. He counted out twenty sovereigns and said, 'Take these and start again somewhere. Try to remember that we are all sinners. Leave the ministry to those who are better fitted to it. Not because they don't sin, but because they don't condemn others. I don't want the money back. Take it as an offering in memory of the hapless girls you have had turned out of chapel in your time. And, if you want my considered opinion for what it's worth, tarring and feathering was far too good for you.'

Luther was already showing him to the door. He said, 'Your feet are in poor shape. You can't go any further like that. I'll get Jack to put the pony in the trap and drive you home.'

When they had gone Sarah gave Luther a coaxing look.

'No, not now,' he said. 'Not after the way I've just been talking to Adams.'

'All right,' she said, 'please thyself. Jack'll be workin' Saturday night anyhow.'

15

The Sunday after Adams had hastened from the district there was a full attendance at chapel. Curiosity was a great motivator.

Joshua Nash, a surprisingly well-read artisan, from the hamlet at Heronsmill, was already seated in the pulpit when Luther arrived and went to his own seat. Blacksmiths most of his family had been, but a carpenter Josh was. Outside of his work he had given the rest of his life to his chapel, and for more years now than Luther could remember had served faithfully as its secretary. Even Adams' devious machinations in conjunction with his new band of the saved had not been able to move him.

Without comment, when he had consulted his watch and replaced it in his waistcoat pocket, he began the service on time and they went through the usual hymns and prayers and readings. When it came to the time before the sermon when he should have stood out to make his announcements there was an air of expectancy.

Joshua Nash folded his hands on the pulpit and said quietly, 'My friends. We arc being tested. There are some things which we shall want to put behind us. That includes the happenings of this week. Shall we do our best to remember all that our Lord had to say about condemnation and idle gossip? The deacons have met and decided to look for a new minister. Until that happens we must carry on the best we can amongst ourselves. If any of you feel like offering yourselves to take a service it would be a great help.'

Luther sensed the disappointment of some and the relief of others. Joshua Nash had been a close friend of Josiah Price. If anybody could keep things steady he could.

The service over, Luther went home. He did not join any of those who remained outside to talk in groups.

It was later on towards haymaking time when Joshua Nash disturbed the even tenor of his ways. Luther had gone to Heronsmill to talk to Watty about the grinding of corn next winter but also to see Tom Harter at Rushyland about new boots. Kit, getting on in years now, trotted along sedately, and Mostyn sat with his chin on the dashboard enjoying the ride as ever. Luther had been quite happy to stick to his little phaeton which suited him nicely.

The dusty hedgerows were thick with growth, and the honeysuckle and wild rose, which never failed to remind Luther of his boyhood and the interest of all creation which Josiah Price had encouraged, were at their best. Along the way there were clumps of dog daisies, wild vetches were in profusion, and the columbines were many-coloured.

He was disturbed from his reverie when Joshua Nash hailed him. Luther reined Kit to a halt.

'The very man I've been waiting to see,' Josh said.

'Me? What can you want with me, Mister Nash?'

'I was wondering how it is you've never volunteered yet.'

'Volunteered? What for?'

'Mister Knox. I've been thinking and praying, which is sometimes the same thing. It's not easy for me to keep the pulpit supplied with preachers and it's going to be a spell before we can find a new minister. You've been faithful to our fellowship all along, even since the Reverend Josiah Price left us and we haven't all seen eye to eye with everything that's been done and said. Could you take a service sometime?'

'What! Me?' Luther laughed out loud.

'Yes, indeed. You could do it well.'

'Good gracious, Mister Nash. I'm not fit to do that.'

'In that case, you could do it a masterpiece. There's none of us fit to do it. The ones I worry about are the ones who think they're there as God's chosen people.'

'No, definitely not. I'll help where I can, but not that.'

'Well, think about it. Just think about it.'

Luther did think about it and was adamant in his own mind. Then, when he had put all such thoughts from his head, he would think again of poor old Joshua Nash doing his best, struggling with the problem with which he had so suddenly been faced. Each time Luther had a twinge of conscience at his own refusal to help.

Joshua Nash did not rush him but, some weeks later, said to him quietly as they came out of chapel, 'Have you given any thought to my suggestion?'

'Oh, indeed,' Luther said, 'I've been thinking about it all the time.'

'Good. That's good. Go on thinking about it.'

Eventually Sarah surprised him one day by saying, 'I hears as thee'rt gwain preach in chapel.'

'Oh, who told you that?' Sarah could see his surprise.

'Isn't it right then?' she said.

'I haven't said. I've been asked, but I haven't said yes.'

'How do'sn't thee say yes then?'

'What are you talking about Sarah? You of all people. You know I'm not fit to go into the pulpit.'

'How not? Thee'rt a good scholar and have always gone to chapel and thee'rt a good livin' man.'

'What d'you mean, good living?'

'Well, thee'rt always willin' to help a body.'

'And what about the way we're carrying on, the pair of us?'

'Lord sowls boy. Nobody else knows about that.'

'But we know. And God knows.'

'Aye, but there's no harm in it. We don't hurt nobody else. Jack isn't interested much an' thee'rt not married.' She smiled. 'It have made me very happy, an' that's truth.'

'But it's wrong, Sarah. You know it is.'

'Of course 'tisn't.'

'All right, then. If it's not wrong, tell Jack and everybody else about it.'

'Thou know'st I daresn't do that.'

'Of course I know. And that's because it's wrong. If it wasn't wrong there'd be no harm in anybody knowing.'

'Well, if thee'rt gwain look at it like that I suppose. But I don't reckon there's much harm in it. An' I thinks 'twould be better for thee to go an' preach than some of the blessed hyprocites as is at it. There's many worse than thee.'

'That doesn't make me any better.'

'Ilisht thee, for the Lord's sake. If everybody talked like that there'd never be nobody in the pulpit.'

Luther smiled. 'That's what Josh Nash said, but he didn't put it quite like that.'

It made him feel better to realise that Sarah viewed the possibility as she did. He had been faithful to the chapel, even since the advent of Suttering Adams, although, soon after his arrival, Luther had ceased to have anything to do with the Sunday school. Perhaps if Joshua Nash asked him again to take a service he would have to agree. Josh asked him the following Sunday.

Luther did not take the matter lightly and believed he could do no better than to remind his listeners of a sermon once preached by Josiah Price, and which had left a deep impression on him and stayed with him over the years. As far as possible, though, although failing time and time again, he had tried to live by Josiah Price's precepts that day. Josiah had talked about the Sermon on the Mount and taken as his text what Jesus had then said at the end of it all, 'Whosoever heareth these sayings of mine and doeth them.'

Luther prepared his notes accordingly. His prayer, which was supposed to be extempore, he wrote out in advance, and that was the most difficult part of his ordeal. For ordeal it was.

Afterwards, there was no great reaction. Those who had been saved were openly disappointed, but Joshua Nash took him warmly by the hand and said, 'Keep on those lines, my friend. Josiah would be delighted. The Word is nothing on its own if we do not live up to it. The negative attitude of the Commandments never bothered Josiah Price. He was always more concerned with the positive approach. Develop that theme next time.'

'What d'you mean next time?'

'Next time will be much easier. And thank you again.'

16

The following summer there was a report in the *Pembrokeshire Herald* that Mrs. Eurwalt Allin, who already had a four year old daughter, Patricia, had given birth to a son. It stirred thoughts within Luther, but it was not so important to him as the fact that Seeny, although it was not mentioned in the paper, also gave birth to a son. He was christened Aaron.

What did warrant a report in the paper was the fact that the Grove ironworks again ceased production.

'But they reckons as things isn't gwain to be so bad this time,' Absie said. 'They reckons that when the railway comes down through Kilgetty for Pembroke Dock as 'twill bring real prospects.'

'Maybe,' Luther said. 'Maybe. But it's just as likely to bring a heap of cheap goods from factories to cut the ground from under everybody's feet.'

'What's thee think we should do?' Absie knew from experience that Luther was so often right.

'I don't know,' Luther said. 'I haven't thought about it. But now you mention it I think I'll try to buy some more land.'

It was a typically instinctive remark and that was what he did, buying some of the better land above Crickdam up towards Catshayes and Tinkers Hill and, for the next two years, farming occupied much of his attention as well as Absie's because it was two years before the Grove went back into blast.

'I was up there last week,' Absie said, 'and Vickerman have spent a heap o' money there again.'

'I know,' Luther said. 'They reckon that Longbournc has pulled out now and Vickerman just about owns the whole lot.'

A year later everything was in full swing.

On the farm, cattle, corn and sheep sold well and so did butter and cheese. Luther, however, having committed himself with Absie in earlier years, retained his interest in the Patches. It was the following year, when Luther was forty years of age, that a black cloud came over his life.

Early that summer Seeny died. It was her fifth child. Never before had she had any trouble, and nobody could have foreseen difficulties this time. But suddenly she and her baby were dead and were buried together in the same grave.

Luther had never prepared himself for such a loss and was shattered beyond anything he could have believed possible. He had loved Seeny. Once he tried to describe for himself how he had loved her and finished up by telling himself there were no words to describe such a feeling. He simply loved her.

That night he could not face the thought of bed. He limped up across the fields in the moonlight and stood above the cliffs looking out over the bay. Sea-pies called with their clear staccato bleep-bleep across a damp patch of sand where the moonlight fell. The waves rolled in gently one after the other and he gazed at them unseeing.

Last summer at Amroth Big Day concert a man and woman had sung a beautiful duet. The couple in the song were supposed to be a brother and sister talking to each other, and the words came back to him now.

> *What are the wild waves saying,*
> *Sister the whole day long,*
> *That ever amid our playing*
> *I hear but their low, lone song?*
> *Not by the seaside only,*
> *There it sounds wild and free;*
> *But at night when 'tis dark and lonely,*
>   *In dreams it is still with me.*

> *Brother, I hear no singing!*
> *'Tis but the rolling wave,*
> *Ever its lone course winging*
> *Over some ocean cave!*
> *'Tis but the noise of water*
> *Dashing against the shore,*
> *And the mind from some bleaker quarter,*
>   *Mingling with its roar.*

> *No! no, no, no,*
> *No, no, no, it is something greater*
> *That speaks to the heart alone,*
> *The voice of the great Creator*
>   *Dwells in that mighty tone!*

Down there on the beach he and Seeny had spent so much time together. Down there, in that cottage which was now no more, they had slept as children on many such nights as this, clasped in each other's arms and lulled into that dreamless sleep by waves such as these. What were those waves saying now? Would he really be with Seeny again one day as they were supposed to believe?

Not for a long time could he remember crying, but now he tasted the salt tears which were upon his cheeks, and he sobbed and lay on the dewy grass until the tempest in his heart was stilled.

17

Seth was now seventeen and tall and strong, like Absie at the same age. Young Jethro was fifteen. Hannah, a well-developed thirteen, said she would have to be mother to them all. Little Aaron was four years old and it was difficult to know whether he yet understood the extent of his loss. Absie and Luther, who had always been close, were somehow drawn even closer in their support of each other during the first awful weeks of readjustment.

How Luther would have reacted to what happened in the early part of September, had it not been for the loss of Seeny, he was not at all sure. He had gone with Absie down to the Patches. Although he was not personally involved, he had a particular interest at the moment because of talk of the tunnel.

'What d'you think of it?' Luther asked.

'Nothin' at all,' Absie said.

'Then why are they doing it?'

'That's just it. It don't make sense. The talk went round about poor owld Dick an' John Wesley donkey an' they reckoned as 'twould be quicker to haul through a tunnel an' out across the courses to the Grove.'

'Never!'

'Aye, well that owld tunnel haven't been used for years. But after Dick an' John Wesley got killed some of 'em said how not open it up again.'

'But heavens above, Absie, what would it cost to open it up again and make it safe?'

'Well, there 'tis then. I'll keep gwain along the beach same as always.'

They were standing above high-water mark where the pollers, amidst a certain amount of clatter and ribald laughter, were picking over the mine, when Luther felt something, not very big, hit him on the shoulder and drop to the ground behind him. He turned quickly and saw a girl of about seventeen, with her head down laughing, amongst a small group of other girls. As he looked, she glanced up, saw that he had spotted her and she put her head down laughing again whilst the others looked at her.

In the brief moment when she had looked up Luther saw she was a round-faced, pretty girl with brown hair and a brown tan from the summer's sun on her well-rounded arms.

'Who's that?' Luther said.

'That's Rose Gwyther, the bell bastard.'

'Is it? She can go one better than me, then.'

They were close enough as friends for Absie to know that Luther took no hurt at references to his birth when they were in good part. Rose was the bastard offspring from old Polly Gwyther's own bastard daughter.

'She's a sight better looking than old Polly,' Luther said.

'Aye, but Rose's mother was a smart girl, wherever she come from. Th' only child as Polly had.'

'What sort of worker is she?'

'Good. One o' the best. Full o' devilment, but a real worker.'

'I wonder if she'd like a job indoors?'

Absie looked at him sharply. 'Ar't thee serious?'

'Yes, I am. Sarah's been on about somebody for help in the house this long time, only I've been a bit slow to do anything because I'm happy as things are.' He could not tell Absie why.

'How's young Martha Jane doin'?' Absie asked. Bessie's daughter had been at Plummtree Hill for more than a year, and in the dairy and milking the cows she excelled.

'Good. I don't know what we'd do without her. Bessie trained her well. But she's outside all the time. And now that there's more work outside there's more work inside. So I said I'd look out for somebody only I haven't done it.'

'Well, thou ca'st ask Rose. There's no law agin that. I'll give her a shout.'

Absie called to her and she walked towards them, not

brazenly, but with a swing to her hips and trying hard to suppress a smile. She was not much more than five feet tall and her rough skirt came down to her ankles.

'You've got a good aim,' Luther said.

'I didn't throw it.'

'No, of course not. 'Twas one of the little green men belonging to the fairies. But never mind about that. The winter's coming on. How would you care for a job indoors?'

Rose looked at him searchingly and he saw she had dark brown, gipsy eyes.

'What sort of job?'

'The usual things, I suppose. Cooking, cleaning, housework. With my housekeeper, Sarah Bowen. D'you know her?'

'Yes, I knows her.'

'Well, how d'you feel about it?'

'Could I live in?'

'Oh, yes. I think that would be better.'

'How much money would it be?'

'I've no idea. As much as you're earning here and your keep on top of it.'

Absie raised his eyes to heaven.

'They've been earning good bonuses here this summer,' he said.

'That's all right,' Luther said. 'If she can aim a stone as straight as that she can surely swing a scrubbing brush.'

Rose laughed. It was a distinctive, merry laugh, and it showed her even, white teeth.

'It wasn't a very good aim,' she said. 'I was tryin' to hit Mister Pugh.'

Absie laughed heartily. 'What ca'st thee do with her?' he said.

It was the first time Luther had heard him laugh since Seeny died.

'Well, what d'you think?' he said to Rose. Suddenly he felt the beating of his pulse and he knew he was hoping her answer would be yes more than he had wanted anything for a long time.

'Yes, I'll come,' she said, 'but I'll have to talk it over with my mother first.'

18

At the end of September, Rose came to Plumtree Hill and
Sarah put her to sleep in the little back bedroom at the head
of the stairs. By the time Luther had worked out what she
had been earning in a year's work at the Patches he found
that her wage would be about twelve pounds a year plus her
keep. Rose was well satisfied, and so was Martha Jane
because, in fairness, she, too, had an increase in her wage.

The only one not satisfied was Sarah. And her dissatis-
faction stemmed from the fact that she could no longer come
to Luther's bedroom on the odd night when Jack went back
to the Grove. The best she could manage now was to try to
get Rose out of the way by arranging for her to have the
occasional half-day to go home to see her mother. Luther did
not mind, but tried hard to show nothing in company, for
Rose had a fierce physical attraction for him.

When he had moved the Estate office to Plumtree Hill he
had built a new room for the purpose onto the end of the
house. Sometimes Rose would bring him a cup of tea there or
come to say there was somebody to see him. At such times
when they were alone he would tease her and she would
laugh and say, 'Don't be cheeky,' and he wondered whether
he could dare to make any sort of move towards what he now
longed for. His common sense told him he was a fool.

Rose had been at Plumtree Hill a couple of months when
Sarah said she was going to Narberth shopping. It was the
Christmas fatstock fair and there were two bullocks to go.
Jack was taking Tom Davey to help drive them and she was
going to take the trap.

'We'll be back in time to feed up,' she said

Luther thought no more than that he might have a chance
to spend time with Rose and to hear her bright laughter.

Jack and Tom set off early with the bullocks, and Sarah
followed in the trap soon afterwards. The weather had been
dry and bitterly cold for several days, but now it had turned
warmer. By dinner time the sky was growing darker. Early in
the afternoon, in a quick flurry of wind, the first silent
snowflakes began to fall, and soon the ground was covered
and it was sticking to the branches of the trees and on the
slates of the roofs.

Before it was dark the snow was deep enough for Luther to say 'You'd better go, Martha Jane.'

'I haven't milked yet, Mister Knox.'

'You've only got two cows to milk. I can manage those.'

'Lord ha' mercy, Mister Knox, do'st thee know how to milk?'

Luther smiled. 'Years ago, long before I was your age, I used to milk the first Fronwen. This one's ancestor. Great, great, grandmother I should think she must have been. I'll work it out for you sometime if you like. But you go now before it gets any worse.'

'If 'tis all right with thee, then. Mamma gets very worried. Especially with Dada gone off as well an' her in the condition she's in.'

Luther was always pleased to see how she had accepted Tom, and she was just as pleased as everyone else at the fruitful fulfilment at last of his union with her mother. They had been married nearly seven years and Tom was so delighted that no amount of leg-pulling could ruffle him. The baby was due in the spring.

Tom had cut and carried plenty of hay the day before, and now Rose had already helped Martha Jane to feed some of the animals. When Martha Jane had trudged off through the snow, Luther settled to milking the two cows. He was not as quick as when he was a boy and he felt the strain on his wrists.

Rose laughed and said, 'My word, Mister Knox, thee'rt lookin' a real farmer sat there under a cow. A bit kift p'raps. But a real farmer.'

'Don't stand there pokin' fun, girl. Get the big can for me to empty this bucket.' The milking bucket, gripped inexpertly between his knees, was already too full for his comfort and peace of mind.

Rose brought the big can and, as Luther rose from under Fronwen and bent to pour the milk into it, he felt his cheek brush against Rose's hair and she did not move her head away.

When he had resumed his position on the three-legged milking stool, he said, 'I'm certainly a bit out of practice. A good job the others are dry.' There were ten more cows and they were due to calve in the spring. But, although not having to be milked, they had to be fed with hay and given water to drink. It was after dark when they finished by lantern light and went into the house. The snow was still falling.

Tom and Sarah should have been home long ago.

'I can't see them coming now,' Luther said.

He could sense the tension between Rose and himself at the knowledge that they would be alone together. There was no back-chat or joking with her now. She said, 'I'd best get some supper.'

Luther ate with her in the kitchen. Hardly a word passed between them and, afterwards, he helped her to clear the dishes and wash them. Eventually she stummed the fire down for the night with balls.

Luther went to the door. Outside the snow lay deep and had banked up against the walls. Great snowflakes were coming down steadily in the slanting beam of the lantern and the silence was eery. He came in and bolted the door. Then he lifted the glass of the lantern and blew it out. It was another step nearer to bed-time. Mostyn and Ham were curled up together on the mat.

Rose was standing by the fireplace. He took her hands and pulled her gently towards him. She resisted slightly, but not completely. He said, 'Won't you let me kiss you?'

'Don't be dreadful,' she said and put her head down away from him.

He lifted her chin in his hand and raised her face. When he kissed her she did not struggle too much and he felt some small response.

'Will you come to bed with me tonight?' he whispered.

She put her hands against his chest and said, 'Don't be so horrible!'

He held her close and whispered, 'I'll come to your room then.'

'Oh, no, thou wou'sn't,' she said.

Luther knew there was a bolt on the inside of her door. She was safe enough from him, if she wished.

Slowly, and with his heart hammering, he undressed in his own bedroom. In the silence he heard Mam Bron's voice say,

'Be careful when it do snow. The snow will be a big time for you, isn't it.'

Every thought in his head told him he was acting madly. But, madness or not, he had to know whether Rose had bolted her door.

Carefully and quietly he lifted the latch and her door creaked open easily in front of him. There was no going back now. He moved quietly to her bed in the darkness and bent over her.

'Go away,' she said 'and leave me alone.' He could tell she had turned her face into the pillow.

In silence, then, he slid into bed beside her. It was a narrow bed and he was close to her. He took her in his arms and turned her face towards him. Then he kissed her.

She responded to his kisses at last and he began, very softly, to caress her body and to explore. Then he knew he would be the first man to take her and he would need to be gentle.

19

By the morning their world was under a great white blanket. As far as the eye could see was white. Here and there a tree stood out stark, there was the edge of the wood in the distance and the occasional pine-end of a farm-house or stable. Round the backdoor the chaffinches, tits and robins gathered to jostle for the food which Rose put out for them.

They fed and watered the animals together and Luther milked the two cows. Then they went back to the house and had breakfast together. They spoke little and Rose was ill-at-ease.

Later in the morning Absie came plodding through the snow. He had come, he said, to help.

'Isn't it funny,' Luther said 'how everybody thinks I'm helpless. Martha Jane thought it was some sort of miracle when I said I could milk.'

'An' how ar't thee gwain manage about cuttin' hay an' carrin' it?'

Luther was on the point of saying that Jack and Tom would be back soon when he realised the seriousness of the situation.

'How bad is it everywhere?'

'Oh 'tis terrible. Not a sign of nobody.'

'The main road closed I suppose?'

'Good God, Luther, what thee talkin' about?'

'Where d'you think Jack and Sarah will be?'

'Narberth somewhere. I don't suppose they'd even set off afore it started. Not if they had any sense any road. Thou wou'sn't see 'em for days.'

Luther hoped Absie would not suspect how he was relishing the prospect.

Like the friend he was, Absie stayed all day. He cleaned out the dung from the sheds, cut and carried hay, and bedded the animals down with clean straw. Rose cooked a good meal which they ate together in the kitchen.

Absie left late in the afternoon and promised to call at Light-A-Pipe if he could and make sure that Bessie was all right. Luther was glad Martha Jane had had more sense than to try to get through the snow and to know that her place for the moment was with her mother. Seth, too, would make sure that Martha Jane was all right. He had had his eye on her for some time.

When Absie had gone, Luther and Rose did the jobs together which they had done the previous evening. Luther milked and they fed and watered the cattle. They did not speak much.

Afterwards Rose cooked supper. When she had made up the fire for the night, Luther took her in his arms and said, 'Are you coming to my room tonight?'

'If you want me to.'

Luther lit a candle, turned out the big table lamp and led Rose by the hand upstairs. They undressed together in his room. Close together in bed they soon forgot the cold. Her shyness of the previous night had gone and she responded to his caresses ecstatically. When at last he possessed her she gasped and murmured and held him tightly in her arms.

Afterwards they talked. Her mother had married now and

her stepfather, she said, was good to her, but she had spent much of her time with her grandmother, Polly Gwyther.

Much of it he knew, but she also talked about herself. She did not know anything about her father except that he was a foreign seaman who had picked up with her mother and used to come in on a cargo boat to Saundersfoot. When she was a small girl, she said, she used to make pictures in her mind of having a nice, clean house of her own.

'Not as Gran wasn't clean mind, but she had funny owld ways. Didn't believe in books an' school an' that.'

'Have you been to school?' Luther asked.

'A bit, but not a lot.'

'You can read a bit.'

'I can't write though.'

'You could learn easily enough.'

'Would'st thee be willin' to learn me?'

'Of course, I'd love to.'

'An' could'st thee learn me to speak nice like thee do'st?'

Luther smiled. 'Not learn you,' he said, 'it's teach you.'

'How?'

He chuckled and gave her a gentle squeeze. It would be nice spending time with her teaching her to write. That might allay some of Sarah's suspicions. He had taught Bessie to read and write at Deerfield years ago and Sarah knew that quite well. He feared there could be trouble from that quarter.

'How old ar't thee?' Rose asked suddenly.

'How old d'you think?'

She ran her fingers through his hair.

'Oh yes,' he said, 'I know there's some grey there.'

'Not much though. An' 'tis nice hair. How owld ar't thee?'

'Nearly forty-one.'

'Thee'rt not!'

'Yes I am. How old are you?'

'Gone seventeen.'

'You're a woman now. Especially after last night and tonight.'

She smiled and nestled close in his arms.

'What if I was to get pregnant after this?' she said.

Luther was startled. 'I don't know,' he said. 'I'd have to marry you I suppose.'

'Would'st thee marry me?'

'Yes, if I had to.'

'But only if thou had to?'

'I don't know, Rose. I haven't thought about it. It's been so sudden.'

They lay quiet for a while after that.

'The snow will be a big time for you, isn't it,' Mam Bron had said.

Rose stirred beside him and he made love to her again. They slept then and stayed in each other's arms until morning. When they woke and daylight came they could see there had been a fresh fall of snow in the night.

Absie came later and Martha Jane was with him. Reports were bad. A few quarry workers had managed to come down from Ludchurch direction and they had said that up towards Narberth it was much worse.

It was on the Thursday that Jack and Sarah and Tom had gone to the fair, but the following Tuesday before they were able to get back to Plumtree Hill. Luther was never to forget those five beautiful nights he shared with Rose.

20

In the event, Sarah showed no signs of suspecting anything. In any case, Luther argued to himself, she had no claim on him. For the most part he managed to avoid being alone with her, because either Rose or Martha Jane were usually about the house. And, by great good fortune, for the time being there was no night-work for Jack at the Grove, where business was reported to be going badly.

Luther had always had a conscience about his relationship with Sarah, and was relieved now to be able to break it off. He already felt that he belonged to Rose and, whilst Sarah was tied to her bedroom by night, Luther was not.

For the rest of that winter Luther spent an hour or two every evening teaching Rose to write and to improve her reading and her grammar. Their relationship was as natural as anything could be and there for all to see. Never by word

or glance was there anything which could give rise to
suspicions of what was really going on between them.

In the spring, when there was so much work to be done on
the land, ploughing, driving out manure and sowing corn,
there was additonal concern because one of the two furnaces
at the Grove had to close down for repairs.

'What we gwain do?' Absie said.

He had come to see Luther the day he had the news from
the manager.

'Hosgood called me in today an' said there'd be a cut-back
in mine as from next week.'

'How long,' said Luther 'before both furnaces are back in
blast?'

'They don't know. Hosgood only said as they'll keep one
gwain for the time bein'.'

'All right, Absie. There's more ways of killing a cat than
stuffing it with cream. How if we went back to what they did
when we were kids?'

'Send it by boat?'

'Why not?'

'Where could we send it?'

'I don't know. I've never thought about it before. But
they've got the electric telegraph at Kilgetty station. We
could soon find out, I suppose, from Burry Port and places
like that. It's worth a try. If we can keep the pollers going at
the Patches over the summer it'll be something.'

Luther knew in his heart that the prospects were not good,
for, now that the railway had come, the coastal trading
vessels must surely die. But, as he had said to Absie, it was
worth a try.

It was exciting, somehow, to see the boats coming in again
after more than thirty years, but Luther realised now that it
was not all as glamorous as when he had watched as a little
boy. The prices, too, were disappointing.

On top of it all came the work and the worry at harvest-
time, and it was one chilly night in late September, only a
week or so after Rose had drawn her year's money, that he
felt the weariness come upon him and went to bed early.
Eventually he went as cold as ice and then he began to sweat.
He remembered feeling a pain spread across his chest and

trying not to cough because the pain was so great, and then, with sweat pouring from him, he felt consciousness slipping away.

He remembered nothing after that except the vague recollection of distant voices and sometimes a rough, cold hand upon his fevered brow. John Wesley donkey was pulling a schooner through the sky whilst being followed by a shearwater, and Mortimer Strong was running after Ieuan Mostyn with flaring torches in each hand offering to light his pipe for him.

For more than a week the delirium lasted and then, when the crisis was past, he slept. By the time he came to his senses and was able to pass his hand over his face there was a fortnight's stubble there.

It was Sarah who brought him his first light feed of bread and milk and told him how ill he had been.

'Yes,' she said, in answer to his query, ''twas I nursed thee through it. Who else would'st thee expect to do it?'

'Is everything all right?'

'Aye, aye. Of course 'tis.'

'Has Rose helped you?'

'Thou was shoutin' for her a lot o' the time.'

'What's she doing now?'

'She've gone.'

'What d'you mean, gone?'

'Gone. Gave her cheek and slammed the door an' I haven't saw her since.'

'When was that?'

'The day after thou was't took bad.'

'Isn't she coming back?'

'She never said.'

Luther thought for a few moments. Josiah Price would have said, '"I will keep my mouth with a bridle" saith the Lord.' Or would he have quoted Proverbs? 'A fool uttereth all his mind, but a wise man keepeth it in till afterwards.'

If Sarah had done this there would be a showdown. All he said was, 'Well, thank you for looking after me. I can but thank you 'till you're better paid as the saying goes. Now ask Jack if he'll come and give me a hand to shave will you, there's a good soul.'

He put his head back on the pillow and closed his eyes to indicate he had no wish for more talk.

21

It was some little time before Luther was well enough to come downstairs, and some weeks before he could go outdoors. The weather was not conducive to venturing too far. He was eating his heart out to see Rose, but there was nothing he could do as yet.

He had lived long enough to have discovered that events rarely happened in isolation. Life had a habit of going along quietly for some time, and then everything would happen together.

As the months went by and he was looking forward to the healing which could come from the spring sunshine, three things happened.

First of all, Bessie came to see him about Martha Jane.

'She's in trouble,' Bessie said. Her nervous fidgetting with her hands betrayed her agitation and it was an effort for her to keep back the tears.

'Seth is it?' Luther said.

'Why aye!'

'Don't say it like that. You sound cross about it.'

'So I am.' She paused then. 'All right,' she said, 'I knows I was no better myself. But I never had no mother to advise me.'

'Seth will marry her won't he?'

'She's only just seventeen.'

Luther thought that was hardly significant when he thought of Rose. And he always thought of Rose.

'What can we do?' Bessie pleaded. 'Tom said to come an' see thee but 'tisn't right for me to keep bringin' my troubles to thee all the time. You been so good.'

'Have you spoken to Seth?'

'Aye, aye, a wants to marry her.'

'So what's the trouble?'

'Where they gwain live?'

'That's quite right,' said Luther and smiled. 'How's your baby doing?'

'Don't talk. Tom got'n home there in the cradle now lookin' like a body pisken led. Daft about the babby a is.'

'Well, that's fine. Let's leave it for a week or two and see what we can think out.'

It was whilst they were thinking it out that the second event occurred.

In some agitation Sarah asked if she could go to Jack's uncle over at Begelly for a few days to help out.

'It's the only relation we got,' she said. 'His missus is bad an' a can't manage. A've gone very owld an' shaky now.'

Within those few days, however, the old lady died and, in some confusion, Jack said, 'My uncle have asked us to move in with'n to th' end of his days an' a's leavin' the place to me.'

'Jack, boy,' said Luther, 'the time to cut a stick is when you see it in the hedge. Or, as the old lady said, the time to kill the fly is when he's in the sugar-basin.'

'Ah, but you been good to us.'

Mentally, Luther asked him for his forgiveness, and felt a sense of shame in his presence, but he was feeling relieved at the prospect of untangling himself and starting again. There was a great weight lifting off his shoulders and it was a joyful feeling.

'Jack,' he said, 'jump at it like a starving dog at a piece of liver.'

As it happened Luther was out the day Sarah came with Jack to collect their belongings and that was a relief, too.

Luther walked up across the fields in the evening and gazed out across the bay. Spring was in the air. Soon now he must see Rose.

When he came back to the house Seth was there with Martha Jane and they looked the picture of happiness together. Martha Jane was making a cup of tea and the three of them sat at the kitchen table.

'Bit of news today, Uncle Luther,' Seth said.

'Oh, what's that?'

'Rose got married yesterday.'

'Rose got married?' Luther could hear his own disembodied voice sounding far away.

'Aye, a chap from Saundersfoot. They reckons a got a bit o' money, but a's no good.'

As in a dream Luther heard Seth say that he was a good-looking young chap with dark, curly hair but wild as a hawk. His people had some money and he had bought a boat trading out of Saundersfoot.

'Thee'rt very quiet, Uncle Luther,' Seth said. 'What ar't thee thinkin' about?'

Luther pulled himself together.

'Oh,' he said, 'I was just thinking that with Jack and Sarah going how would it be if you two moved in here to look after me?'

22

There was trouble for everybody that year it seemed.

If spring sunshine was to be the medicine for Luther he had a surfeit of it. May was an especially warm, dry month.

'But that's it,' Absie said, 'it isn't so good is it? We can't go long without rain. Thou know'st what th' owld people used to say, ''Wet an' windy May, plenty o' corn an' hay.'' An' we haven't hardly had a skit o' rain since the corn was sowed.'

Thus the summer blazed on. Hay crops were light, the corn did not fill in the ear and cattle had to be driven long distances to water.

Just before Christmas Martha Jane's baby was born, and died within the first few hours.

The Grove had been working only intermittently and, by the New Year, had closed again.

Cattle had done well enough in the sunshine of the summer, where they could have water, but now that hay was running low the position was serious. The prudent had hay left over from the previous winter but that, too, was now having to be used up.

''Tis a job to know what to do for the best,' Absie said. 'I got horses there now eatin' their heads off an' nothin' for 'em to do.'

'Well,' Luther said, 'you know I've always had my doubts. But now that the railway's come it's going to be worse. You can see it already. There's good anthracite coming down here from Glamorgan and Carmarthen cheaper than the pits round here can dig it. If you want to know what I think I wouldn't be surprised if the Grove never opens again.'

''Tis no good tryin' to sell horses just now.'

'Well, I can help you out with a bit of hay until the spring if that's any good. Be thankful the farming is all right.'

'Aye, but store cattle an' sheep is down terrible.'

'That's only because of the drought. Good times will come again.'

The following summer, however, the drought was even worse and, this time, even the prudent knew they would have to face the winter with no reserves carried over from the year before.

In that summer the new minister came to Ebenezer and was known as Evans Half-a-Man because his services were shared in a joint pastorate with Zion.

'Better half a loaf than no bread,' they said.

In spite of his nickname, even if he was not in the same class as Josiah Price, the Reverend Shadrach Evans had come to do his best. And anybody, for Luther, would be an improvement on Erasmus Adams. He lived up to his Old Testament name, too, and was a cheerful soul.

The only trouble was that, under the new arrangement, there were some services he could not take. Luther had helped out occasionally since that first time and now Joshua Nash asked him if he could call on him on a regular basis. Luther was firm in his refusal but agreed to take the occasional service. He had no aspirations towards being a preacher. He tried to live up to what he believed, even when he knew he was failing. If his conscience no longer troubled him as much as it had previously, at least he recognised his unworthiness and told himself he was prepared to be judged accordingly in the final reckoning. But, at least, even to himself, he did not want to be a hypocrite. In the pulpit, that was what he felt, and so he ensured that his presence there was as infrequent as possible.

In any case, he had plenty to occupy his mind with the affairs of those tenants of the Estate who had smallholdings. On their land they were feeling the effects of the drought, and at work they were faced with the closure of the Grove ironworks and the Patches, and poor wages in the pits. The farmers with more land suddenly found that labour was no longer either plentiful or cheap. The coming of the railway had made a sudden exodus from the area much easier. Many of the working classes took one-way tickets to the industrial areas and many kept going until they reached Canada or New Zealand or Australia.

Luther was glad to have Seth on the place full time, with Tom to help when he was needed, and Martha Jane was a treasure. Jethro, a couple of years younger than Seth, spent some time with Absie but he, too, found work at Plumtree Hill. It had suddenly become a place of young people and Aaron, seven years old, usually found his way there most days after school.

Aaron already showed signs of developing the good physique of his father and two older brothers but, like Hannah, he had Seeny's features and colouring. Luther had determined, when Seeny died, that he would see the boy right in life.

23

Whether it was the heat, or the passing years, another casualty was poor old Mostyn. Luther knew a great sadness when he came down one morning and found him apparently asleep on his favourite mat where he had died quietly during the night.

Fourteen was a fair age and he had enjoyed every minute of his life. Seth had lifted him fondly and took him away and dug a hole under the shade of the big old plum tree in the garden and buried him there.

So much had happened in those years since Mostyn had come into his life at Llandeilo Abercowin, where he had found the crude details of his own birth recorded in the church register, and learned something of his first journey by boat as a helpless babe in the arms of an unknown woman. Unknown. So much was unknown. And Mostyn had come and gone, having lived a good life of greater than average span, and still Luther knew no more than that day at Abercowin. But that was it, and Ieuan Mostyn had said, 'If the Lord wants you to know, it will come all in His own good time.'

Well, maybe the Lord was taking His time or maybe He did not want him to know.

Luther limped up to the cliff road and down the track to Crickdam. Only the ruins were there now, and the memories. Down on the beach it was warm, but he did not have the spirit to go for a swim. Along the Patches under the cliffs everything was dead, where once there had been so much activity. Where he had spent so much time with Seeny. Where he had first set eyes on Rose.

He went on towards Wisemansbridge and, at the inn, sun throwing back hot from the white-washed walls, he went in and, seated on the oak skew, called for a sleever of ale because he was sweating and thirsty. And, because he drank rarely and little, the ale tasted that much better. But, although it quenched his thirst, it did nothing to ease the sorrow and the loneliness.

That day Ham wandered unhappy and disconsolate, mewing occasionally, round all the favourite haunts where he and Mostyn had played and known such happiness. He ate his supper, but without any show of interest, and left some of his milk. The back window, by which he came and went, was left open as usual, but in the morning, he was nowhere to be found. Nor that night, nor the next morning. He was never seen again.

It was hard, not to know what had happened to such a loveable character, but life had to go on, and then the news was spread abroad that Mrs Radley up at Deerfield had had some sort of stroke and was paralysed down one side and her speech had been affected. Luther was never to see her again either.

Summer passed into autumn without any sign of rain. The fields were bare, the haysheds were empty, and then it was rent day.

Some of the smallholders could not pay, and some could only pay part of it and promised to pay next spring or when they could. Luther said that would be all right because that was the way it had always been with him.

Some he would call on before rent day and some afterwards. Some always presented themselves at Plumtree Hill on the day itself as the custom was, just as it had been the custom in former days for them to present themselves at Deerfield. All the tenants had gone to Deerfield in Protheroe's time, but with Luther, being one of them and living amongst them, it was different.

He knew they could not sell their few cattle because, with no grass and no hay, the price of store cattle had hit rock bottom. The Grove was silent, and the money underground, for those able to find work, was small. Some rents, he knew, would have to remain unpaid this half-year.

Those who came to Plumtree Hill did not find him unsympathetic or unhelpful. There was one caller that day, though, whom he had not expected. Her name was Mrs Rose Barlow, the stepdaughter of Albert Saunders, who had a smallholding beyond Kilgetty.

Luther had no idea how it had come to be part of the Rhydlancoed Estate. Albert had come on rent day in the spring and explained his troubles after last year's drought and with no employment. Luther knew better than to expect any rent from him this time, after another season's drought, and still being out of work. Having heard that Albert, to add to his misfortunes, had broken his leg, he did not even expect to see him. He certainly did not expect to see Rose.

Luther thought he had managed to forget her or, at any rate, to forget what she had meant to him. It was two years since he had seen her, and now, as she stood in the doorway, more mature but prettier than ever, all his old longing for her came back.

'Rose!' He said.

Her full-skirted, ankle-length cotton dress was a simple check pattern and she wore a bonnet. Her shoes were dusty below the hem of her skirt.

'Have you walked from Saundersfoot?'

'Of course.'

'You must be tired.'

'Oh, no. It's not far through the tunnels.'

'But you must be thirsty.'

When she did not answer, he said, 'You'd like a cup of tea I expect.'

'There's no need to trouble.'

'It's no trouble. Martha Jane will be only too pleased to make you one. Come in and sit down.'

Luther led her into the sitting-room and gave her a chair, then he went through to the kitchen. Amidst the turmoil of his feelings he had already sensed a certain coldness towards him.

'Rose,' he said when he had come back and shut the door behind him, 'this is a wonderful surprise.' He held his hands towards her but she ignored them.

'I didn't want to come,' she said, 'but I decided to sink my pride for the sake of others.'

Her speech and grammar had improved considerably during the year he had helped her. She had been an apt pupil. Now, she spoke rather nicely, and her speech was enhanced by a trace of her Pembrokeshire accent. 'Pride?' he said. 'What pride are you talking about?'

'I told you once that my stepfather'd been kind to me. With my bringing up that means a lot. And he's been good to my mother.'

'And is that what you've come here to tell me?'

'Not exactly, but.....'

There was a rattling of the door-knob and Martha Jane came in with a tray bearing a teapot and cups, milk and sugar, and a fruit cake.

'Lord sowls,' she said, 'there's a nice surprise for us. But how hasn't thou been to see us afore this?'

Rose laughed and said, 'You're looking well Martha Jane.'

It was all small talk and Rose was ill-at-ease. When Martha Jane had poured the tea, cut the cake and left the room, Luther said,'Tell me about this pride you're talking about, Rose.'

She dropped her eyes. 'All right,' she said. 'If I must. Even if I never meant much to you I thought it would have been enough for you not to do such a thing by Albert.'

'Why?'

'Well, because he was kind to me. You knew that, because I told you when we. . .when we were. . .together.'

'Yes, I remember well.'

'Then why have you done it?'

Luther took her cup and put it on the table. Her hands, fidgetting nervously with her bag, told of her agitation. Presently a tear rolled down her cheek.

'How could you do it?' she almost whispered. 'The past is gone, but I always believed you were a kind man. How could you do it?'

'All right,' he said. 'Now tell me what it's all about. What am I supposed to have done?'

'What d'you mean?'

'I said, what have I done?'

'How can you sit there looking so innocent?'

'Easy. Because I am innocent. Until you can persuade me otherwise. What have I done to Albert?'

She looked him straight in the eye.

'You're the agent aren't you?'

'Yes, I'm the agent.'

She opened her bag, took out a letter and threw it, with an attitude of disgust, on the table.

Puzzled, he picked it up and opened it. As he finished reading it he raised his eyes to hers and saw that she had been watching him.

'Rose,' he said, 'will you take my word for it that this is the first I've heard of this?'

'If you give me your word.'

'I'll do more than that. I'll give you my word and do something about it.'

'Will you?' Her voice was eager and, for the first time, she relaxed.

'So you don't feel too hard about me?' he said.

She dropped her eyes again.

'Tell me, Rose,' he said. 'Can't you raise the rent between you?'

'No.'

'It's quite right what it says here. It's ten pounds altogether. Two pounds owing from last autumn, four pounds for the rent in the spring, and another four pounds due now. That's ten pounds.'

'I know.'

'I know your stepfather's had a rough time. He's the only tenant with anything owing from last autumn. There are plenty owing something from the spring, but he's the only one owing from last year. It can happen to the best of us and I wouldn't have troubled him yet. I don't have the last word, of course, but I should have been asked before the solicitors wrote to him.'

The letter from Phillips, Lloyd and Vaughan was on the table in front of him. He tapped it with his finger. He said, 'There's nothing in this which could make you think I was responsible for it.'

'It says on your recommendation.'

He smiled. 'No, Rose. Not my recommendation. It says the agent's report. Obviously I have to report every half-year who has paid and how much is owing and all the rest of it.' He smiled at her, 'You should have thought better of me. But you haven't told me yet. Why can't you raise the money between you? Couldn't your husband help?'

'He could, but he won't.'

'I see.'

There was a long pause. Then he said, 'Tell me, Rose. Are you happy?'

'No, I'm not.'

'Oh, I'm sorry. Truly sorry.'

'Well, that's how it is. I've made my own bed and I've got to lie in it. Can you really do something about it?'

'I must. I'm due to go to Deerfield next Wednesday. Would you like to call again on Thursday?'

'And what do I tell Albert about this letter?'

'Tell him to forget about it. And come and see me on Thursday.'

His old fierce physical longing for her was still there.

That evening he suggested to Seth and Martha Jane that they should take the trap and go to Narberth the following Thursday.

24

As Kit trotted gently along Pleasant Valley on the way to Deerfield there were many thoughts in Luther's head, and Rose was the centre of most of them. In between, he thought of Squire Radley and of how little he had seen of him or had to do with him. He had figured largely in his life from the time one of those drunks years ago at Amroth Big Day had laughed and shouted, 'Nor a don't look much like the Squire neither.' For nearly twenty years he had been his agent and at one time had even entertained foolish notions of marrying his daughter. Yet he could count on his fingers how many times he had ever seen him. If needs be today would be the last.

Along Pleasant Valley everything was tinder dry and Ford's Lake had become little more than a trickle. Up on the hillside there was activity at the Grove pit but, down in the valley, the ironworks stood, silent and deserted, the graveyard of so many hopes.

There were a few horse-drawn drams heading for Saundersfoot on the railway line, but the activity was not what it had once been. Aaron had already gone with Absie on a dram-load to see the boats in the harbour. They fascinated him.

Luther reached Deerfield at last and, as always, remembered his apprehension as he had limped up the drive that first day when he came to meet Toby Protheroe. Affie Day had died the year before, and the place was looking less well kept than of old. The paint on the window-frames was peeling, and there were weeds where no weeds had grown when Luther had first come to know the place.

Luther tied Kit to the railing and went round to the back door. It would never do not to pass the time of day with Mrs Powell. Squire Radley could wait.

After he had greeted her, Luther tapped the door to what had once been Protheroe's study and walked in without waiting to be asked. Iorwerth Vaughan, who had come by train to Kilgetty, was already there.

Luther dumped the canvass bag he was carrying on the table. The bigger farmers had paid by cheque, the smallholders in sovereigns.

'Any questions?' he said.

Vaughan was taken aback by his abruptness.

'What sort of rent roll has it been?' he said.

'Considering the drought,' Luther said, 'quite good.'

'But have they paid?' Squire Radley demanded, 'Have they paid?'

'Anxious are you?' Luther said. 'Lost a lot at the Grove have you?'

'Damn it all, of course I have.'

Luther's truculence seemed to have been lost on him.

Luther had not really given much thought to what would be said. He remembered Josiah Price long ago saying, 'Never forget what the Master said, ''Think not what ye shall say, for in that hour it shall be given unto you''.'

'I have work to do,' he said, of a sudden. 'Will you now please tell me why you sent that letter threatening Albert Saunders?'

'It was the Squire's wish,' said Vaughan.

'I told you a long time ago,' Luther said between closed teeth, 'that as long as I was the agent to the Estate I wouldn't be concerned with what you or the Squire thought and that I would deal with the tenants.'

'Saunders?' Radley said, 'is that the scoundrel who owes money since last year?'

'He is not a scoundrel and he owes nothing. He has paid up-to-date. But that's not the point. Do you not understand that people are now leaving the rural areas at such a rate you will soon have cottages on your hands? Empty. No tenants. No rents. Unless I continue as your agent you'll be lucky to find tenants for some of the cottages.'

'By jove, that sounds serious.'

Luther exchanged glances with Vaughan.

'Mister Vaughan,' he said quietly. 'I would have expected better of you. You should have known better.' Each time he emphasised the 'you.' 'Let me repeat. Albert Saunders' ten sovereigns are there in the bag. How he found them I don't know. But I carry on as agent to this broken-down outfit on one condition. You write to Saunders telling him your letter was all a mistake. When you've done that and sent me a copy of the letter, I'll let you know whether I intend to continue as agent. And if you don't do it, be quite sure of one thing. You can start looking for a new agent as of now.'

Without bidding them good-day Luther went from the room and slammed the door behind him. He could not know then but, although he was to remain as agent to a shrinking Estate, it was to be the last time for him to see Squire Radley.

25

The following day, always happy to have a day off together, Seth and Martha Jane set out for Narberth. Martha Jane had left a pie, cold meat and a tart, she told Luther. She did not mean him to go hungry.

Time hung heavy when they had gone. Rose had said she would come, but he could not be sure. Each time he took out his watch only another five or ten minutes had dragged by, and a hundred doubts assailed him.

He had almost given up hope, near to mid-day, when there was a timid knock on the door and he opened it to see Rose standing there.

'I thought you'd changed your mind,' he said. 'Come in. The kettle's boiling.'

Rose took off her bonnet and sat down. They were in the kitchen.

'It's almost like coming home,' she said.

'Then why did you walk out in the first place?'

'What? Walk out? I was turned out.'

'Who turned you out?'

'Sarah, of course. When you were ill. And you didn't want me back.'

'What d'you mean, didn't want you back?'

'Well, you didn't answer my letter.'

'I didn't have any letter from you. When did you send it?'

'The day after I left.'

Luther put his hands over his eyes. 'Dear God,' he said, 'I was in a sog for a fortnight. If a letter came from you it was Sarah who had it and I never saw it. What did you say in it?'

'I just said what had happened and if you wanted me to come back to let me know.'

'Did you have much of a row with Sarah?'

'Jesus! Don't talk! She hated the sight of me.' Rose burst into laughter.

'I wonder why?' Luther said.

'I didn't like her either.'

'Why not?'

'Because she was so bossy. Used to watch me like a hawk. She must have been pretty keen for me not to come back for her to have hid my letter from you.'

'Hidden,' Luther said.

'All right, Mister Knox. Hidden. But I haven't done bad have I?'

'You've done wonderfully well.' He was glad to be off the subject of Sarah.

'Have you any news?' she asked.

'Yes, I saw the Squire yesterday and the solicitor to the Estate. Albert should have a letter from him in the course of the next week or so explaining that the first letter was a mistake.'

'But what about the rent?'

'Tell him not to worry about that. Tell him he can give it to me when he can manage it.'

'Did the Squire say that or the solicitor?'

'Neither of them. I did.'

'Are you sure?'

'Rose. You came to ask me to do something about it. I've done it. You've come here today for my answer. You've just had it.'

Rose looked at him for a few moments. She dropped her eyes and said, 'Thank you.'

'What's more,' he said, 'there are no strings attached. Now then, I expect you're hungry. Seth and Martha Jane have gone to Narberth for the day, but Martha Jane has left enough grub to feed the multitude.'

Rose laughed. 'You bugger! You haven't sent them off to Narberth?'

'Yes, I have.'

She laughed again, 'What if it came to snow?'

'In that case we'd find better things to do than eat.'

'Don't you believe it. There won't be any of that nonsense.'

'Don't you believe it either, and it isn't nonsense. Let's have something to eat.'

They washed up the few things together afterwards, just as they had done in the time of the snow nearly three years ago. Then he took her in his arms and kissed her.

'That's all you ever wanted with me,' she said.

'Don't say that Rose. You know it isn't true.'

'Isn't it?'

'Of course it isn't.'

He kissed her again and felt her respond.

With his heart beating just as wildly as it had always done he took her hand and she followed him upstairs.

26

As they lay in each other's arms afterwards, Rose was the first to speak.

'Oh, Luther,' she said, 'I love you.'

Never before had she used his Christian name. 'I do love you. And I've missed you so much.'

'I've missed you, too. More than you'll ever know.'

'Then why didn't you send for me or come to see me?'

'But Rose. It was a long time before I was well enough to go out. The next thing I heard you were married.'

'I must have been mad.'

'You're not happy you said the other day?'

'If I was I wouldn't be here with you would I?'

He held her close. 'What's the trouble?' he asked.

'He's useless. Oh, very charming. Especially in company. But he's weak. Loves to spend money in the pubs to make out big, but he keeps me screwed down to the last ha'penny. And when he comes in drunk he's revolting.'

'Then why don't you leave him?'

'Don't be silly. Where could I go?'

'What about his family?'

'They think the sun rises and sets on him. They don't know half. They set him up with a beautiful boat because he said that's what he wanted, but he loses a lot of work because he's in the pubs half the time. And now the railway's come he'll lose a lot more. But you always said that didn't you?'

'Why did you marry him?'

'Wanted a home I suppose. And he was good looking like you.'

'Like me?'

'Well, dark curly hair and brown eyes and smart. That's the trouble, I think. He never had a chance.'

'How d'you mean?'

'You. I learned a lot from my Gran. She reckoned that a girl's heart will always be with the man she first gives herself to no matter who else there is. And that's you. I always think of you and especially those nights in the snow.'

'They were wonderful nights weren't they? What I've often wondered since is how you never became pregnant.'

'I didn't want to then. Sometimes now I wish I had, but at the time I was afraid to.'

She saw the puzzled look on his face. 'Oh, it's all right,' she said, 'that's something else I learned from Gran. If you know the right time of the month it's safe enough.'

'And what about today?'

'That's just it. It's the wrong time.'

'You mean you could become pregnant after today?'

'Very much so. More than likely. I hope so anyway.'

'What!?'

'There's nothing more in the world I'd like better than to have your child.'

She cried then and he held her close. When she had quietened down he made love to her again.

Luther made a cup of tea before she left. Whilst he was waiting for it to brew he went through to his office and came back with a receipt which he had made out for the ten pounds rent.

'Give this to Albert,' he said.

'It's all right,' he said, when he could see she did not understand, 'I paid it myself. He can pay me when he can. The Estate don't know that. All that concerns them is that it's paid.'

'But why did you do it?'

'It's a free country isn't it? And I didn't tell you before because I didn't want you to think I was doing it just to get you into bed.'

She said no word as she put the receipt into her bag.

When it was time for her to go Luther wanted to drive her home.

'No,' she said, 'people will talk. He's jealous as hell about me as 'tis without any reason. And I'm not going to give him any.'

He kissed her once more and then she was gone and he was alone again.

The autumn leaves were already falling, although September was not yet out, so dry had it been all through the summer. It would be a hard winter for the tenants.

27

It was not only hard for the tenants. They had further cause for concern one night just after Christmas when Squire Radley had too much to drink, even by his standards, and finished up in a ditch, where he lay undiscovered until morning. This affected the Estate in so far as he did not recover from the chill which turned to pneumonia. He died a week later.

Only the gentry and a fulsome report in the *Pembrokeshire Herald* paid tribute to his sterling qualities and bewailed the passing of such a fine gentleman. The tenants, most of whom knew better, turned out dutifully and respectfully, even so, for the funeral, as did the agent, Mr Luther Knox. Mr and Mrs Jonathin Allin came to Deerfield for the occasion, but Luther was not summoned to see them. A few days after the funeral he went to see Mrs Powell. She was getting on in years but wearing well.

''Tis nice to see thee, honey,' she said, 'but I don't know what's to happen here now for all.'

'I haven't heard anything yet.'

'I'm all right for myself mind.'

'Are you? What are you going to do?'

'Oh, Miss Eiry, bless her l'l' heart, have said there's a cottage down by her I can have to the end o' my days. Missus Radley have gone already.'

'Gone where?'

'Oh, they took here back with 'em. She's helpless now.'

It was no more than Luther would have expected of Eiry, to do the right thing. He was sorry not to have seen her, but it was probably just as well. There was no point in opening old wounds.

It was odd really. He had loved two women in his life and gone to bed with two others, neither of whom had he loved.

It was purely physical as far as Rose was concerned, yet she had always been so much in his mind. Now she had come back into his life again, if only for a brief and passing moment, but he could not pursue a married woman, however unhappy her marriage may be, and it was doubtful whether she would come to him again.

Well, it had been physical in the first place, but then they had known the companionship of his teaching her to write and improve her reading, and he was not so sure that it was only physical after all. He wondered how things were going with her and longed to see her again. That was physical anyway.

It was in the spring that Iorwerth Vaughan wrote to him and told him that Deerfield, along with the home farm, was to be sold. Some other farms would have to be sold as well and he wondered whether Luther would be kind enough to go to Carmarthen to see him.

Sad though some had found it to see the passing of the stage-coach, there could be no comparison with the speed and comfort of the travel by train. It was no longer an adventure to go as far as Carmarthen.

Luther walked to the solicitor's office in a narrow street leading away from the river which ran near the station.

'It's good of you to come all this way,' Vaughan said, 'but there are so many plans and maps here that it's the only place really where we could talk usefully about the problem.'

'Is it a big problem?'

'Bigger than we thought. Radley owed money nobody else knew about. Some gambling debts. He lost most of the money he invested in the Grove when he sold Rhydlancoed, and his other investments at the same time were hardly much more successful. And his high living didn't help.'

'So what d'you want me to do?'

'I thought if we could get some figures on paper you could give me a better idea than anybody which properties it will be best to sell and which to keep. You will know those who will be most interested in buying their own places.'

'Yes, I can see that.'

'And I'm anxious that we do the best we can for Missus Radley. She's in a pretty helpless state and entirely dependent on her daughter and son-in-law. I'd like to think that what little is left of the Estate will be managed to the best possible advantage for her.'

'Yes, of course. And I give you my word I'll do that.'

'I was sure you would. In spite of your occasional threats over the years.'

Luther smiled. 'Did they sound very bad?'

'I'd have done the same in your position. And what you said last September is coming true with a vengeance. They tell me a hell of a lot of workers have left the land this last year.'

'There'll be more yet.'

'Well, don't let's get miserable about it. I'll take you out to lunch now, and we can spend the afternoon on the maps and figures. There's still a great deal I don't pretend to know. Waldo Lloyd was really the Radley's solicitor, you see. He was one of the Lloyd family of Derllys, related to Missus Radley. She was a Lloyd. Nobody else in the firm handled their affairs, and when he died a great deal of knowledge died with him.'

'Are there no family papers?'

'Oh, yes, plenty of them. But I've no time to go through them. I handle the Estate business and that's the beginning and end of it. It's the same with most firms. A certain amount of personal knowledge dies with a particular partner. That is your value to the Estate. Personal knowledge.'

Luther smiled to himself. He knew well enough what Iorwerth Vaughan meant, but personal knowledge of himself was exactly what he did not have. He would have given much for the chance to look through those papers.

28

In that summer of 1869, in haymaking time, just before the end of June, he heard by chance that Rose had given birth to a daughter. Her husband saw it as a good excuse to buy everybody in the pubs their fill of drink on the strength of it.

III
Plumtree Hill

Whether we be young or old,
Our destiny, our being's heart and home,
Is with infinitude, and only there;
With hope it is, hope that can never die,
Effort, and expectation, and desire,
And something evermore about to be.

Wordsworth *The Prelude*

1

Anna was six years old when Aaron brought her to Plumtree Hill. He was fourteen.

His reason for bringing her was to see the calves and chickens and the new Springer puppy. So he had said. Luther, smiling and indulgent, had known it was a good excuse for him to take the phaeton on his own to Saundersfoot. Kit, ancient now, would not lead him into any harm. A steady, gentle trot with her it was, and as sensible as they came.

It was an odd experience, waiting to come face to face with his own child. Only he and Rose knew that, of course, and he had seen nothing of her, nor had any word from her, since that day she had come to Plumtree Hill seven years ago.

They had been quiet years, free from great incident on the domestic scene. Seth was doing well on the farm, Martha Jane had given birth to two babies, and she had two girls to help her in the house and in the dairy.

At the Grove it seemed that Vickerman had at last had enough for, in 1872, it became known that, having bought Hean Castle and the estate round Saundersfoot, he was selling his industrial interests in the area. In addition to the ironworks, he was selling the Saundersfoot Railway and Harbour Company, and his Bonvilles Court and Kilgetty collieries, to a Mr James Carlton of Knutsford in Cheshire for £144,000

'Is that a lot of money, Uncle Luther?' Aaron asked.

'It would be for me, son,' Luther smiled. 'It would be for me.'

'Will it make any difference to the harbour?'

'I don't think so, Aaron. They won't dig it down or blow it up, will they? So I can't see it'll make much difference to working people like us.'

The harbour was of much concern to Aaron. He had been going there with Absie since he was quite small. He had always loved the boats and more recently he had become friendly enough with some of their owners for them to take him on the occasional trip. It was thus he had come to know a good many of the harbour fraternity, including Will Barlow and, through him, his wife Rose and their little daughter Anna.

The year after Vickerman was reported as having sold out, the new Bonvilles Court Coal and Iron Company was established. It was the month of May.

With the new Company came new hope, but it was short-lived. To start with, the iron ore was being imported from Spain. It was not the only aspect of the new developments to damage Absie's interests, for the railway track was pulled up and relaid, so that a steam engine could replace the horses.

The Grove pit was closed and a new pit was sunk at the Lower Level near Stepaside. Even Absie was not too optimistic.

'They reckons as this new Bessemer process have killed th'owld fashioned blast furnaces,' he said.

'Well,' Luther said, 'you know the old saying. ''A dying pig will kick.'''

'Do'st thee think they'll do any good?'

'No, I don't. And apart from the state of the iron trade, you know as well as I do how the men are complaining.'

'That's just it. Bein' stirred up by that damn owld Cutty Hier. Their money's pretty good. Some of 'em's gettin' up to half-a-crown an' three an' six a day.'

'Why did the men elect him to a union job?'

'Well, there 'tis isn't it? Most of 'em is with the Amalgamated Association led by Thomas Halliday, but Cutty's with the National Association. An' a's like a damn owld rat. Where a'll get his head a'll get his body. But a won't do 'em no good. Thou ca'st venture to reckon on that.'

The following summer Absie's words came true. The Company announced a ten percent cut in wages to take effect at the end of May. The men protested, the cut was deferred for a fortnight and the great Thomas Halliday himself came down from Glamorgan to see the general manager, Mr Foley, and then a mass meeting was held on Kingsmoor Common.

'Foley's a decent sort,' Absie said afterwards. 'If he can do anythin' he will. Any road, Halliday said as Foley had agreed to a five percent cut for a month an' they'll negotiate for a closed shop agreement.'

'Will the men settle for that?' Luther said.

'I d'n' know. Halliday's advisin' 'em to settle, but they're meetin' tomorrow an' Cutty Hier is gwain round sayin' not to accept it.'

The following day the men came out on strike and the one furnace in blast was blown out. A fortnight later Cutty Hier was one of the first to return to work down the pit and accept a five percent cut in his wage. The Grove furnace, however, was not relit, and it was to prove to be the end. Neither employers nor workers had gained anything and the Union had suffered a serious reverse.

'*Duw, duw,*' Tom Davey said a few months later, in October, when news came that Hugh Williams had died, 'that's the man they should have had to organise things whatever.'

'Did you know him, Tom?' Luther said.

'Know him? *Duw, duw,* of course I did know him.'

Hugh Williams was the solicitor from St Clears, generally believed to have been one of the brains behind the successful Rebecca Riots more than thirty years previously. Now, at the age of seventy eight, he had died.

'And was he a good man?' Luther asked.

'Well, what d'you think? Married for the second time when he was sixty-five, to a girl of twenty-six. Gave her four babies whatever and the last when he was seventy-six. Wouldn't you call that good? *Duw, duw,* bloody marvellous I do call it.'

Luther laughed, 'That's even better than you, Tom.'

'*Duw, duw,* who's talkin' now then? You haven't managed one yet, *bach.*'

It was the following summer that Aaron brought Anna to Plumtree Hill.

2

Very smart Anna looked in her lace-up boots and black stockings. A frilled petticoat showed beneath her red print dress, which was full round the bottom and had a sash. Her long hair was not as dark as Rose's, which had been a lovely brown. Rose's gipsy eyes had been brown, too, but Anna's were lighter altogether.

It was difficult to tell with a six-year-old. She had something of Rose's prettiness, but there was, too, an indefinable something which, try how he would, Luther could not place. Not by any stretch of the imagination could he see anything of himself in her. Nor was there anything of Seeny or even Mam Bron. His own mother, Meg, he had never seen, but folks had said she was much like Seeny. It would be funny if Rose's husband had been Anna's father after all. Yet, in his heart, Luther knew better. Otherwise, what was that something which stirred memories from somewhere when he had never set eyes on Rose's husband? If only he could know who his father had been.

Some years were to pass before Anna would come to Plumtree Hill again, but she enjoyed herself that day. Much as she liked seeing the calves, and feeding the chickens, it was the puppy who was her favourite, and she named him Gipsy.

'Why have you named him Gipsy?' Luther said.

'My Mammy said that years an'years ago you had a dog called Gipsy.'

It did not strike him as odd until much later that Rose should have been talking to her child about him, especially of things which had happened long before Rose had known him. Gipsy at Deerfield had lived most of his life before Rose was born. What had struck him most of all at the time was that Anna was quite nicely spoken.

Gipsy had not yet been named because he had come to Plumtree Hill without a name only days previously. Tom had brought him back from Llandeilo Abercowin where he had gone to pay his last respects when the Reverend Ieuan Mostyn was laid to rest.

Luther was delighted. He had never found a replacement for his beloved Mostyn, and he knew that the loveable old vicar would have been very happy to think of this one taking his place, especially as the farmer at Abercowin had assured Tom that the puppy was out of a bitch who was herself one of the litter that had resulted from the mating of her mother when she had gone down with the vicar in the boat to

Crickdam. So this young Gipsy was a grandson of his old Mostyn through its mother. Nice thought. And he was as like Mostyn had been at the same age as two peas in a pod.

3

In the autumn of the following year Aaron came to Plumtree Hill after a visit to Saundersfoot and said, 'You knows somethin' Uncle Luther? You was quite right what you said a couple o' years ago when I asked you was a hunderd an' forty four thousand pounds a lot o' money.'

'Was I? What did I say?'

'You said, 'twould be for you.'

'Did I? Well, so it would.'

'Aye well, so 'twould be by all account for this covey James Carlton.'

'How's that then?'

'Well, it's all the talk down the harbour as a can't find it. A never paid Vickerman in the first place.'

The miners in the area were suffering terrible poverty. In the face of further wage cuts, with no reduction in their rents and cost of food, there was another prolonged strike which resulted only in the destruction of their Union. Neither side had learned a lesson.

Within weeks the Company went into liquidation and the liquidator decided to run the collieries only.

There was, too, a dark cloud, albeit a small one, on the farming horizon, and it was Absie who first voiced his misgivings. For well over a decade farming had prospered, and even Absie had seen the wisdom of sticking to the land. The vicissitudes at the Grove, and at the pits, had all been cushioned by the money he had made on the farm. Lack of work for his horses was an aesthetic worry only. Financially there was no concern.

Now, however, corn prices, which had taken a tumble a couple of years previously, remained low.

'It looks bad,' Absie said.

'It had to come,' Luther said.

'But how have it took so long? They said 'twould come

when they abolished the *Corn Laws*, but that was thirty years ago.'

'Well, up to now, the corn coming into the country hasn't amounted to much. But now the steamships are taking over it's a different story. Especially with the railways bringing corn down here a lot cheaper than we can grow it.'

'So what's thee reckon 'tis best do?'

'Don't grow any corn. Raise cattle instead and buy corn cheap.'

Absie reflected for a while. 'Sounds all right,' he said.

''Tis the best I can think of. And 'tis what I'm going to do. I've always had a few black cattle and now they've started this new Welsh Black herd book there could be a future for them. Build a herd all descended from old Fronwen. As good as anything you'll find even down at Castlemartin and they don't come any better than that.'

If such adjustments could be made on the land, however, there was no such expediency available to the struggling and antiquated coal industry in the area, where those who did not emigrate knew only poverty and hunger.

Two years later the Company's liquidator put the company up for sale by auction. Vickerman offered £10,000 and was the only bidder.

'Still, fair play,' Luther said, 'if he was never paid in the first place, he's hardly getting such a wonderful bargain.'

'Apart from th' improvements an' the new engine an' all that,' said Absie. 'A've named th' engine Rosalind after his daughter, so they says.'

'Let's hope the change of name will bring a change of luck.'

It did not.

Nor was the suffering confined to the miners, for the land now faced two disastrous summers when rain followed more rain. And more rain after that.

It was the worst Luther could remember since he had gone to Narberth with Mam Bron forty years ago to buy that suit to start work at Deerfield. Even though he was no longer growing much corn the loss of the haycrops was a disaster. He had always saved his money, as well as being willing to use it. Now he needed it. Others were not as fortunate and had little behind them to see them through.

It was to be another two years before farm prices began to improve, but the miners were receiving a wage of one shilling and sixpence a day, which was only half of what they had been earning before the strike. Vickerman, unable to find a buyer for the Company he no longer wanted, was having all sorts of surveys, and exploring all sorts of possibilities, without anything happening.

4

Luther was in his late fifties and the decade in its early years. When he looked back later in life he realised that it was at that time that things had really begun to happen.

For so long, everything had gone on quite smoothly. True, old Jethro Pugh, Absie's father, had died, but he was an old man, and old people were entitled to die if their time had come. His grandson and namesake, young Jethro, was well over thirty and showing no signs of wanting to marry. Even little Hannah, as Luther continued to think of her, was over thirty, and seemed to be satisfied in life to look after brother Jethro and their father. Absie was a contented man.

Sometimes Luther wondered whether she might regret giving her life to them as she did, but if she ever spoke of it herself it was only to say how much better off she was than those women who had to go to the pit-head to earn a living. Like poor old Rita, for example. Whatever she may have been in her time, it was rough on her to have to come to that.

Seth and Martha Jane were a steady and settled couple, rejoicing in their two children growing apace and now, after a gap of nearly ten years, she was filling out round the waist again.

Tom, in his seventies, was looking like a two-year-old, with a growing lad of seventeen to keep him young in heart. Bessie's other boy, who had been a babe in arms when his father was killed along with John Wesley donkey, had long since set out to try his luck in Tasmania with some sort of notion of trying to find out something of his father's servitude in that far away land.

It was early in the summer of that year, 1883, that Aaron surprised Luther by saying, 'Tell me, Uncle Luther, how'd you like to buy a boat?'

'A boat! What the devil would I want with a boat?'

'Well, you've always said that when you were young you wanted to go to sea. You've always spent a lot of time watching the boats from up the cliff there.'

Luther looked at him keenly. There was so much of Seeny in him.

'What are you getting at, son?'

Aaron was a little ill-at-ease. He said, 'There's a lovely boat for sale in Saundersfoot.'

'What sort of boat?'

'A sixty ton ketch.'

'You're not serious?'

'How not? I could run her for you.'

'I'm sure you could. How much do they want for her?'

'Eight hunderd and fifty pound.'

'Oh, aye, just like that. Like Carlton buying up the Grove, and then Vickerman having to buy it back.'

'No, no, 'twould be a good business.'

'Would it? Then tell me, how much money would an outlay like eight hundred and fifty pounds bring in?'

'I don't know.'

Aaron was not interested in business affairs. It was enough for him to love the sea.

'Aaron, boy. Work it out for yourself. The coastal trade is dying before our eyes. Look at the stuff coming by rail, with the railways cutting the price of everything.'

'There's still coal and limestone.'

'For goodness sake, boy, you know the state of the collieries round here. Look at the way they're closing down. And the sailing ships are finished. Another few years and 'twill be all steam. You know that.'

'I suppose you're right,' Aaron said.

His face was the picture of dejection and disappointment.

Relenting a little, although he knew it was foolish of him, Luther said, 'Whose ketch is it anyway?'

'Will Barlow's.'

Aaron could not know the reason for his thoughfulness.

But it had put a new complexion on things. 'Why is he selling?' Luther said.

Aaron looked uneasy. 'You won't say nothin' if I tells thee?'

'Anything you tell me is the same as burying it in the grave.'

'A've got into debt.'

Luther had heard bits of the story from time to time. Will Barlow's parents had died and it had taken little time for him to go through what money they had left. He had spent most of it for them before they had died. He had, however, set up a shop which Rose had been running fairly successfully.

'I see,' Luther said. 'So he wants to sell the boat to clear the debts. What'll he do then, d'you know?'

Aaron did not answer, and Luther said, 'What's on your mind, boy?'

'Look, Uncle Luther. Nobody knows about this. I've never spoke to Anna about it nor her mother. But one of the men on the boat towld me as Will Barlow have put a girl in the family way and wants to clear off. A's only a drunken waster.'

'I'd heard something to that effect,' Luther said. 'What about the crew?'

'They're good. Two men and a boy. 'Twas they towld me as a was tryin' to sell.'

'And he's reckoning to abandon the girl as well as Anna and her mother?'

'They'd be better off without'n. And Anna's mother'll still have the shop.'

'Supposing he pockets the money and clears off with the debts not paid?'

Luther could not help but smile at the blank look on Aaron's face.

5

The following day Luther went to Carmarthen.

Iorworth Vaughan was old now and only spent odd days in the office. His son and a young nephew were running the practice, but the old man said he would be pleased to handle this little business for Luther.

'Might I be permitted to ask what your particular interest is?' Vaughan said.

'I'm doing it mainly for my nephew. He's my sister's son. She and I were very close. When she died, my nephew was only a little boy and I said I would see him right in life.'

'That I can understand. But why the rest of the business?'

'More difficult to explain. I've never met the man in my life, and don't particularly want to. But his wife worked for me when she was a girl, and I'd like to see her right in life too. Once Barlow gets his hands on the money he'll be gone and his wife will be left to face the music.'

'So what d'you want me to do?'

'I want you to write to him asking for a full statement of his affairs and telling him you'll hold yourself responsible for settling his debts and will send him a cheque for the balance.'

Vaughan laughed. 'He'll never agree to that.'

'You think not?'

'Well, damn it all man, talk sense. Would you agree to it?'

Luther shook his head. 'No, I wouldn't agree to it. But, then, I'm not planning to do a moonlight flit.'

'And if he refuses?' Vaughan said.

'Then tell him the deal is off. I'm paying him his asking price, which is a sight more than he'd get from anybody else. Not even a partnership would pay him that much, and I doubt if he'd find a single buyer anywhere.'

Luther smiled at Vaughan. 'You're a solicitor,' he said 'and I've never heard of anyone accusing your fraternity of acting quickly. Maybe you can send Barlow something to be going on with. Keep the balance for a time and then, when he's gone, see if you can work out some way of paying it to his wife. Just a thought.'

'And which way d'you suggest I do that?'

'I haven't a clue. Not a clue. But what was it Squire Radley said to us once upon a time? Something about not keeping a dog and barking yourself. I have no doubt your bill will be commensurate with the service you perform.'

6

Before haymaking was over, Will Barlow had gone, Aaron had taken possession of the ketch and, after a discussion with Luther, changed her name to the *ASENATH*.

It needed little calculation, once some trading figures were available, to convince Luther that he had indulged in an act of madness, and yet the knowledge only made him smile. It had two redeeming features.

For one thing, it had brought much happiness to Aaron. But far, far more important was the fact that it had done much to help Rose. He would not have contemplated such folly merely to satisfy Aaron's whim. To do something for Rose was a different story.

Even at that, the loss need not be too great. He could still sell shares in the boat. Most coastal traders belonged to anything up to a dozen shareholders, with farmers and shopkeepers and even, in some cases, gentlemen being part-owners. Will Barlow had been a fool. Few young men had ever had the good fortune to have such a boat in their sole ownership.

All of this was not to say that things could be allowed to continue as they were without some effort being made to cut down on the losses and operating costs. There was only one thing to do and that was to find out for himself.

Before the end of July Luther, for the first time in his life, put to sea. He did not count the time he had been brought as a baby by boat from Llandeilo Abercowin to Laugharne ferry. As a boy he had longed to go to sea. All his life the sight of the ships with their canvass spread above them out in the bay had stirred a longing within him. Now, as the breeze sang in the riggings and the prow threw out a surging wave of white foam, he felt the deck rise gently beneath his feet, looked up and saw the full mainsail quiver ever so slightly as it towered above him, and he knew a feeling of exultation and fulfilment. Whatever the loss in which this crazy venture involved him it would almost be worth it just for the intoxicating splendour of such a trip as this. The selling of shares in the *ASENATH* could wait until another day.

A steamer which had left Saundersfoot on the full tide before them was already far beyond Monkstone and off

Caldey. They had a load of culm aboard for Cresswell Quay lime-kilns but were due to call at Tenby for some deck cargo on the way.

Luther was glad to see that the two men and the boy on the boat were well disposed towards Aaron. They all wore fustian trousers and seaman's heavy blue woollen ganzies and caps. The oldest of them, white-haired and bearded, smoked a stained clay pipe. His name was Thomas George Childs and he was known as Thomas George.

'I sailed from Saundersfoot when I was a crut,' he said 'afore the harbour come. From th' open beach 'twas then. After that I went away to sea an' I been all over. But them days is gone an' I'm satisfied as I am.'

'D'you think Aaron'll do all right?'

'How not? A got a nice way with people an' a's sober.'

'But Will Barlow didn't do so well.'

'A was drunk half his time.'

'They say he was a nice man though.'

'Who towld thee that?'

'I don't know really. Just somebody talking I suppose.'

Thomas George took his pipe from his mouth and spat over the rail on which they were leaning.

'A was a bad bugger. Oh, aye, hail fellah well met an' a big man throwin' his money about in the pub, but when a'd took enough drink aboard 'twas there for anybody to see. No man can run a boat like that. There's good business to be had with owld Tom Mathias at the chemist, but a wouldn't have Will Barlow to car' a pound bag o' sugar. Got drunk in the Globe there one night an' gave his cheek an' Mister Mathias had'n put out an' that was th' end of it.'

Luther knew well enough what trade was carried on by Thomas Mathias. He by no means confined his activities to dispensing medicine for humans and livestock. The Globe Inn, at the back, was only another small part of the business. In addition, he imported cattle food, corn, flour, fertiliser and paraffin, and dealt in seeds, ships chandlery, china and glass. In his spare time he had an insurance agency and a sub branch of the Midland bank. He was also a shipping agent for the West of England Manure Company and others.

'Tell me, Thomas George,' Luther said, 'is this run to Cresswell Quay worth doing? It seems a long way to me.'

''Tis worth it if there's enough business on the way. But Barlow'd shot his bowlt. A was owin' money an' that's no good. A only kept doin' this run for a had a 'ooman there. An' o' course a daresn't go near Bristol. There's a bloke as is waitin' to tear his guts out the minute a set foot on the quay. An' if thou casn't go to Bristol thou might's well pack up.'

'So you reckon there's business to be had?'

'O' course there is, master. Only look after it when thou'st got it.'

'What shall we have coming back?'

'Limestone from West Williamston quarries. But that's a slow owld job with the barges bringin' it out. An' then back to Stackpole Quay with it for the kilns there. They uses a lot o' lime down that way.'

'And what's after that?'

'Home then.'

'No cargo?'

'That's just it. We could be bringin' corn from there. Wonderful corn land all down along Castlemartin, but like I towld thee, master, owld Tom Mathias wouldn't deal with Will Barlow. So there 'tis. Come to that, there be no need to frig about with the limestone. We could wash out th' howld an' go on up river to Blackpool mill for corn. Right up to th' upper reaches o' th' Eastern Cleddau. That be a beautiful trip. Or there be Carew mill for that matter, or there's Harfertwest right up the Western Cleddau. Oh, aye, there be plenty o' business for them as wants it an' knows how to look after it.'

Luther had visited Tenby but had never seen it from the sea. A fine sight it was, with the big houses and the hotels looking out across the bay from the cliff tops, and the church spire rising to a point high above them and visible for miles. The big houses, of course, were more modern, but the old part of the town had a history going way back. An important and busy trading port it had been as long ago as Tudor times and even earlier than that.

The whole place this time of year was busy with holiday-makers, and the bathing machines along the beach were

doing good business. In the harbour area there were more
pleasure craft than cargo boats, and there was a keen interest
in the activity from the gentry and their children. From there
the *ASENATH* sailed towards Caldey and then headed west
towards St Margaret's.

At the jetty on the eastern side of Caldey a steamer was
loading limestone from the quarry. As they sailed along the
coast they had a clear view of the houses down by the shore
on the island. It was a delightful bay but a sandbank had
started to build up. Further up the island they could see the
farm buildings and the leaning stone tower of the ancient
priory and, beyond that, the gleaming white of the lighthouse. Then they were under St Margaret's. A little girl on
the cliff waved to them as they sailed between the island and
Giltar Point and they waved back.

Luther remembered these details later, as well as other
things he noticed along the way, but the abiding memory
was of the seabirds.

These were birds he had never seen before, but he had
learned enough from Josiah Price, and read enough, to
recognise them. The first of them, eligugs and razorbills,
flew across their bows as they approached Caldey and then,
low and strong-winged above the water, were the great
cormorants. These he had seen off-shore from Crickdam but
never had he seen the clown-like puffins which tumbled
from their cliff-top burrows on St Margaret's and whirred on
their clockwork wings down to the water.

There were other boats about, but Luther paid little heed
to them. He was too occupied drinking in the splendour of
the towering cliffs, limestone in some places and red
sandstone in others, the beauty of the thrift and sea-
campion drenching them in pink and white. For a time a
great bull seal, which had pushed his head out of the water
beyond Caldey, followed them. His curiosity satisfied at
last, he dived and was gone, and Luther returned to contem-
plating the coastline, beaches of golden sand, and bays
dotted with white-washed cottages and farms.

Further out to sea a raft of shearwaters drifted. A fishing
boat sailed close and disturbed them and they took to the
air, sweeping round and showing their light underparts as

they turned on their long, scything wings. Luther had not
seen one of these birds since the one he had rescued as a
small boy. Presently he caught sight of half-a-dozen big
white birds which he did not recognise. Their great pointed
beaks were steel blue and then, with their black-tipped
translucent wings spread to a six foot span, they circled the
boat and flew on.

'Them's gannets,' Thomas Goerge said.

'Well look at that,' Luther said. 'I should have known.
Where have they come from?'

'From Grassholm I expecs. That's way out beyond Skomer
and Skokholm islands.'

'I didn't know gannets nested there.'

'Oh, aye. They been there about twenty year now an'
they're breedin'. Settled there from Lundy so they reckons.'

As they watched, one of the birds rose in the air,
plummeted downwards at tremendous speed and, with its
great wings close-folded, pierced the water like an arrow.
Moments later it surfaced with a fish in its beak and then the
others dived. Closer in to the cliffs was a small boat from
which two fishermen were setting lobster pots. The gannets,
Luther knew, would be no friends of theirs.

Aaron, at the wheel, was engrossed in his job, but Thomas
George talked on, telling Luther the local legend of the
Huntsman's Leap, naming the headlands and bays from
time to time, Manorbier, with its ancient castle, Swanlake,
Freshwater East, Trewent, Stackpole Quay, Barafundle and
St Govan's with the tiny chapel tucked into the side of the
cliff. And then, between St Govan's and Saddle Head, there
was enough wind against the run of the tide for Luther to
start wondering whether God in His infinite wisdom had,
after all, been taking care of him all along much better than
he could have realised in not letting him be a sailor.

Aaron, he saw, had a broad smile on his cheerful face.
Thomas George said, 'Lord ha'mercy, master. This isn't
nothin'. Come you out in the winter sometime when the
breeze is freshenin' a bit. There be some noble waves here
then. But if 'tis waves you be wantin' hold hard a bit an' see
how you likes it under Saint Ann's.'

They sailed on in quieter water again towards the west and
Aaron took the ketch in close under the towering Stack
Rocks. Never could Luther have imagined that such bird life
existed. In their countless thousands the eligugs and
blackbirds, as the fishermen called them, thronged the cliffs.
These were the guillemots and razorbills of which Josiah
Price had told him when he had found the shearwater and
they had talked of the islands and the seabirds. On the water
they swam and dived. In the air they circled ceaselessly. On
the cliff-ledges they sat in rank upon rank, groaning in a
great thunder o{ protest at this intrusion. It was the most
awesome sight he had ever seen in his life.

'Aye, 'tis a sight all right,' said Thomas George, looking
up. 'I seen a fellah fire off a gun here once, an' as the bords
rus up in th' air th' whole place went black from the sunlight
bein' shut out.'

When, at last, they reached St Ann's Head at the mouth of
Milford Haven, however, Luther decided it must be a lucky
day for him. The sea was calm, but he had heard from those
who should know, that in certain conditions the waters there
could be amongst the worst anywhere in the world.

As they came about off St Ann's, ready to run into the
Haven, Luther could see islands away to the north-west. He
had learned something of their marvellous bird-life from
Josiah Price, who had been so well-versed in country lore,
but, until now, they had been no more than names to him.
To see them filled him with a feeling of excitement and
discovery.

'That smallest island be Skokholm,' Thomas George said,
'an' that's Skomer up above that. Lovely island that.'

'Is there anybody living there?' Luther asked.

'Not on Skokholm. Not now. There was a man livin' there
by the name o' Cap'n Harrison. Used to skipper a boat
sailin' copper ore from Cuba to Swansea afore a retired there
to farm th' island. But a died a couple o' year ago. I can mind
it well, for I seen the fire they lit to signal to the mainland.'

'What about Skomer?'

'Oh, aye, there's folks there. Another owld sea-cap'n,
name o' Cap'n Davies. Wonderful good sailor by all
account. Used to command a sailin'-clipper between

Bombay, Calcutta an' Hong Kong. I knowed a man as come round the Cape o' Good Hope with'n in one o' them coffin ships in a storm. A packed it up after that an' took over from his father-in-law on Skomer.'

'And is he farming the island?'

'Why, aye. A good farmer, too. Grows wonderful corn there. I've saw it with my own eyes an' fetched some from there, but it's a bad owld place to go in with a boat. That's the place to go if thou wants to see bords. Lord ha' mercy, I've never saw nothin' like it in all my born days.'

'They tell me there are a lot of puffins there.'

'Puffins? That's what they calls them l'l' sea-parrots is'n't it?'

'Yes, that's the ones.'

'Oh, aye, there's millions of 'em there.'

'Millions?'

'Well, maybe more than that for all I knows. The fields an' slopes above the cliffs is white with 'em like daisies. An' the cocklollies. We was anchored off there one night for shelter an' I've never been so feart in all my born days, like as if the devil hisself was screamin' all round a body. An' all down the cliffs there's the eligugs an' blackbords.'

'Well, where's Grassholm then, Thomas George?'

'Oh, that be way out miles beyond Skomer. Thou ca'st see it on a clear day. That's only a small l'l' island like St Margaret's, but there's millions o' them sea parrots there an' now some o' them gannets. Bad buggers they be for the fish.'

'Nobody lives there?'

'Lord ha' mercy, no. 'Tis too wild for that an' no water. But the fishermen from Marloes goes out there to set their lobster pots an' keeps some sheep there.'

They came in under St Ann's then and began the long journey up the Haven.

Without anything else that, in itself, was an experience as they tacked up through this magnificent natural harbour over which Lord Nelson and so many others had enthused down through the ages. Mighty schooners and leviathans of steamships went past disdainfully, dwarfing the *ASENATH*, which had looked so impressive in Saundersfoot Harbour.

On their port bow there were the new docks being built at Milford and then, to starboard, was the naval dockyard all stir and bustle, and with great steam ships at anchor being fitted out. For mile after mile as they had sailed there had been rich farmland running down to the water's edge, herds of sleek Welsh Black cattle grazing, and fields of waving corn turning colour ready for harvest. The corn growers, Luther knew, were having a bad time, but the cattle men were still doing well enough. Dairy produce was not so good, and he understood why when he looked at the great vessels which were bringing in so much from abroad.

When Luther was a boy, Josiah Price had told him that no part of Pembrokeshire was further than seven miles from salt water and now, as they sailed on up this vast waterway, which ran up through the heart of the county, he began to realise what Josiah had meant. They changed course eventually and left the Daucleddau to sail east up the Cresswell River. To starboard was the estuary of the river coming down from Carew and above them, on their port bow, they looked up at Lawrenny Castle where a herd of deer were in the park which ran down to the water. The boatyard at Lawrenny had closed.

''Twas a fine yard at one time,' said Thomas George, 'but there've been nothin' much built there now this last forty year.'

Luther knew as they passed Pembroke Dock that the days of sail were numbered. It was all part of the pattern.

The tide was on the flow and they were making good time but, as their way narrowed, and there was more evidence of mud-flats and marshland, so was there evidence of teeming birdlife, not only waders, but duck of many varieties waiting to feed upon the corn fields.

How Ieuan Mostyn would have loved such a place. Luther could just imagine him now with his *Tarfgi* on the cold winter nights waiting for dawn and the swift flight of the geese, with the flood tides creeping in across these muddy creeks. Or perhaps, with the full moon rising at dusk, straining his eyes to see which way the bubbles were floating and waiting for the call of the geese which would make his heart to leap and his *Tarfgi* to tremble.

They had set sail early enough from Saundersfoot that morning, but dusk was falling when they tied up at Cresswell Quay. Young Jimmy Wilks cooked them a hunger-satisfying meal of sausages and bacon, boiled potatoes and thick slices of wholemeal bread and butter, washed down by mugs of strong tea.

Luther and Aaron went with the others for a drink at the Cresselly Arms. Hunting prints were on the walls and masks of foxes gazed down glassy-eyed upon the assembled gathering. There was no interest in the *ASENATH's* change of name and ownership. It was of far more concern that some heathen, as yet unidentified, had shot one of Squire Allen's foxes.

The lifting of the culm from the hold the following day was carried out by labourers using a two hundredweight basket which was raised by means of a pulley fastened to a spar on the ketch's mast. The next day there was the even slower job of loading limestone floated out in barges through the narrow channels to the main waterway from the quarries at West Williamston, and then followed the return voyage to Stackpole Quay and another day unloading.

Luther's bunk bed had been comfortable and he had slept well, but he could not help pondering on their trip, the days it had taken, and what Aaron could expect to make out of it. Most assuredly they would have to sit down and do some serious thinking and talking if there were to be any hope of making even a moderate success of the venture. How much more time-consuming and costly the whole operation would be in winter, with its less favourable weather conditions, he could scarcely bear to contemplate.

As Luther admired the marvellous skill with which the *ASENATH* was berthed at the tiny harbour at Stackpole Quay, the conviction came to him again that Josiah Price had counselled him wisely when he had said, 'Stick to your books, my boy. Stick to your books.'

Sailing past the lovely beach beyond Stackpole Head at Barafundle he had seen some black cattle in the fields above, and the next morning, whilst the unloading of the limestone began, he went ashore and walked along the cliff-top fields, taking with him some bread and cheese. He was glad of it later because he went further than he had intended until he came to a place where he looked down on a beach of such beauty as he had never seen in all his life. The sparkling blue water was crystal clear, and the waves, white-ribboned, rolled gently up the golden sand where no foot had been to leave a print, nor doubtless would all day.

He did not descend to the beach but, skirting above the sand-dunes which backed it, went through the fields until he looked down on a valley given over to a series of lakes, where many duck and waterfowl were to be seen amongst the white and green spreading patches of water-lilies. This, he knew, must be part of the grounds of Lord Cawdor's seat at Stackpole Court and he headed back towards the Quay.

He was making his way slowly through a field, where there were some of the most handsome Welsh Black cows it would be possible to see, when he saw a man coming towards him. Wearing breeches, he had all the look of a farmer about him. As he came nearer Luther could see he was young and certainly not yet thirty. He was not tall, but was broad-shouldered and strong.

'I hope I'm not trespassing on your land,' Luther said.

'It isn't my land,' the young man said, his weather-beaten face lit with a smile, 'it's Lord Cawdor's and he'll let anybody go anywhere.'

'I thought you were a farmer.'

'I am. I'm the tenant at Stackpole Quay.'

'Are these your cows?'

'Oh, aye, they're my cows.'

'That's really why I came up. Just to have a look at them. I saw them from the boat yesterday.'

The farmer looked at him with more interest.

'Do you mean the ketch back there unloading limestone? She's from Saundersfoot isn't she?'

'Yes, that's right. My nephew has just bought her.'

'Isn't she Will Barlow's boat?'

'She was.'

'What's happened to him?'

'Gone abroad I believe.'

'Best place for him. He's no good to anybody.'

'So they tell me.'

'So what's your interest in cows?'

'I've been interested in Welsh Blacks for years. I'm trying to build up a small herd of them.'

'Well, these are all in the new herd book.'

'Are they indeed?'

'Yes, all of them.' His enthusiasm was evident.

'I went up to Caernarvonshire in the spring to see some of the Welsh Blacks up there. Useful cattle some of them. But they don't milk like ours down here in the Castlemartin area. His Lordship is very keen on them.'

'Tell me,' Luther said, although he had never given the matter any thought until now, 'could you find me a bull calf to rear for my own herd?'

'Yes, indeed, delighted.'

'My name's Knox,' Luther said. 'Luther Knox.'

'Good God,' the farmer said, 'aren't you the agent to the Rhydlancoed Estate?'

'To what little is left of it, yes.'

'Well, fancy that. My name's John Roblin.'

Luther took the hand which the young man held out to him and felt a firm handshake.

'But how would you know me?' Luther said.

'I don't, but my wife does. At least, her mother did. My wife was Patricia Allin. Her mother was Eurwallt Radley from Rhydlancoed. A beautiful and lovely lady.'

'You said was.'

'Yes, indeed, very sad. She often spoke of you. She was very fond of you she always said.'

'Tell me, then. Is she dead?'

'Yes, she died suddenly last winter.'

Luther was aware of a great sadness, yet it was not the sadness he had known when Seeny had died. Perhaps it was because he had not seen Eiry for so long. It was no good trying to explain these things, even to himself. All he knew was that he had loved both of them.

'Here's a good cow over here,' John Roblin was saying, 'and she's in-calf to the old bull.'

Luther's mind was only half with the Welsh Blacks. He agreed that the bull was half the herd and it was important always to use a good one. And he did indeed like that particular cow with her broad muzzle and bright eyes, deep body and well-attached udder. And yes, if she had a bull calf next time, he would be very pleased to buy it. But the rest of his mind was far away on a secluded seat in the garden at Rhydlancoed, and there were butterflies and birdsong, and Eiry was resting her hand on his and saying, 'Dear Luther, don't be bitter.' He felt again the softness of her lips as they brushed his cheek and he turned to look out across the blue sea away to the Gower coast in the far distance so that his tears would not betray him.

7

'Pat will be very disappointed she missed you,' John Roblin said, as they ate a good meal of cold beef and ham and boiled potatoes and pickles. 'You'll be off on the evening tide, and she'll hardly be back by then. Grandma Louisa likes her to stay as long as she can. And Pat adores her anyway.'

'How is Missus Radley keeping these days?' Luther asked.

'Oh, very frail. Can't speak much and hardly leaves her bedroom. Yet there's something about her.'

'I'm sure there is. I think she must have been the most beautiful and loveliest woman I ever met in my life.'

'You knew her when she was young, of course?'

'Yes, I did. And she was really beautiful. But I couldn't claim to have known her.'

Luther thought for a moment and smiled.

'I would have liked to have known her much better,' he said, 'but I was only a clerk in the agent's office. I knew my place. But I came to know her a bit better later on.'

It was John Roblin's turn to smile. 'You can forget that now,' he said. 'Old man Radley thought he was making a wonderful marriage for Eurwallt when he married her off to Jonathan Allin, but that was the biggest mistake he ever made. Nice enough chap, mind, but no money there. If it hadn't been for Lord Cawdor accepting us as tenants here we'd be in poor shape.'

They talked then about the farming and from that they turned to the prospects for the sea trade.

'Obviously,' said John Roblin, 'it's not going to be what it was. But Pembroke station is still a long way for a lot of us. We're not using as much lime now, of course, because it's easier to use phosphates. But they can be brought in here just as easily as culm and limestone. And we'll go on growing corn and hoping times will improve.'

'You think then that Aaron could do business here?'

'Why not? The railways's made a tremendous difference in many ways, but it's still out of reach of a good many.'

'Well, it needs thinking about. So does this bull calf.'

'As soon as Duchess calves I'll let you know.'

When Duchess calved, however, she had a heifer calf. So impressed had Luther been by her that he wrote to tell John Roblin that, rather than have a bull out of any other cow, he would wait until Duchess calved again next year.

8

The following year Duchess duly obliged and, at three weeks of age, her bull calf came, by courtesy of Aaron Pugh and the *ASENATH*, from Stackpole Quay to Saundersfoot and thence, in collusion with the descendants of the first old Fronwen, to set about establishing a Welsh Black herd at Plumtree Hill. That, however, would take time. Another year had to go by before he was ready for service and, around that time, came the news that Will Barlow had been stabbed to death in a fight with a foreign seaman over a woman in a drinking place in the dockland area of some foreign port.

Full marks to Rose, Luther thought when Aaron told him as much as he knew about it, she had made no hypocritical show of wanting more details or pretending to be upset. She had crossed him out of her life long ago and had as much as she could do to look after her business.

For a time Luther wondered whether he should write to Rose but, in his heart, he knew there was nothing he could say. Then he had the wild notion of going to see her and he felt again that fierce longing for her. She would always be a part of him but, after such a long time, he could think of no plausible excuse for making a move.

The news of Will Barlow's death made no great impact in the village. It was of far greater moment to people in the area that Mrs Vickerman had died at Hean Castle. By this time even Absie had given up hope of ever seeing the Grove being opened again and of driving more iron ore from the Patches.

'I don't suppose Vickerman'll have much interest left now. It's a big blow when a man loses his partner,' he said.

'And d'you think Vickerman's as human as that?' Luther said.

'Oh, I knows a's a hard man but a'll feel it.'

'I'm glad to hear you say it. I've often thought he's been misjudged.'

'Mind thee, 'twas shameful the way as a turned them widows out when a bought them farms round Sandersfoot.'

'Don't believe it, Absie. He left it all to his agent. The widows were turned out by the farmers who had sub-let the cottages. Vickerman was miles away in Essex and knew nothing about it.'

'Well, I only knows what I hears.'

'And that isn't to know anything. All I know is, that's what he'll be remembered for. Shakespeare had it right when he said, "The evil that men do lives after them, the good is oft interred with their bones." That was about Caesar. He was an ambitious man. So was Vickerman. Do you think posterity will take account of the money he sank in this area?'

'Well there isn't much left to show for it now for all and times is bad. Do'st thou think that young Aaron'll make a go of it with thicky boat?'

'No harm for him to get it out of his system whilst he's young. I'm more concerned about all the foreign meat that's coming in with these refrigerated ships. We're in for some hard times I think.'

By the following year the farmers were really feeling the effect of what was happening. In Pleasant Valley, whatever hopes may have been entertained, they knew now for sure that the death knell had been sounded, for the rumour was that, having failed completely to find a buyer, Vickerman had decided to dismantle the ironworks. Enough was enough.

Important as all this was, however, it paled into insignificance for Luther at the end of the summer when Aaron brought Anna to Plumtree Hill for the second time. But now she was a young lady, up to the latest fashion with a hat, and very smart in her silk dress with a bustle.

When she was a child, Luther had seen something in her face which had stirred memories and troubled him because he could not place it. Now she was growing up and her features had matured. When he looked at her now he knew whose features they were and he was even more troubled and perplexed.

'Uncle Luther,' Aaron said, 'we haven't told Father yet. We wanted you to be the first to know apart from Anna's mother. Anna an' me's gettin' married.'

9

That night Luther went to bed with his mind in torment. He had protested to Aaron that they could not dream of such a thing. The only reason he could put forward was that Anna was too young, but Aaron had laughed and said, 'She'll grow out of that fault every day. She's seventeen mind.'

Aaron was twenty-five. Only Luther of the three of them knew what had happened with Anna's mother when she was the same age, and Luther had been far older than Aaron was now.

The one good thing was that they had said there was no hurry, but that they were going to be engaged, and perhaps marry the following year. Somehow or other he would have to find a way to prevent it.

He knelt by the side of the bed to pray. For the first time in years, perhaps for the first time in his life, he would pray. Every night since he could remember he had said his prayers, but tonight would be different. Tonight he would tell God about his troubles and listen for a change to find out whether God had anything to say.

'Leave it at that,' Ieuan Mostyn had said that day when he brought Gipsy's grandmother to Plumtree Hill to be mated. 'If the Lord wants you to know, it will come all in His own good time.'

Well, God knew how, and how often, he had fallen by the
wayside, but he believed in his heart he had done his best in
life. It was something of a trial being a chapel man, and one
who went into the pulpit at that. It would make it very
difficult for him to tell Aaron that he was in fact Anna's
father. Yet he would have to know. Aaron was his nephew.
More correctly, he was his first cousin, for Aaron's mother
and his own mother had been sisters. The relationship was
far too close. The Church and the law would not counte-
nance such a union. The risk to unborn children was too
great. Life was hard enough for those who were born with all
their faculties. How could he stand by, just to protect his
own miserable good name, and say nothing, and allow
imbecile children to be born?

His head jerked suddenly on his hands and he came
awake. His knees ached from their long time pressing on the
floor and he was cold and shivering. He crawled into bed.
Like it or not, tomorrow he must face up to going to see
Rose. Perhaps she would have some influence or better
ideas.

Funny thing, he thought, it was in this bed the trouble had
all started. He went to sleep then.

10

In the cold light of day he was not so sure about going to see
Rose. Eighteen years it was since he had last seen her and he
fancied that she might be just a little difficult to deal with. He
looked in the mirror as he dressed and was conscious that
there was very little black amongst his hair. Still, he hadn't
lost it, which at sixty-one wasn't bad.

There was also the fact that Rose had her shop, and there
were still a few late summer visitors about. Perhaps she
would be too busy to talk to him. So he would have to go on
Sunday. Perhaps it would be just as well to write to her
apprising her of his intention.

It had never taken him so long to draft a simple letter but,
in the end, it was written to his satisfaction, and posted in
plenty of time for her to write back, if she so wished, and tell
him not to come. There was no reply.

Kit had long since moved on to whatever green and Heavenly pastures await faithful equine servants, and her place had been taken by a bright and happy natured little grey roan mountain pony, who had already been named Tegwen before she came to Plumtree Hill. Luther saw no reason to change it. The phaeton was still giving good service.

At the sight of Tegwen coming out of the stable with her harness on, Gipsy was all excitement, but when Luther said, 'Not today, boy. You can't come today,' his ears and tail dropped. He loved going in the phaeton as Mostyn had loved it in his time. It was some compensation for him that he would be fussed for the rest of the day by young Robert, Martha Jane's last baby, who was now a rumbustious three-year old.

As he set off, wearing his new suit of broadcloth, Luther's pulse quickened at the thought of seeing Rose again, and yet he would have given much to defer the confrontation.

Autumn tints were already upon the trees and wayside hedges, the last of the swallows had gone and all the valley was hushed and still. The Grove had been born within his lifetime, lived and died, along with all the hopes that had gone with it. One day the scars would heal and Pleasant Valley would again be a fitting name.

As the phaeton crossed the bridge over Ford's Lake, Tegwen pricked her ears and threw up her head moment-arily as five wild geese rose from the water with a great beating of wings and honked their way down to the beach beyond Crickdam. Only once, many years ago, could Luther recall geese having come so early in the year and it had been followed by an early winter.

As in a dream he reached Saundersfoot and turned Tegwen's head towards Rose's place. It was neat and clean, as he would have expected, knowing Rose, and it also looked prosperous. He was glad of that.

The door of the stable, round the side of the house, was open and there was nothing inside. Luther took Tegwen out of the shafts and led her into the stall where there was some nice, fresh hay. The omens were propitious. He went round to the back door and knocked. He heard movement at last,

the door opened and Rose was standing there and he knew
not what to say.

He noticed vaguely that she was wearing a pretty dress
with a bustle and that her lovely brown hair was piled high.

'Well, Mister Knox!' she said. 'Fancy Mister Luther Knox
coming to the back door.'

Her tone was flippant and there was the same mischievous
smile of old playing around her eyes.

'Come in,' she said, and led him through a spotless kitchen
to a spotless, comfortably furnished sitting room. The table,
he noticed, was laid for two. Then he realised that Rose's
hands were restless. She, too, was a little unsure of herself,
and her flippancy was a pose. It made him feel better. Time
had dealt kindly with her. She was still pretty and looking
much younger than her thirty-eight years.

He looked round the room and said, 'Well, Rose, you
certainly have the nice little home you said you used to
dream about as a small girl.'

'I've worked for it.'

'I'm sure you have. Are things going well with you?'

'Yes, thank you. Very well.'

'Should I say I was sorry to hear about your husband?'

'Not unless you're an even bigger hypocrite than I
thought.'

He ignored the barb.

'I was glad when you were able to set up on your own.'

'I had the shop before he went off.'

'Yes, of course. But when Aaron was on for buying the
boat there was talk of a lot of debts.'

Rose laughed. 'Oh yes, but the solicitor from Carmarthen,
Mister Vaughan, fixed all that. Charming old gentleman he
was.'

'I'm glad to hear that. What did he do?'

'He came down and explained that he would have to treat
it as a joint concern in order to settle the debts. He gave Will
two hundred pounds and he was gone. When it came time to
settle the balance, good God these solicitors are slow aren't
they?'

'Yes, aren't they?'

'You've found that have you?'

'Oh, aye, terrible. So what happened then?'

'Well, it was nearly a year before it was settled. Mister Vaughan wrote and asked me for Will's address, and I wrote back and said I didn't know and didn't want to know. It was a bit cheeky perhaps, but I didn't care. I just wanted to wash my hands of him.' She laughed. 'And what d'you think? Mister Vaughan wrote back and said that he wanted to see the matter settled and as he had already paid my husband two hundred pounds he was quite sure he could pay the balance to me.'

'And did he?'

'Why, aye. Sent me a cheque for nearly two hundred pounds.'

'That was a bit of luck.'

'You can say that again. It's made a world of difference. Now then, let me make you a cup of tea and something to eat.'

'But Rose, I want to talk to you.'

'Be quiet a minute. I know what you want to talk about. Have something to eat first.'

Rose had her best cutlery out and the fine crockery was as good as anything he had ever seen at Rhydlancoed or Deerfield. She served him with cold meat and thinly cut bread-and-butter, apple tart and fruit cake. When they had finished eating he leaned back in his chair and smiled.

'Like old times,' he said.

'No, not old times. That can never be.'

'Oh, why not?'

'I loved you then, but you didn't want to know.'

'What d'you mean?'

'You could have married me and it would have been marvellous. But I don't want to talk about that. Talk about what you've come to talk about. Anna and Aaron.'

'Yes,' he sighed, 'it's difficult.'

'What's difficult?'

'You know they can't get married.'

'Oh, and why not? Isn't my daughter good enough or something?'

He could see her temper rising.

'Rose,' he said, 'it's out of the question.'

She pushed her chair back and got up from the table. 'Christ Almighty,' she said, 'what have you come here to preach about now? D'you know something? You chapel people make me bloody sick. You, of all people! Chapel on Sunday, up in the pulpit telling other people how to live. Too bloody sanctimonious to be true, and you can father a married woman's child and let her palm it off on her husband.'

'Rose,' he said, 'calm down a bit. I don't pretend anything. I only ever take a service because I've been railroaded into it. I know I'm no better than I ought to be and nothing like as good as I should be.'

'You can say that again.'

'Do you really hate me that much?'

She was standing with her hands on her hips and her foot was tapping the floor.

'No, I don't hate you. You're not worth hating. You just make me sick.'

'You've said that before.'

'And I'll say it again. You're a bloody hypocrite.'

'It says in the Book, Rose, "Stolen waters are sweet, and bread eaten in secret is pleasant."'

'H'm,' she grunted. 'Trust you to have an answer.'

'Maybe. But I don't know the answer this time.'

Rose sat down again.

'What's got into you in your old age, Luther?' she said. 'What difficulty is there?'

'This business of Aaron and Anna wanting to get married.'

'What's wrong with that?'

'The relationship. The blood relationship.'

She looked at him, bewildered.

'Do I really have to spell it out to you?' he said. 'Anna is my daughter isn't she?'

'The world doesn't know that.'

'Never mind about the world. You and I know, don't we?'

'All right, so what?'

'Aaron is my nephew. Or if you want to be exact, my cousin. His mother and my mother were two sisters. With blood as close as that there's every chance they'd bring imbecile children into the world. Do you want that to happen?'

She looked at him in amazement. 'Good God above,' she said, 'you don't really believe that do you?'

'I do. We can't stand by and say nothing just because we don't want people to know what was between us.'

Rose started to laugh.

'Say that again will you?' she said.

'No, I won't.' He was beginning to feel angry. 'I've said it once and that's enough.'

'You poor fool! You really believe you were Meg Knox's child?'

'What d'you mean, really believe? I know! I've seen the entry in the church register.'

'I don't care what you've seen. Megan Knox was no more your mother than I'm Queen Victoria.'

It took time for what she was saying to sink in.

'I thought you knew better than that,' Rose said.

Luther just looked at her.

Rose said more kindly, 'Gran told me years ago.'

'Gran?'

'Yes, my Gran. Polly Gwyther. She was there when you were born.'

'Where was I born?'

'I don't know. But Gran was a young woman at the time and brought you from there in a boat.'

Luther sat, speechless and stunned. At last he said, 'That's right anyway. I knew about that. But I didn't know who it was.'

There was another long silence. He ran his fingers through his hair. 'Tell me,' he said, 'who was my mother?'

'I don't know.'

'Then who was my father?'

'I don't know that either.'

Already he was thinking of Anna and the likeness he had seen.

'All I know,' Rose said, 'is what Gran told me. And that's what I've just told you now.'

'How old is your Gran?'

'She's ninety.'

'What's her mind like?'

'Her mind and her body are both good. I go there once a week to do a bit for her, but she's tough. Oh, aye, her mind's all right, don't you worry about that. And if she said you're not Meg Knox's child you're not. Go and ask her if you like.'

Luther rose from the table. 'I think I will,' he said.

Rose brought him his hat. He kissed her on the cheek and she did not pull away. As she opened the back door for him, she said, 'Go and ask her and sort it out.' Then she smiled and said, 'Then come and talk to me again sometime.'

He was in too much of a daze to think of the invitation in her voice, and of all the promise it might hold, but he thought about it later.

11

Luther drove home with his mind in a turmoil and heeded nothing of the sea and the lovely countryside as he went. It was no use trying to think straight. Long ago there were questions he would have asked Protheroe, but he had shot himself before Luther could have the chance to ask him. Waldo Lloyd had died soon afterwards. He, too, would have known the answers to a few questions.

Then there was that crazy old Mortimer Strong. He had lost his mind completely just when he could have shed useful light in dark places.

What was it Tom Davey had said about the woman who had gone with them with the baby in the boat? 'Never spoke much but she was sharp when she did,' he had said. 'Not bad looking but keep out of her way like.' And Tom's father had said, 'She could turn the milk sour if she looked at it twice.' Yes, that could be Polly Gwyther all right. Even John Roblin had found it difficult to believe that Louisa Radley had once been beautiful. Maybe time was when Polly had not been such a bad looker and not just the dragmallin as he had always known her.

When Mam Bron had died Polly Gwyther was there. What was it she had said? 'There's things as I could tell as lots of folks would like to know about. So don't thee ask questions young Mister Knox.'

Maybe she would not have answered questions at that time, but perhaps she would now. Rose had said she was fit in mind and body. That was as maybe, but it would be a pity for her to die or go crazy, the same as the rest of them, before he could ask her. He headed Tegwen towards Sardis. It would be a little out of his way to go home that way, but there was no point in waiting until tomorrow.

He tied Tegwen to the gatepost and knocked on the cottage door. There was the sound of clogs shuffling on the hard dirt floor and the door opened.

Old and bent, with a shawl wrapped round her, Polly Gwyther looked at him keenly with eyes that were still surprisingly bright. Then she grinned and showed her ancient yellow tusks and said, 'Well, well, if it isn't Mister Knox in his best Sunday suit. Come thee in my little curly headed gentleman.'

Her cottage was much as he remembered his own home at Crickdam, but it was clean and dry and the ball fire was burning merrily. Polly shuffled to her chair by the corner of the fireplace and motioned Luther to the skew opposite.

'Well, well, young Mister Knox, ''tis nice to clap eyes on thee again. I often wondered if thee'st 'ud ever come an' try an' hawse owld Polly.'

'I've just come from Rose's.'

'She's a good girl is l'l' Rose.'

'She told me that you told her that Meg wasn't my mother.'

'No, no, indeed honey. Meg was never thy mother for all. Worried about the childern marryin' is it? No, no, don't worry. Nobody else knows, but owld Polly knows, though 'tis mortal strange l'l' Anna don't look like thee.'

'You know about that do you?'

'Why, aye, owld Polly knows lots o' things. I knowed the date as Rose went to see about poor Albert's rent when he'd broke his leg. No, no, honey, Meg was never thy mother.'

'Why d'you say that?'

'I was there, honey. I was there.'

'Where was it?'

'Oh, I'd'n'know that. 'Twas a long time ago.'

'Sixty-one years.'

'That's a mortal long time for all. But I remembers well.'
'What happened?'
'I'm not supposed to tell. I was swore to secrecy, but it
don't matter now. I've never towld nobody else, nor never
shall. I only ever towld l'l' Rose a bit of it for she was so keen
to know the why, when, how an' what for about thee. God
love her, breakin' her l'l' heart for thee she was, but thou
wa'st too blind to see it. Any road, Toby Protheroe come to
me an' fixed up about it. Meg come home from Rhydlancoed
just afore her time was up an' I went with her by night in the
Squire's coach. Hours it took an' 'twas a bumpy owld road
at th' end. 'Twas a owld place as we was at, an' when it come
daylight I could see it was down by a river lookin' out to sea,
but I was never towld where 'twas. 'Twas up in
Carmarthenshire somewheres, an' they was all jabberin' in
Welsh, they're all blessed foreigners up that way, so I never
spoke to none of 'em. Any road, the babbie come an' I
delivered her an' passed her to Meg an' she loved her.'
'Her!? Was it a girl Meg had?'
'Aye, 'twas a girl right enough an' a couple o' days after
that the Squire's coach come an' took the pair of 'em for Meg
to be drove to London with the babbie.'
'So where did I come from?'
'I d'n'know that neither. But the day after Meg was drove
off with her babbie another coach come an' they gave thee
to me, but thou wa'st a lot owlder than Meg's babbie with
black hair an' brown eyes. Ha'st thou ever saw a newborn
babbie with brown eyes? Perhaps thou'st never saw many
newborn babbies. But owld Polly have an' they alus got blue
eyes, then they changes.'
Luther closed his eyes and thought. Old Mortimer Strong,
in his crazy rambling, had mentioned the brown eyes of the
baby he had christened and wondered why he had
remembered it. So that made sense at last. He said, 'Who
was my mother or where had I come from, d'you know?'
'I d'n'know. But Squire Radley was the father of Meg's
babbie. She was the very image of'n. Any road, I had thee in
a shawl an' I was took in a boat with a couple o' blokes who
only talked in Welsh an' I never said nothin' to 'em. When
they put me ashore, the Squire's coach was there an' drove

me with thee in my arms all along the coast road through Pendine an' Amroth to Crickdam an' I gave thee to Bronwen Knox. She looked at thee an' looked at me an' I could tell she knowed thou wasn't Meg's babbie, but she never said nothin' to me an' I never said nothin' to her. So I gave the belongin's as was sent with thee an' there was a lovely tea-caddy an' half a spade-guinea in a l'l' velvet pouch an' off I went an' shut my mouth. By-an-by Toby Protheroe come to see me with a solicitor an' his name was Lloyd. They paid me well for what I done an' towld me as I could keep my cottage rent free to th' end o' my days so long as I never said nothin' to nobody but the minute as I towld anybody I'd be put out. Then they read out a piece o' paper to say that's what 'twas an' I made a mark an' they both signed it. An' if I never muv from here alive again I've never towld a livin' sowl apart from the bit I towld Rose, an' I don't suppose it matters now any road.'

The old woman went quiet then and Luther gazed into the blue and yellow flames of the ball fire. A trickle of hot ash broke the silence.

'Tell me,' he said, 'was Squire Radley's father alive then?'

'No, th'owld man had died afore that. Th' young squire was livin' a wild life. A was the father of Meg's babbie for all. An' a took Meg up to London an' kept her there with her babbie an' I heard tell as a had a couple more by her. Mad over her a was.'

'Was he my father, do you know?'

'Lord ha' mercy young Mister Knox, I don't know. Nor I don't know who thy mother was. But I knows 'twasn't Megan.'

'Did you ever know anybody by the name of Christopher?'

Polly Gwyther gazed, unseeing, into the fire.

'No, honey,' she said, 'I've never heard tell of no Christopher.'

12

It was night by the time Luther arrived back at Plumtree Hill. He stabled Tegwen and fed her, and left her in the stable for an hour or so whilst he had some food himself, and before turning her out. Then he limped quietly up across the fields.

The harvest moon was hanging, big and bright, in a clear sky, lights twinkled along the valley, and cattle were calling in the near distance. Against the sky, trees were silhouetted and some slight cloud was riding high and darkening far out over Caldey. The night was cold.

Excited, as always, to have his adored master home again, Gipsy hunted through the fern and sent the nocturnal rabbits scurrying for sanctuary. Down on the beach below Crickdam everything was still, and the music of the waves soothed him and he heard again their chorus, '*What are the wild waves saying?*'

Since time out of mind he had been bothering about who his father was. Now he was further away than ever from coming to the truth. Now he did not even know who his mother was. But it explained why Meg had never bothered about him. She had not been the hard-hearted, uncaring sort to abandon her own child as he had always thought. She had her own child with her all the time. Somebody must have been having a good laugh to themselves somewhere once upon a time.

Then another thought struck him. If Meg had not been his mother, Seeny had not been his aunt or half-sister or anything at all. For years he had been in love with her. So often he had felt a sense of guilt at the intensity of his feelings for her, and there had never been anything to be ashamed of at all. He could have married Seeny. Fond as he was of Absie, he would never forget the heartache when Seeny had married him. Dear old Absie. He had loved her, too, and had never as much as looked at anyone else.

What did any of it matter anyway? Who cared who his father or mother had been? Rose had said, 'Sort it out, then come and talk to me again sometime.'

In all probability he would never sort it out now. But he could go to see Rose. She had asked him.

13

For the second time in his life, when he should have been going in search of Rose, he was confined to the house. It was no more than a heavy cold at first, but it took some weeks to shake off. He thought it even more of a coincidence because it was only the second time in his life that he had ever been really ill. But this was nothing as bad as the first time. It was merely inconvenient.

He was just getting out and about again and had strolled as far as the cliff road. Shuffling along, head down, was one of the familiar strags who passed that way annually. A bundle was on his back and a billy-can hung from the string round his waist. Not all of his fraternity were the thieves and desperate characters who for years had been a plague upon the rural areas, especially since the Irish famines. Luther had a sympathy for many of them in their plight. So had Mrs Laura Powell in her time at Deerfield, and so had Eiry and Mrs Radley.

White-bearded Irish Seven Waistcoats had been tramping the coastal road for as long as Luther could remember.

''Tis a cold mornin' sir,' was his greeting now as he saw Luther.

'But nice to have it dry, Irish. How are things going with you?'

'Old now, sir, gettin' old. The bones is creakin' now, sir, an' the blood runs thin it does. 'Tis terrible when the blood runs thin so 'tis.'

'Still on the same beat?'

'Sure I am sir, still on the same beat. I'm too old to be after changin' now.'

'What's the news down country?'

'Her Ladyship's gone, sir. I suppose ye'd be after hearin' o' that, sir?'

'Her Ladyship? You mean Missus Radley?'

'Indeed, sir. A fine lady she was, sir. She'll be with Mister Christopher now I trust an' pray, safe an' united for ever, may their souls rest in peace.' He crossed himself as he spoke.

'Mister Christopher? Who was Mister Christopher?'

'Ah, that was before your time, sir. The sailor gentleman as was her sweetheart and was drowned. A sad job it was so.'

'But what was his other name?'

'Now that I can't recall, sir. But it's on the church wall isn't it? That's the family, sure 'tis indeed. That's the family.

The name's on the stone in the corner of the wall so 'tis.
I expect 'tis written down in the church records 'tis sure
enough.'

'What church is that then?'

'Ah, sure, sir an' I wouldn't be able to pronounce such a
name even if I could remember it, but 'tis down by the river
with the parson gentleman and the nice friendly little spaniel
dog so 'tis. But he's gone, too, along with his little dog. Pray
to Our Blessed Lady, may his soul rest in peace.' He crossed
himself again.

To Irish's amazement Luther put his hand in his waistcoat
pocket and gave him a sovereign.

Irish looked at it in disbelief. 'Well, sure, sir, 'tis a fine
gentleman I always knew ye to be, but like they says in this
part of the country there's a difference between scrapin' yer
arse an' tearin' the skin off. But 'tis from the bottom of an
old man's heart I'm after thankin' ye, sir, an' I'll be makin'
my way along now so 'tis.'

'Before you go, Irish,' Luther said, 'tell me one more thing.
What did he look like, this Mister Christopher?'

Irish stared at him, and there was an astonished look on his
face. 'Well, Holy Mary, Mother o' God, an 'tis feeble-
minded I am that I've never thought of it before. If ye were
after bein' a younger man ye might be his double. An' sure
I remember thinkin' such a thing when ye were a young
gentleman years ago up at her Ladyship's big house. An'
why in the name of God did I never remember it before?'

14

It was only a matter of days later that Luther received a letter
from Huw Vaughan saying that now Mrs Radley had died
there was some confusion in clearing up her affairs, particularly with regard to what remained of the Estate. There was
much that he did not know. Since his father had died, he
said, only Luther had been aware of what was happening
and the writer would be grateful if he could go to Carmarthen to see him and try to sort some of it out. Luther had
his own reasons for going willingly.

'It will take some time,' Luther said to Huw Vaughan as he opened the big, tin box of Estate papers.

'Well, any help you can give me I'll be glad of. There are more than twenty cottages and smallholdings which have disappeared off the face of the earth.'

Luther looked at the list Huw Vaughan had drawn up and smiled.

'That's simple,' he said. 'They've disappeared. More or less. Workers emigrated and there was nobody left who would take even these miserable hovels. So they just fell down.'

'And the land?'

'Put with other holdings.'

'How about the rent?'

'Readjusted.'

'I suppose you'll know most of the details?'

'I know all of them.'

'Well, that's a help to start with. But there are papers here going way back before Protheroe's time which nobody ever seems to have sorted out.'

'I don't suppose I can do it all today. Can I take some of them home with me?'

'By all means,' Huw Vaughan said, almost with an air of relief, Luther thought. 'Take what you like and let us know what you find.'

Once before, Luther had been near to some of these papers and would have given much to have been able to look at them. They went into his leather case now to be studied at leisure.

15

When Luther came home that evening it was to find that Aaron and Anna had called during the afternoon.

'They looked pretty pleased with theirselves,' Seth said. 'Anna's stoppin' the night at Bellman's Close an' they're gwain call again tomorrow mornin'. Aaron brought a box for you from Stackpole Quay.'

'Box?'

'Aye, an' a letter. The letter's in the sittin'-room with the box.'

'I'll have a look at them after, then.'

Tired though he was, Luther also knew a feeling of excitement at the thought of going through the papers he had brought home with him and, supper finished, he settled to the task. Before he did so he opened the letter Aaron had left with the box. It was a big box and a fair weight.

The letter was from John Roblin. He said that on going through her grandmother's belongings his wife had found this box with a note she had written years previously, just after her husband had died. The box contained some silverware which, she said in the note, she wanted Luther to have in appreciation for all he had done for her. Why it had been overlooked and not been sent to him at the time John Roblin could not think.

That was a nice thought anyway. He would go through the contents of the box afterwards. First of all, he must turn to the papers.

Much of it he knew. And most of it was tedious. The clock had long since struck eleven when he came to one paper which made the search worthwhile, and he smoothed it out on the heavy green tablecloth in the soft light of the big brass lamp.

Only a copy it was, but he had seen the original in Mam Bron's box. It was the letter setting out the financial arrangements for her to support Megan's bastard child, Luther Knox, until he was twenty-one. If a copy of that letter was there, then there could be other such letters.

He turned back to the remainder with a quickened interest. And it was only moments before his patience was rewarded. Next to it was another paper concerning Megan and her bastard child. The date was the same, in the year 1825, but this one was in more detail and it concerned the financial arrangements for the support of Megan Knox and her female child by Vaughan Radley Esquire.

Luther was not Meg's child. Polly Gwyther was right. Not that he had doubted it. The thought had been in his head since the day Anna had come with Aaron recently. It had been there when she had come as a six-year-old, but he could not pin it down. But when she came now, as a young woman, he knew. He did not think there could be anything about it in these papers. But there was. It was all there in the marriage settlement.

How people could be so cruel and detestably proud he would never be able to understand. That sort of hardness was not in him. How could he know when he had been so attracted to Louisa Radley that she was his mother? But there it was.

She had had her child before she married and under this hateful settlement he was to be farmed out and she was to renounce all recognition of him. Breaking her heart at the loss of the child's father, no doubt controlled by parents who saw a suitable marriage, she would have been little able to resist. All very convenient. No scandal. Financial security.

There was much now which he would never know, but he remembered something of the letters through which he had only glanced quickly that time at Deerfield. Letters from his father to his mother. From his father to his mother.

What was the name on the stone in the church wall? He had read it that day when he had gone to see Ieuan Mostyn but, rack his brains though he would, he could not recall it. Still, that was not important just now. He could always go there again and maybe find out some more when he knew the name for which he was searching.

The night he had come back from talking to Polly Gwyther to the realisation that he had been so much in love with Seeny, and that she was no relation at all, the thought had come to him that, if other people, with their lies and agreements, had not fouled everything up he could have married her.

Tonight it suddenly occurred to him that Eiry was his half-sister. In law he could have married her. Now, as he realised, there would, in fact, have been everything against it. Perhaps Squire Radley was not the fool he was taken to be. Nor as hard either. He had discouraged their association and so had Eiry's mother.

Luther had known all along that his feelings for Eiry were not the same as they were for Seeny. What was the point of thinking of it anyway? There would never be any proof.

He had bought a bottle of whisky when he had his cold, and had hardly touched it. He fetched the bottle now, and a glass, and poured himself a generous measure. The first mouthful stopped his breath and then he felt the warmth tingling through his body and he swallowed some more.

No, there would never be any proof, but that was of no consequence. What was it Ieuan Mostyn had said? 'Let the dead bury their dead.' Quite right. Rose had said to sort it out and then go back and talk to her again. He reckoned he had sorted it out quite well. He poured himself some more whisky.

Now that he was at it, he might as well see what his mother had sent him. His mother. Not Meg. Not Mam Bron. His mother. Well, at least he had known her and thought she was beautiful and had not wanted to hurt her and she had kissed him on the cheek. He was a lucky man. He raised his glass and drank a toast to his mother.

The silver in the box was carefully wrapped in soft paper. There were two beautiful candlesticks and some cutlery. It looked very expensive stuff to Luther.

There was another small parcel. Luther opened it. There were letters tied in a bundle and he did not need a second glance to recognise them, for he had seen them before. They were the letters from his father to his mother. He handled them lovingly. He could read them now and they might tell him much. He suddenly remembered that there had been some mention of the colour of her hair and a gold coin.

Along with the letters was a little velvet pouch. Luther opened it and found that it contained a coin. But when he extracted it he found that it was only half a coin. Gold it was, in all its pristine brightness. For some reason, and he knew that reason now, somebody had cut a spade-guinea in half, with the cut running clearly from top to bottom of the spade on the one side and the monarch's head on the other.

Yes, there had been something about the two halves in the letter.

Luther fetched the half which had come with him when he was a baby from Llandeilo Abercowin and which he had found in Mam Bron's chest. They fitted perfectly. The coin had been cut down the middle and the 17 in the one corner matched up with the 94 in the other to make the date 1794 in the reign of GEORGIUS III DEI GRATIA MEF. ET. H. REX and he couldn't understand the other letters, so he drained the glass.

Who cared about proof anyway? What would Rose say about all this? Sort it out, she had said, and then come and talk to her again.

He put on his coat and wandered aimlessly up through the fields until he was standing on the cliffs above Crickdam. Gipsy was hunting the bushes. It had been blowing hard for a couple of days, but now the wind had fallen. Far below he could hear the waves breaking and rolling the pebbles back down the beach, gathering them for a fresh charge.

It was on such a night, cuddled up with Seeny on their straw palliasse, that she had told him that Mam Bron was not his mother and he had wondered who his father was.

Suddenly out of the night there came a wild shriek as if from someone pursued by all the fiends of Hell. It was the first time he had heard a shearwater since that night something like fifty years ago.

What had they said it was? 'The tormented souls of them lost at sea,' Mam Bron had said. Absie's father had said, 'Possessed by the spirits of the sailors as have been drownded and roams the face of the deep in torment.'

Luther did not think of himself as superstitious. His father's soul was not in torment for he and his mother had already been reunited.

What proof did he want?

He had another drink of whisky when he got back to the house, just to keep out the cold, and crawled into bed.

He was asleep before his head touched the pillow.

16

Luther lay in bed in the morning thinking. It was a funny business this thinking. One thought led to another.

He wondered what Absie would think if he knew that he was to have his, Luther's daughter, for a daughter-in-law. He might find that not too difficult to understand, but how would he feel at the knowledge that Anna was also Mrs

Louisa Radley's grand-daughter? Luther might never have any proof that she was his mother, but Anna's whole face and bearing were living proof of their particular relationship. He had loved Mrs Radley. It would be even easier to love Anna. His daughter.

It was odd to think how it had all happened.

Right back at the beginning he had gone off the rails with Sarah. He had always regretted that sordid and squalid relationship. It had never been anything else. He had asked God's forgiveness many times. Yet, if all that had not happened with Sarah, he would probably never have had the confidence to make that first approach to Rose as he had.

Later on, of course, it was because of his relationship with both of them that Sarah had got rid of Rose when he was ill. The result was Rose's disastrous marriage and, following her visit to Plumtree Hill, the birth of Anna. If it had not been for the fact that Anna was his child he would not have gone to see Rose when Aaron said he was going to marry Anna.

Then again, had it not been for that visit to Rose, he would not have had a row with her, and she would not have sent him to see Polly Gwyther. And had he not gone to see Polly Gwyther he might never have known that he was not Meg's child. His name was not Knox, but it had suited well enough for long enough, so it was hardly worth changing it now. There were more important things to think of.

Yes, he had many regrets at having gone to bed with Sarah, but never for one moment had he regretted what had happened with Rose. Certainly he did not regret Anna.

He needed Rose now. He wanted her. Who was it had said there was no fool like an old fool? The only trouble was he had been a fool all his life.

He had spent his time worrying about his feelings for Seeny and for Eiry and had never recognised his feelings for Rose. Right at the start he had been physically attracted to her, that day at the Patches, and so he had gone on thinking of it as having been physical. Now he began to realise how much he had always missed her and thought of her, recalling moments of happiness together and remembering some of her endearing ways. For years he had loved her and had been too blind to see it. Fool was too kind an epithet for him.

That day when Rose had come to Plumtree Hill after she had married, and as they had lain in each other's arms in this same bed, she had said she loved him and had missed him. Even then, all he had said was that he had missed her too. He had not told her that he loved her. He had not had enough brains to do that.

Years ago, when it all started, in this bed, she had hinted at marriage and a nice home of her own. What sort of fool had he been?

Maybe it was not too late. When he had seen Rose a few weeks ago she had told him some rather unpalatable home truths, and she was more than entitled to. But she had said good-bye with a smile and told him to come again.

Yes, maybe it was not too late. Rose was thirty-eight now and he was only sixty-one. Only sixty-one. What was it Tom Davey had said about that Hugh Williams character? Married when he was sixty-five and gave his wife four babies, the last of them when he was seventy-six. Yes, he was only sixty-one. There was still time. Time? It was time to get up.

17

Aaron and Anna called at Plumtree Hill shortly after breakfast. Seth had said, 'They looked pretty pleased with theirselves.' It was no wonder.

Anna was smiling broadly. The ring was of gold with three rubies surrounded by small diamonds. Very modern. Very smart.

Luther took her in his arms and kissed her and held her close.

'There y'are,' Aaron said. 'I told you didn't I? 'Twas just because a's a bachelor an' was took a bit by surprise. Don't know much about these things like.'

Luther led them into the sitting room.

'We mustn't stop long, Uncle Luther,' Aaron said, 'we're catchin' the tide an' sailin' for Bristol.'

'We?'

'Aye, we. Anna's comin' too.'

'And what d'you plan to do when you're married?'

'Well, that's just it. We wants to talk to you about that an' about the *ASENATH*. We wants to settle down.'

'Oh yes?'

'We been talkin' to Father an' a reckons that the coastal trade is finished an' th' only thing with any future in it is farmin'.'

'Absie said that?'

'Aye, that's what a said.'

'You know what a terrible time farming is suffering?'

'I know. That's what I said, but Father said good times'll come again an' the country'll never manage without the farmers.'

'Now I find that very interesting. What else did he say?'

'Well a said, sometimes corn is up an' sometimes down, an' the same with beef an' sheep an' pigs an' with horses. But a reckons that to make farmin' pay year in, year out, you always wants to make sure you got a good milkin' cow an' a good layin' hen. Always put your faith in the land, a said.'

'Indeed. Very interesting. Well, I'm sure if Absie said that it must be good advice. What about the *ASENATH*?'

'That's what we wanted to talk to you about. I knows 'twas only because of me you bought her in the first place an' I won't let you down. You said all along there'd be nothin' in the coastal trade an' the business is finished, an' that's right enough. There haven't been much in it for all the work an' risk an' everythin'. But if you'd like to sell her, there's a man in Bristol will buy her. Says she's just what a's lookin' for. There's several of 'em wantin' to have shares in her an' a's willin' to pay eight hunderd pounds for her.'

Luther went to a drawer and took out the *ASENATH*'s papers. 'Here,' he said, 'do the deal. The sooner the better.'

He went back to his chair. 'Tell me one thing,' he said. 'Do you have enough money to start farming?'

'We've saved a bit. An' Anna's mother have said she'll help us as much as she can.'

'You couldn't have a better friend,' Luther said.

'That's what she said about you.'

'She did?'

'Good God, Uncle Luther, she thinks that in the Day of Judgement God'll sit on your right hand.'

'The last time I saw her she gave me a piece of her mind.'

Anna burst out laughing. 'You don't take any notice of that. That's her. Ever since I can remember she's said that Mister Knox used to say this and Mister Knox used to do that.'

'Mister Knox?'

Anna smiled. 'Sometimes when she wasn't thinking she'd say Luther.'

'Well, what about the *ASENATH*, Aaron?' Luther said.

'We're sailin' for Bristol straight after dinner an' I'm seein' the man tomorrow with your answer.'

'Your answer.'

'No, your answer, she's your boat.'

'But when you start farming, eight hundred pounds will come in useful won't it? You're my sister's son, mind.'

They both looked at him incredulously. Then Anna came and sat on his knee and put her arm round his neck and kissed him and he knew such happiness as no money in the world could have bought. He knew something once again of the feelings Eiry had aroused in him, only stronger.

'Isn't he lovely,' Anna said, and hugged him.

He would love to be able to tell her one day that she was his daughter.

18

Aaron and Anna were sailing for Bristol straight after dinner. Rose would be on her own. Too often he had left it too late. Why, oh why, had he not told her that he loved her and asked her to marry him years ago?

The weather did not look too good. It was a bit risky to set off for Saundersfoot just now. Snow it was going to be for sure. The wild geese had come early this year.

If he set off for Saundersfoot now he would get there all right, but the chances were that he would be stuck there. And Rose was on her own.

He harnessed Tegwen and put her in the trap, looked again at the glowering sky and wondered.

It was at Crickdam that he had first set eyes on Rose.

It was during the snow, alone in the house, just the two of them, for five long, beautiful nights, that he had first possessed her.

It was before the snow at Crickdam that he had had that strange vision of the funeral.

'Be careful when it do snow,' Mam Bron had said. 'The snow will be a big time for you isn't it.'

It was too late to think of that now.

Tegwen was stepping out smartish towards Saundersfoot.

Glossary of Pembrokeshire words

a: he or it. Sounded as a wide *a*, as in *father*.

afeart: afraid.

afore: before.

bach: small (Welsh).

balls: small oval lumps of *culm* mixed with clay and water and kneaded by hand in the shape of balls for use as fuel.

banter: to haggle about price.

beam: a large timber, such as the body of a plough.

bell bastard: the illegitimate child of a woman who is herself illegitimate.

bidding: invitation to a wedding.

bleeze: bladder.

bosh: wooden cask.

budram: gruel consisting of oatmeal steeped in water.

burgage: a small field near the house.

caffle: confusion, entangled.

carren-gull: the greater black-backed gull.

clom: a mixture of clay and straw used for building walls.

cockel,cocklolly,cockly nave: the shearwater.

coppit: proud.

croggan: Welsh people who visited the sea-shore in summer.

crut: a boy, lad.

culm: the slack of anthracite.

cutty: small.

cutwyn: a windlass.

drabble-tail: a slovenly dressed woman.

dragmallin: a poor, hard-working woman.

druke: a turning handle.

dull: foolish, silly.

Duw: God (Welsh).

fetch-funeral: a supernatural or ghost funeral foretelling death.

filty fine: smart, well-dressed.

firkin: a small cask.

for all: in spite of.

fox: a single fine day during poor weather.

gambo: a cart with side-poles instead of a box.

gant: a gander.

garget: inflamation of the udder.

griskin: lean pork slices for frying.

gwain: going.

haggard: a rickyard.

hasty pudding: gruel made of meal instead of oatmeal.

hawse: to seek to draw information from.

hayes: a small field.

heck: to hop on one leg.

hisht: be quiet.

honey: a term of endearment. Often abbreviated to *hun*.

how: why.

kift: clumsy, awkward.

lab: gossip.

licker: something which would take some beating.

lootch: a wooden spoon.

maddock: a pick-like tool.

mewk: a small sound.

maid, mide: a young girl, lass.

main: very, much, greatly.

mine: iron ore.

molly-hawn: slut.

patches: places where iron ore was dug.

pine-end: the gable-end of a house.

pisken led: led away by fairies.

pollers: people who picked iron ore.

rabbats: rabbits.

rammas: a long, tedious story.

scraping: scratching.

sea-pyat: the oyster-catcher.

servant sir: salutation from a social inferior.

skew: a settle.

sleever: a liquid measure used for beer—about ¾ of a pint.

snib: a bashful young man.

sog: a semi-comatose condition, drowsiness.

springle: a snare made with a pliant stick and a noose of horse-hair.

sprotting: animals breaking out when in season.

strag: a tramp.

stum: to smother, to bank the fire at night with *culm*.

tack: a person or thing.

taler: a man who keeps count of the presents at a wedding.

tallet: the hay-loft over the stable. The unceilinged loft of a cottage.

tammat: as much straw or hay as a man can carry.

tamping: angry, very annoyed.

thicky: this one, that one.

tide: the sea.

truckle-bed: a low bedstead on castors.

wash-in-the-tide: to bathe.

washporo: oatmeal allowed to ferment and boiled to a jelly and served as a dish.

waskat: waistcoat.

winchester: a bushel.

wood-cush: the wood-pidgeon.

worrit: to worry.

yeat: to eat.